One Poison Pie

WITHDRAWN

One Poison Pie

A Kitchen Witch Mystery

LYNN CAHOON

KENSINGTON
PUBLISHING CORP.

www.kensingtonbooks.com

KENSINGTON BOOKS are published by

Kensington Publishing Corp.
119 West 40th Street
New York, NY 10018

All Kensington titles, imprints, and distributed lines are available at special quantity discounts for bulk purchases for sales promotion, premiums, fund-raising, educational, or institutional use.

Special book excerpts or customized printings can also be created to fit specific needs. For details, write or phone the office of the Kensington Sales Manager: Attn.: Sales Department. Kensington Publishing Corp., 119 West 40th Street, New York, NY 10018. Phone: 1-800-221-2647.

Kensington and the K logo Reg. U.S. Pat. & TM Off.

First Printing: February 2021
ISBN-13: 978-1-4967-3031-2
ISBN-10: 1-4967-3031-3

ISBN-13: 978-1-4967-3034-3 (ebook)
ISBN-10: 1-4967-3034-8 (ebook)

10 9 8 7 6 5 4 3 2 1

Printed in the United States of America

Here's to all the people who make the world seem just a little more magical by the hope they bring to us all.

ACKNOWLEDGMENTS

There's a magic shop in Seattle's Pike Market. Or there was the last time I visited. The first time I visited, I was in high school in Seattle for the Future Homemakers of America national conference (don't judge, it was a great place to learn about goal setting and achieving). After wandering through the market I found the bookstore and the magic shop. I was looking for real magic, not how to be a magician, so I left the store with one thing: a prediction from the fortune-teller in the glass box. I don't remember the exact fortune, but I remember the feeling it gave me. Hope for a better future.

I'm long overdue for another visit.

CHAPTER 1

Karma sucks.

Mia Malone slapped the roller filled with cottage yellow paint on the wall. She'd missed another spot. Her lack of attention was one more thing on the long list of karma credits she could blame on her ex, Isaac.

If karma didn't smack down the lowlife soon, she had several ideal spells just waiting to be used on the rat. Maybe he'd like to develop a rash? Or be turned into a toad to match his true personality? A line of yellow paint dripped off the roller and onto the scratched wood floor.

She set the roller in the paint pan and, with a rag, wiped up the paint before it could dry. Maybe a run would be more productive right now. She could burn off this pent-up energy tingling her fingers. Teasing her with all the curses she could inflict.

She took a deep, calming breath. Magic came back

threefold. She needed to control her impulses, keeping her anger in check. As much as she wanted Isaac to pay for his betrayal, she didn't need any help in the bad luck department. Sighing, she sat cross-legged on the floor in the middle of the half-painted schoolroom and tried to envision her new life.

A noise echoed through the empty schoolhouse. *Had the door opened?*

"Mia," her grandmother called. "Are you here, dear?"

"To your left, Grans." Mia stood and dusted off the butt of her worn jeans, imagining dusting off Isaac and his bad energy at the same time. Keeping her karma clean seemed to be a full-time job since she'd left Boise.

Mary Alice Carpenter, tall and willowy, stood in the doorway to the foyer. The curl in her short, gray hair was the only physical trait Grans and Mia shared. Mia stood a good five inches shorter than the older woman, and Mia's curves would have made her prime model material, oh, about a hundred years ago.

Besides her curly hair, she'd inherited power from her maternal grandmother. While her mother had turned away from the lure of magic, choosing instead the life of a corporate lawyer's wife, Mia had embraced her heritage.

Her grandmother took one look at her and groaned. "I knew he wouldn't stay gone. That boy is worse than spilled milk. You just can't get rid of the smell."

"I can handle Isaac." Mia gave her grandmother a hug. "You don't worry about him."

Grans's eyebrows rose. "Are you sure, dear? I've done a few transmutations in my time that may be quite appropriate."

Mia bit back a laugh and glanced around the large room. "Seriously, don't get involved. That part of my life is over. I've made a fresh start."

"You've bought a run-down money pit that's going to bankrupt you just trying to keep the place warm." A second woman followed her grandmother into the room, shoving a cell phone into her Coach bag. "Sorry, had to take that. Apparently, my long-lost nephew is gracing us with his presence at my birthday party. Probably needs money."

"Adele, so nice to see you," Mia managed to choke out after a death stare from her grandmother.

Adele Simpson stood next to Grans and glanced around the room, noticeable disgust covering her face. "Mary Alice, *this* is what you fought so hard with the board to save?"

"The building should be on the historic register. You and I both know it would have already been protected if it sat in the Sun Valley city limits. Magic Springs is always an afterthought with the historical commission." Grans slipped off the down coat that had made her look like a stuffed panda.

Mia watched the women bicker. Adele, the meanest woman in Magic Springs, was the dark to Grans's light and, for some unbeknownst reason, Grans's best friend. She was also Mia's first and only client for her new venture. *So far*, she amended.

Gritting her teeth, Mia forced her lips into what she hoped was a passable smile. "Ladies, welcome to Mia's Morsels." She glanced around the room, sweeping her arm as she turned. "Currently, you're in the reception area, where staff and students will gather before classes, and where we'll do most of the daily work scheduling. Here, customers will be able to sample dishes and peruse a weekly menu of available meals."

"You sound like a commercial," Grans chided. "It's just us. You don't have to put on the sales pitch."

Mia smiled. "Just trying it out. I've got a lot of work to do before I can even think about opening." She nodded to the half-painted wall. "Do you like the color?"

Her grandmother nodded. "It's friendly without being obnoxiously bright, like so many buildings. Day-care colors have swept through the decorating studios. I swear, the new crop of interior designers have no sense of style or class."

"Fredrick just did Helen Marcum's living room in pink." Adele sniffed. "The room looks like an antacid commercial. I swear, the woman shows her hillbilly roots every time she makes a decision."

"I don't believe Helen's Southern, dear." Grans focused back on Mia, closing her eyes for a second. "Color holds a lot of power. Pull out your books before you go too far. Although if I remember, yellow represents the digestive system."

Mia loved listening to her grandmother talk about the representations of power. Being kitchen witches was different from being Wiccan, or what normal people would think of when you said *witch*. They didn't wear black, pointy hats or fly around the moon. Mia's magic was more about the colors, the food, the process of making a house a home. That was one of the reasons her career choice was such a natural extension of her life. Food made people happy. She liked being around happy people. Sometimes magic was that easy.

"You are not doing woo-woo magic stuff again, are you, Mary Alice?" Adele shook her head. "Next you'll be telling the girl to open on a full moon and wave around a dead cat."

Grans looked horrified at her friend. "I would never tell her to desecrate an animal that way. We've been friends for over forty years. You should know better."

"Oh, go fly your broomstick."

Grans and Adele had been the swing votes on the board, allowing Mia to purchase the property based on her pledge to save the building's history. The losing bidder had presented a plan to bulldoze the school and replace it with a high-end retail mall. Instead, Mia had a place to start over. Grans always said the best way to get a man out of your head was to change your routine.

Mia may have gone a little overboard.

Her arms and back ached from painting. Another two, three hours, the room would be done. Then she could move on to the kitchen, the heart of her dream. Right now, all she wanted was to clean up the paint supplies and return to her upstairs apartment for a long soak in the claw-foot tub. The unexpected visitors had her skin tingling, a sure sign nothing good was about to happen.

Catering Adele's birthday party had been an order more than a request, even though her business wouldn't be completely up and running for a month or so. The planning for the event had gone smoothly, like an aged Southern whiskey. The final prep list for Saturday's party sat finished on her kitchen table in the apartment. James, the chef at the Lodge, had allowed her time to prep in his kitchen tomorrow evening. By Sunday she'd have a successful reference in the books for Mia's Morsels. Now, without warning, the triumph she'd hoped for was slipping through her fingers.

"Add one, maybe two more, to the guest list. Who

knows who he'll bring from Arizona to help me cele-brate." Adele shoved a piece of paper toward her.

Mia glanced down. A name had been scrawled on the torn notepaper, William Danforth III. She hadn't known Adele had any living relatives, no less a nephew. "How nice. Are you close?"

A harsh laugh came from the woman. "Close? I wasn't kidding about the money. He's checking on his inheri-tance. I'm pretty sure he thought I'd be dead by now."

"Now, Adele, at least he's visiting." Grans picked up Mr. Darcy, Mia's gray cat, who'd wandered into the room. He'd probably been sleeping in one of the empty southern classrooms, where the afternoon sun warmed the wood floors. He curled into her neck and started purring. Loudly.

Unfortunately, during a late summer visit to Grans's house, Mr. Darcy had picked up a hitchhiker. The spirit of Dorian Alexander, who had been Grans's beau before his untimely death, had taken up residence with Mia's cat. A fact that weirded Mia out at times, especially at night, when Mr. Darcy slept on the foot of her bed. Mia really needed to get Grans focused on a reversal spell. But this wasn't the time to be chatting about spells and power. In-stead, she focused on Adele and her party.

"I'm sure he's . . ." Mia stopped. What had she been going to say? That Adele's nephew was nice? If the guy had any of Adele's temperament, the guy would be a royal jerk.

Adele waved away her words, her hands showing her impatience, "Let me worry about Billy. You're serving beef tomorrow." The words weren't a question.

"I'd planned to serve squab with raspberry sauce and

wild rice for the main course." Mia held her breath. *Please no last minute changes—please.*

"That won't do at all." Adele watched as Mr. Darcy crawled up on Grans's shoulder. She reached out a hand to pet the cat, who hissed at her. Dropping her hand, she focused her glare on Mia. "My parents ran the Beef Council for years. You had to have known we had the largest cattle operation in the Challis area, maybe even the entire Magic Valley."

"I sent you the menu a week ago." Mia thought about the prep list she'd spent hours writing out last night. A list that would have to be completely revamped if Adele made this change in the menu. "I'm sure you responded."

"I've been busy. You should have called rather than sending paper." Adele stepped farther away from the hissing cat. "I don't remember everything. That's why I'm telling you now. Oh, and no cake; pie for dessert. Several different types, of course; you'll know which ones to serve with the beef. I've never liked cake."

"You already approved the menu," Mia repeated through clenched teeth. Apparently sensing her distress, Mr. Darcy jumped out of Grans's arms and walked over to Mia. He curled on her feet, watching the women.

"I doubt that. No matter, you need to serve beef. It's a tradition. I'm surprised you didn't know." Adele pulled out a beeping phone and, after glancing at the display, focused on Grans. "We need to leave now if we're going to keep our court time."

Mia sighed. Trying one more time to win a battle already lost, she asked, "Are you sure you don't want squab?"

"The homeless eat pigeon. Porterhouse. Or whatever

cut you think is best. You're the expert." Adele turned toward the door, pulling Grans along with her.

That's what you keep saying. Mia said, "I'll try, but the
party is this weekend."

"I'm sure you'll do your best." Grans shook off
Adele's grip and turned back to Mia. She planted a kiss
on her cheek.

Mia followed them to the front door. Daylight filtered
through the dirt-covered windows. Another item for her
to-do list: hire a window cleaner. Mr. Darcy's soft footsteps padded behind her. "Thanks for stopping in," she
called as they left the building. After the door closed she
added, hoping her grandmother wouldn't hear, "And ru-
ining a perfectly good day."

If she was being honest, though, the ruination of her
day had started with Isaac's call. She reached down to
stroke Mr. Darcy. He meowed his wishes.

"Sorry, your dinner is going to have to wait. I've got to
get to Majors Grocery," Mia told the cat, who looked horrified at the thought. She hauled the painting supplies to
the kitchen. Her mind whirled as water rinsed cheery yellow paint out of the roller and down the drain. Her de-
tailed plan of attack for the event had disappeared with a
flick of Adele's perfectly polished, bloodred nails.

Mr. Darcy wove through her legs as she stood at the
sink. Finishing the cleanup, she laid the tools on a towel
to dry and double-checked the lock on the back door.
Then she climbed the two sets of stairs to the third floor
and her apartment.

Christina Adams, the almost-twenty-year-old sister of
her ex, jumped up from the couch when Mia entered the
apartment. "I thought you were going to paint this afternoon?"

"I thought you were coming to help just as soon as you finished lunch?" Mia studied the girl. Last month Christina had returned to Magic Springs. She'd shown up on Mia's doorstep with a police escort. Mark Baldwin, the town's only officer, had found her loitering in the small downtown park. Her long, blond hair screamed cheerleader, but the bars in her eyebrow and her lip along with the row of piercings in her ear hardened the look.

Christina had been planning on starting college this semester after spending last year in Las Vegas, trying to make it as a dancer after some bad advice from her substitute dance coach. Now, after one more fight with the family, she'd tracked Mia down and asked if she could live with her for a while. Mia didn't have the heart to turn her away, even if Mia wouldn't be part of the Adams family, now or ever.

She had the decency to blush. "I'm not really good at all that painting stuff. Maybe I could just help you with the cooking rather than the remodeling."

"Don't worry about it. I have a feeling we're going to have to pull an all-nighter if we want to finish prep before the party. And now we have to bake pies as well." She went into the kitchen to get her list. "I'm heading over to Majors. Be ready to work when I get back."

Mia heard the television come on as her only answer. Training Christina to be a sous chef might be harder than she'd imagined. Running her fingers over the cookbook she'd left out that morning with the prep list, she remembered Isaac's call. Could there be another reason Isaac's sister had come to live with Mia? She locked her cookbook in the safe in her room. She'd been stupid before. Today she'd take paranoid.

Where was she going to get thirty servings of steak by

tomorrow evening? And the side dishes had to completely change. Adele was paying for both grocery orders, no matter what Grans said.

She hoped the small country store had enough meat on hand. Or an idea.

As she opened the front door, she tripped over an envelope. The delivery service must have dropped it off late yesterday. They'd been busy in the kitchen, doing a trial run-through of the menu. The return address on the top was smeared, but the envelope was clearly addressed to Christina. Mia shoved the envelope into her purse. She'd give it to her when she got back. Or after the party, when she wouldn't mind losing her apprentice.

A dusting of snow had fallen the night before, coating the town in white. Magic Springs looked like a Dickens-novel Christmas. The roads had been plowed. Someone had run a small blade—probably on the front of a four-wheeler—over the sidewalks in front of the school and down the two blocks toward Majors. Small towns, Mia mused. No way had the city paid for this type of service. It had to be one of the homeowners in the village who donated their early morning service for the pleasure of driving their toy around the snow-covered streets.

Mia took a deep breath, trying to focus on solving her menu problems rather than being filled with the quiet beauty of the town. Beef. Maybe a garlic mashed potato? Or a scalloped? Or would Adele consider the menu too homey for her party? Would there be any way Majors could pull off an order of fresh asparagus? It was April, even though the town wouldn't acknowledge spring for a few weeks at the earliest. There had to be asparagus ready to harvest somewhere.

Stomping the snow off her boots, she pushed open the

glass grocery slider. A bell rang over the door, echoing in the seemingly empty store. No cashier stood at the register, no shoppers filled the aisles. Mia glanced at her watch: 5:15. The store closed early during the winter, but she'd just made it.

She grabbed a cart and headed to the butcher block in the back. The meat case stood empty and her heart sank. A bell sat on the top of the case and she rang it once. No one came through the doors. Maybe Adele would just have to suck it up and eat the food Mia had planned to serve.

Mia could see her grandmother's frown. Again, she banged on the bell, harder this time, picturing Adele's unsmiling face each time she hit the silver chime.

"Hold up," a man's voice called from the back. "I heard you the first twenty times. I have my hands full back here."

Mia jumped back from the meat case. Her hand still reached out in front of her. She called toward the door, "Okay, I'll wait here."

That was dumb. Of course she would wait. Now that she'd had some time to think, Mia pulled out a slip of paper and started making a quick shopping list. Peaches, asparagus, more butter, fresh horseradish, potatoes; she continued to write as she waited. Finally, she looked up from her list satisfied. She only needed to add thirty quality steaks. Maybe she should serve a soup too. That would give her more time to grill and prep the main course.

Loud voices were muffled by the swinging doors. Was that an argument? She inched closer, trying to see through the window in the door. Two men stood by a large metal table. One, dressed in a suit, shook a finger at the other.

Now she could hear the actual words. "I'm not making this offer again. I'll wait and get the property for pennies when it goes to auction."

"I'm not losing this store. Majors has been in the family since the settlers came to Magic Springs. It's part of the community, the town's history. We're just going through a bad patch. Everyone is." The man dropped a box on the table. "I have a customer waiting for me. Unless you're here to shop, get the heck out of my store."

"You'll regret turning me down." The suit walked toward the door and caught sight of Mia watching. "Of course you'd be here. Are you trying to ruin all my business?"

"I'm sorry, do I know you?" Mia stood back, stunned at the man's outburst.

"Why would you?" The man glared at her, then stomped around the counter and almost ran from the store.

CHAPTER 2

A voice behind her caused her to jump. "John seems to hate you worse than he does me at the moment. I guess I should thank you."

Mia turned and spied a man watching her from behind the counter. His light brown hair curled around his face and a set of the greenest eyes peered out at her. A smile sat lightly on his lips. Just looking at him caused Mia to shiver, thinking thoughts not exactly PG. She bit her bottom lip and focused. She was here for meat. Not a man.

"Who was that?" Mia's voice cracked on the question. "Why doesn't he like me?"

A smile played on the man's lips. "I think you got what he wanted. Anyway, not for me to gossip. What can I help you with?"

Mia shook off the negative energy lingering from John's departure. "I'm Mia Malone and I . . ."

The man interrupted her. "You bought the old school. How do you like the apartment? My brothers and I did some renovation for the principal a few years ago. He turned one bedroom into a bath and a closet. Never knew a man to love his closet as much as Albert did."

"I love it. The apartment's great. But I have a favor to ask." She took a breath.

Again she was stopped. "I hear you're putting in some kind of cooking class business. You really think there's enough of a market for that type of company up here?"

"It's not just a cooking school. I'll start out delivering made-to-order dinners for customers. For when you want a great meal, but don't want to cook? I'm also catering. In fact, that's what I need help with. . . ." Mia watched the man walk around the still-empty meat case, ignoring her.

"Sounds like a lot of work for such a little girl." Now the man stood over her. His six-foot-something frame made her feel small, but his words ticked her off.

"Look. Can you help me or is there someone else who can? I didn't come in to be insulted about my height or to be told how my business won't survive. I need steaks." Mia's face burned. But she knew she couldn't stomp out. The next-closest store was fifty miles away. She'd never get all the prep work done if she had to make the drive.

"Boy, you can tell you're from the big city. Relax a second. Doesn't hurt to make small talk with your best supplier." He held out his hand. "I'm Trent Majors, owner of this fine establishment."

Mia hesitated, then sighed and accepted the offered gesture. "Sorry. I've been thrown for a bit of a loop. I've got a dinner party for thirty tomorrow and my customer just decided she wants input on the menu. Now I need thirty steaks. Any suggestions?"

"You planning on grilling?"

"I'm going to have to." Mia frowned, trying to remember the setup from her last visit to her temporary kitchen. "I'll be cooking at the Lodge. Tell me the kitchen has a grill."

"James has the best grill in three counties; you'll be fine. Now, meat, that's going to be a challenge. My supplier comes on Tuesdays."

"I don't suppose you happened to order thirty extra porterhouses this week?" Mia's voice was hopeful.

"Nah. In fact, I tend to order short on the more expensive cuts this time of year because most of the houses are empty for the next few months." He glanced at Mia, "Now don't you worry, I'll get you those steaks. Maybe even play grill master for you."

"You're a chef?"

"Amateur. James and I are friends. I sub in when he needs an extra hand." Trent grinned. "When I'm not fishing."

Mia groaned. Her first big gig and she would have to count on a teenage Goth sous chef and an I'd-rather-be-fishing grill master. Why not? She was only doing the birthday party for the meanest, most demanding woman in the county. She'd mentioned Adele's name to the florist when she ordered the flowers for the evening and the clerk visibly blanched. The woman didn't have a real friend in town. Except Grans.

That alone was good enough for Mia. This party would be perfect if it killed her.

Two hours later she was back at the apartment and packing up the food they'd prepared for the party. Christina and Mia carried tub after tub of ingredients to the van for the five-minute trip to the Lodge. Then the two would finish the prep, put everything into the fridge, and hope Trent showed up with meat. Otherwise, she'd have to steal protein and improvise from the Lodge's kitchen because she'd frozen the squab. Adele might just get sliders for her birthday.

James met them at the back door leading to the kitchen. "Trent just called. His supplier had enough porterhouse, but he had to drive into Boise. He'll be back into town late tonight and drop off the steaks first thing tomorrow. Can you be here by eight?"

"Eight's a little earlier than I'd planned, but yeah, I'll be here." Mia toted a plastic tub into the kitchen. Glancing around the kitchen, already buzzing with activity, she hesitated. "You sure about us doing prep here? We won't be in your way?"

"The dining room's pretty empty. Everyone's planning on attending Adele's party tomorrow, so a lot of our in-town regulars stayed home." James put the tub he'd been carrying on a table near the back of the kitchen. "You can set up here. Your business sounds like a great addition to the community. I wish I'd thought of it. We do a lot of takeout, but people always want delivery, and I just don't have the staff."

"I hope you're right. I really appreciate the use of your kitchen. I know it's an imposition." Mia started unpacking the produce, putting things into piles of ingredients by course. "I'm sure the Lodge would rather that you cater the party."

"Believe me, I would have let anyone use my kitchen rather than work for that woman again. Last year she changed the menu three times before we finished. And even then she didn't like what I served. She thinks servants should be able to read her mind."

"Let me guess: when she set it up she said she didn't care one way or another about the menu." Mia smiled. She had known taking this job wouldn't be easy. She just hadn't known that everyone else had been smart enough to say no.

"Worse, she told me to do whatever I wanted. . . ."

Mia broke in, "Because you're the professional."

James laughed. "Sorry, I should have realized that's why Trent's on the scavenger hunt."

"I felt bad imposing, but I was desperate." Mia shoved the tub she'd just emptied under the table and opened a second one. The catering setup system was time-consuming, but she never forgot an ingredient or lost a utensil. She liked buying her gadgets at the specialty cooking stores even though she could find a cheaper version somewhere else. Expensive gadgets had a habit of walking off if she wasn't careful with both her hiring and her inventory system. She thought about the grocer who'd offered to grill her steaks. Too cute and he knew it—she didn't need cute in her life right now.

"Trent doesn't do anything he doesn't want to. You must have made quite the impression." James nodded to a line cook who was waving him over to the flattop. "Got to save the world from another undercooked salmon. We'll compare notes later."

Christina burst through the kitchen door and dramatically dropped a tub on the table. "That's the last one. Now what?"

Mia watched James walk away. She hadn't considered the fact that Trent might be doing this for any other reason than she, as a customer, had asked. Boy, she'd been out of the dating game way too long. Now what indeed?

She turned and surveyed the half-unpacked boxes, a familiar ease coming to her mind. She grabbed two aprons and threw one at Christina.

"Now we cook."

By nine all the prep they could do a day before was complete. Three different types of fruit pies cooled on a table in the back, and the chocolate cream pies were in the cooler, waiting for fresh whipped cream topping to be piled on tomorrow. Everything was stored away, and James's kitchen, at least the part they'd been working in, was clean and back in order. The dinner rush had started more than an hour ago. Mia wanted to get out of their way.

"Time to head home." She pulled her car keys out of her purse. Her fingers brushed over the envelope she'd found that morning and still hadn't given Christina. She pushed the envelope deeper into her purse. Tomorrow was too important for drama. Or to lose her only help. Besides, Christina really was good at cooking. "What do you say we stop and pick up a pizza on the way?"

"As long as I don't have to chop anything, I'd eat a frozen dinner." Christina rubbed her hands together. "I have aching muscles in my fingers I didn't even know existed."

Mia laughed. "Cooking's not for the weak. You did an excellent job today. You have real potential."

Christina beamed but waved away the compliment. "Let's get out of here."

"After you." She followed Christina to the van. "I hope you like kitchen-sink pizza or we're going to buy two."

"The more toppings the better." She covered her mouth, but Mia still saw the yawn.

On the ride back home, Mia listed off her new prep list for tomorrow and Christina wrote. She'd key it into the computer and print out a couple of copies in the morning before they left. Getting to the Lodge that early, they should have time for a break in the middle of the day. Maybe she'd even treat Christina to lunch and a tour of the grand building.

Tomorrow would be absolutely perfect.

When they arrived home an upscale SUV was parked in what she'd come to think of as her spot. The plates on the black monster read SELL4U. John Louis, the other bidder on the school and the man who'd almost run her down in Majors Grocery, had come to call.

Mia handed Christina the keys to the front door. "Go head on upstairs. I'll be there in a minute."

She didn't move from her seat but looked at the other car. "I can come back down after dropping this off. Maybe say you have a phone call?"

"I think I'll be fine. But if I'm not up there in ten minutes, come get me." Mia put her hand on the door handle. "I'd hate for my dinner to get cold."

"Deal." Christina bounced out of the car and headed to the front door. Mia saw her sneak a peek into the driver's window, then speed up when the car door opened.

Mia climbed out of her van and stood at the front of his car. "Kind of late for a social call." She nodded to the retreating Christina. "We were just about to have dinner."

John paused, then walked toward her and leaned against the front fender. "Not really a social call. I just wanted to apologize for my rude behavior before. Trent can rile me up a tad."

Mia felt the waves of insincerity flow off the man. And a touch of anger, mostly aimed at Trent, but not all of it. The man had the temperament of a walking time bomb, just waiting to be set off. She wondered if there was a Mrs. Louis, and if she accepted the brunt of her husband's rage. "No need to apologize." Mia took a step toward the door. "Thanks for coming by, though."

He put up his hand, stopping her. "Hey, I'm not done."

Mia raised her eyebrows at his brusque tone and he lowered his hand.

Her silence must have given him the idea she wanted to continue the conversation, so he pushed on. "I know you didn't realize what a money pit this building was when you bought it. I can't see a single woman on her own living in this dump. And even if you intended to open a catering business, there are plenty of cleaner, newer places in town I could lease you for less than this place would cost to get up to code."

"I don't want to lease . . ." Her words were cut off by John's flowing hands.

"Don't make a decision today." He shoved a business card at her. "I'll take the place off your hands for what you paid plus a reasonable profit for your time. Just call me when you're ready to sell."

He turned back toward the driver's door.

Confused, Mia glanced at the business card. "What makes you think I'll ever want to sell?"

He paused halfway into the front seat and turned back to glare at her. His stare burned into her. "Lady, you have no idea what you've gotten yourself in to. There's no way you can pull this off. I'm going to make sure of that."

Mia stepped out from behind the car when he started it

up and watched him angle the car down the driveway. The smile on the man's face had chilled her more than the night air, and she rubbed her arms against the cold.

"Aren't you coming in?"

Mia jumped at the sound of the voice, putting a hand on her heart to slow the rhythm. "Christina."

"Sorry I scared you, but I didn't like the thought of you out here with that guy. He gives me the creeps and I've never even talked to him." She peered at Mia. "He didn't hurt you, right? You're okay?"

Mia put on a shaky smile she didn't feel. "I'm fine. Starving, but fine." She put her arm around Christina and led her up the path. "Let's tear into that pizza."

As Christina started chatting about the day and all the people she'd met in James's kitchen, Mia tried to keep up, but her mind was on John's pronouncement that he would make sure she wasn't successful.

A rumor can swirl through a small town faster than a forest fire could burn an acre. She'd talk to Grans tomorrow to see if John's campaign against her could hurt as much as he believed.

Tomorrow; she'd think about it tomorrow. She locked the front door and checked to see if the lock held before following the chatty Christina upstairs.

But she *would* think about John.

The sound of a phone ringing woke Mia out of a deep sleep. Grabbing the cell, she croaked, "Hello?"

"Good morning, sleepyhead. I take it you're not up yet?" a male voice teased.

"Isaac?" Mia ran her hand across her face, trying to

brush away the cobwebs. It wasn't Isaac on the phone. This voice was deeper. Friendly, even. She still couldn't make her mind work to place the name. "Who is this?"

"I'm crushed. This is Trent. You were supposed to meet me at the Lodge at eight?"

Mia sat up. *Trent.* Crap. What time was it? She grabbed the alarm clock. Eight thirty. So much for today being perfect. She was already almost an hour behind schedule and she wasn't even dressed. She stared at the phone still in her hand. Putting it back to her ear, she answered, "I'll be there by nine, nine fifteen at the latest."

"No worries. I'm just drinking coffee with James." Trent chuckled. "See you soon."

Mia clicked off the phone, slipped on her robe and her blue-and-gold Boise State slippers, and sprinted to the hallway. Pounding on Christina's door, she yelled, "We overslept. Get up and get dressed. We're leaving in ten minutes."

It had been closer to thirty minutes, and Mia was still steaming. The van had taken forever to warm up and they had to wait for the shuddering heat to clear the iced-over windows. Christina sat dozing in the passenger seat. Mia parked the van in the back lot at the Lodge. Turning off the engine, she shook the girl's arm. "We're here."

Christina blinked, then opened her door, climbed out, and stretched, "Maybe I could be a night cook somewhere. Then I could sleep later."

Mia sprinted toward the Lodge. "Come on, it's not that early."

She found James and Trent at a table in the dining room, an assortment of muffins, and a carafe of coffee staged on the table between them. She pulled out a piece of paper and a pen to start prep work. "Sorry, we're late."

"No worries. Have breakfast with us. I baked huckle-berry muffins this morning." James pointed to the two extra chairs."

"Man!" Christina fell into a chair and pulled off her parka. "We didn't have time for breakfast."

Mia slipped the prep sheet back into her purse. She glanced at the oversize clock on the dining-room wall. "I guess we can sit for a few minutes."

"There you go. City girl can learn a lesson." Trent handed her a filled cup. The warm, dark smell was comforting.

"Thanks. And thanks for getting the steaks. I'm assuming they look good?"

Trent frowned at her. "No shop talk at the breakfast table. Who raised you? Wolves?"

Christina laughed as she buttered a still-warm muffin. "She's always been this way. When she lived with my brother the first and the last thing they talked about each day was the catering schedule. I don't think the two of them said one sentence that didn't relate to food in some way."

"That's not true," Mia sputtered. "We talked about a lot of things besides food."

"Like remodeling the house?" Christina offered.

"Yeah, like that." Mia broke open her muffin, smearing a light coating of butter on the inside. Was Christina's memory more accurate than her own? Had she and Isaac turned into the work couple so soon? Or had it always been about the job? Mia's musing broke when Fredrick burst into the dining room.

The decorator scanned the room, and then his gaze landed on Mia. His eyes wide, he ran to their table. He carried a basket of apples and they fell out onto the floor as he ran.

"Oh. My. God." Fredrick's breathing was heavy. He pulled over an extra chair and fell rather than sat down. He shoved the basket onto the table in front of him. "Oh. My. God," he repeated. The man's entire body shook.

"What's the matter?" Mia's imagination went wild. The flowers were the wrong tone. The ballroom needed repainting. Or the tablecloths were that pink color Helen Marcum adored. The one thing she didn't imagine was what Fredrick actually said next.

The decorator put his hands on the table to steady himself. Then he glanced around the table, his voice low and quiet. "Adele Simpson is dead in the ballroom."

CHAPTER 3

The police had cordoned off the ballroom with yellow tape. Lodge guests were diverted to the far entrance of the dining room, where a breakfast buffet had been hastily pulled together. Officers wanted to talk to the staff on-site sooner rather than later. Mia pulled on an apron and, with Christina by her side, went to the kitchen, helping the line cooks get the meal ready.

That was the thing about working a kitchen; no matter what, people had to be fed.

She'd finished the last batch of scrambled eggs and Christina was working on cutting up a fourth bin of fruit when James returned to the kitchen. "Thanks for helping out." He leaned against the cooler door, his face ashen. "I can't believe she's dead. I mean, yeah, she was old, but why couldn't she be normal and die in her sleep? Somewhere besides my dining room."

"Probably measuring the table height or counting the threads in the tablecloths." Mia wiped her hands on her apron and came around to the front of the kitchen. "You know Adele; she left everything to the professionals until it didn't meet her expectations."

James barked out a short laugh. "You're probably right. I bet she decided the colors of the candles didn't match the napkins and had a massive stroke thinking about the shame the decorations would bring on her family."

"Might be true, but so not funny." Mia smiled at the chef. She'd enjoyed cooking next to James's staff. He'd trained them well.

"Then why are you smiling?" He stepped closer and patted her arm. "Seriously, you were a lifesaver. They wouldn't let the rest of my kitchen staff in until the investigation is over, so I would have been screwed. We're full up with guests this weekend. Most of them are attending the birthday bash tonight."

"*Were* attending the party," Mia corrected. "I don't think it would be in good taste to celebrate her birthday on the same day she died."

"On the day she was murdered," a male voice corrected her.

She turned to see Officer Baldwin standing in the kitchen.

"Funny the two of you are here," he added, pointing a glance at Christina.

Mia fumed. The guy didn't like Christina and she'd done nothing wrong. "Not funny at all. Adele hired me to cater her birthday party tonight. We arrived at about nine fifteen this morning to finish prep. Ask James."

The chef shuffled his feet. "Nine thirty, actually."

She shot him a glare. "Fine, we overslept. Nine thirty."

"I just wanted to be accurate. You don't have to bite my head off," James mumbled.

"I'd like to talk to you." Officer Baldwin pointed at Christina. "Now."

Christina shot Mia a look of pure fear. "I'm working," she stuttered, holding up the piece of fruit and knife, as if to prove her point.

Mia reached back to untie her apron. "Can I at least be with her? She's just a kid." Officer Baldwin had been watching Christina since she showed up at the bus stop a few months ago, first trying to arrest her for loitering, then dropping her off on Mia's front door with a warning that the Magic Springs Police Force wasn't a taxi service. The man had it in for the teenager. He wouldn't make this interview pleasant.

Officer Baldwin looked at her for a few long seconds. "Sorry, you haven't been questioned. I can't have her answers leading you to say something to uphold her story."

Trent's voice cut into the discussion. "You've questioned me already. I'll sit with her."

Relief flowed through Mia's body. At least she wouldn't be alone with the cop who hated her. She glanced at Christina. "Trent will go with you, okay? And then I'll talk to the nice officer and we'll get out of here." She shot Baldwin a look with her words, hoping he'd take her warning to be at least professional if not nice.

Christina looked like a scared rabbit. Mia prayed Christina wouldn't say or do anything foolish, like run, but, finally, she nodded and laid the chef knife on the cutting board. Mia hadn't noticed she'd been gripping the knife like a weapon until she saw the release. Apparently, Officer Baldwin had, however, because now he moved his hand away from the gun on his belt. Seriously, this man needed to get laid or something so he wouldn't be this jumpy. Christina wouldn't hurt a fly and he treated her like public enemy number one.

Trent put his arm around Christina and nodded to Mia. "We'll be right back."

Mia poured coffee and followed them out of the kitchen. She chose a seat where she could watch the door to the makeshift interview room. She saw another man standing in the hallway, and he'd nodded to Baldwin when he entered the room with Christina.

James sat next to her, his coffee cup in hand. And he'd brought a carafe of the stuff. She nodded to the third man. "Who's that?"

"Sheriff Cook. He's here, technically, as an adviser to the police, but everyone knows he runs both the Blaine County office and Magic Springs. Hell, I wouldn't doubt if he had pull in most of the little towns around here. Except Sun Valley. Those guys can't stand him, and they have the money to keep him out of their investigations."

Mia shivered suddenly.

"You cold? I can get a chef jacket from the supply cabinet." James looked at her, worry in his gaze. "It might be shock. You haven't had the best of mornings."

Mia shook her head and sipped her coffee. The liquid warmed her throat, easing her jitters. "I'm fine. I guess I'm just realizing Adele's dead." The face of someone who wouldn't be fine crossed her mind. "Oh no. Grans."

Mia leaned back and closed her eyes. Her grandmother would be heartbroken at the loss of her friend. No matter what kind of pill Adele had been to most of the world, she'd also been Grans's best friend.

James nodded. "I hope you don't mind, but I've already called her. She wanted to come here to be with you. The police aren't letting anyone into the Lodge, so I told her she might as well stay put. She said she'll meet you at the school when you're done."

"Probably with a kitchen filled with food." Mia thought about the years she'd lived with her grandmother. The hours spent in the kitchen cooking and talking. "Grans's response to any adversity is cooking. I guess we're a lot alike that way."

James smiled and sipped his coffee. "We all have our coping mechanisms. For me, it's hiking. Rain, snow, summer heat, doesn't matter. If something's bothering me, you'll find me on the trails. Last year, when I had to deal with the fallout from Adele's party, I took a week and flew to the Grand Canyon. I had to buy new walking shoes after that."

"I hear it's beautiful. I've always wanted to go." Mia watched as the door opened. Christina walked out of the room, her face white. Mia stood to meet her, but she spun left and headed to the restroom.

She cornered Trent. "What happened? Why is she upset?"

Baldwin stepped in front of Trent, blocking Mia from Christina. "Not yet. You need to give your statement."

Mia raised her eyebrows. "You better hope I don't find out you were badgering her. I don't know why you're so hard on her."

"I think Miss Adams is the least of your concerns. This way." Baldwin motioned to the open door.

"Fine, then after this, we're leaving." She glanced back over her shoulder at Trent. "Tell Christina I'll be right out."

Trent nodded. But before the door closed on the dining

room, Mia thought she saw an emotion flash in his eyes. Pity? Worry? She sighed, then walked over and sat at the one table in the tan room. The hotel used it as a small conference room. There wasn't much in the room except for a built-in counter where food or beverages could be set up and a small lectern. Mia quickly calculated that the room would comfortably seat ten, maybe fifteen, depending on the table arrangements. Smiling to herself, she wondered if she'd ever lose the caterer mentality.

Baldwin cleared his throat and she focused her attention back on the matter at hand.

"So, what do you want to know?" She leaned back in her chair, suddenly tired from all the prep work and then the craziness of the morning.

"Let's start with where you were last night at about eleven." Baldwin's brown eyes seemed to drill into her.

"What? You think I had something to do with this?" The blood pumped in her ears, causing her to sit forward, not sure she'd heard him right. "Are you sure Adele was murdered? Maybe she just had a heart attack or passed because she was old. Old people die."

Baldwin smirked. "The county coroner hasn't made a formal determination, but it's pretty clear she didn't stick a knife into her own chest."

Mia gasped. "Adele was stabbed?" She sank back into her chair. "Who would want to kill Adele? Okay, well, maybe anyone she'd ever talked to, but just because the woman could be aggravating."

Baldwin leaned forward. "You found Mrs. Simpson aggravating?"

"Had you ever met her?" Mia looked at the police officer across from her. *Shut up, Mia. You didn't kill her; stop giving him rope to hang you.*

"Interesting." Baldwin slowly wrote in his notebook. "Now, please answer my question. Where were you at eleven last night?"

"I don't know. Asleep?"

"Miss Adams said she got up to go to the bathroom and your bedroom door was open and your bed was empty." He read the information off his notebook. "So where were you?"

Mia thought about last night. She'd gone to bed about ten, the same time as Christina, but then she couldn't sleep. She'd never slept well before a big catering assignment—too many things running through her mind, lists to write down, and supplies to check—and last night had been no exception. This party would have been the calling card getting Mia's Morsels into the homes of the Magic Springs elite. She'd been worried about the change in menu and had run downstairs to check a recipe from her cookbook, making sure she'd ordered all the seasonings she'd needed.

Then she'd pulled on her snow boots and a coat and left for a walk around the park next to the school grounds. Alone.

"I went out for a walk," Mia admitted.

Baldwin's eyebrows rose. "The temperature dropped to twenty-two last night. You decided to take a stroll?"

"I bundled up. And I didn't stay out long." Mia sighed, picking up a pen from the table and twisting it in one hand. "I worry before big events. I'm always thinking about what could go wrong and trying to make sure I prepare for everything. I'm a caterer. That's what we do."

Baldwin didn't answer; he just watched her for a long moment. Mia didn't break the silence. She hadn't done anything wrong and he wasn't going to make her feel like she had.

"Well, everything besides my client winding up dead under the head table," she admitted. Her first real catering gig on her own, and now Mia's Morsels was in jeopardy. This needed to be cleared up and put behind her so she could start fresh. Again. She realized Baldwin hadn't said anything while she mused about her infant company's demise, just watched her. According to the cop shows she watched on television, giving the suspect time to squirm in silence was always their trip up. People couldn't stay silent. Well, she could. Because she didn't have anything to say about Adele's death.

Finally Baldwin stood. "You're free to go; just don't leave town."

Mia laughed, his words catching her off guard. So typical of the old cop shows on television. She'd been right about the silent treatment. The guy took his investigation skills from the boob tube. Adele's killer would never be found if Baldwin was in charge of the investigation.

He cocked his head, his face turning a bright red. "You find me funny?"

"You've seen the building I bought? I've got tons of work to do before I can even think about opening. Where do you think I'll go? Cancun?" She thought about John Louis's card sitting on her desk in her study. She'd almost thrown it away. But it was an out. He'd buy the building and give her enough to start over somewhere else. And as much as she'd blustered about not selling last night, well, that was before this had happened this morning. She pushed aside the thought of letting the weasel win and felt anger bubble up inside her.

"We take murder seriously around here, Miss Malone." Baldwin tapped his pen on his little black notebook. "And somehow you're always in the middle of things when bodies are found lately."

"I'm not a killer. But I am glad to hear you take this seriously. Just go find the murderer and leave me alone." Mia spun around and headed to the door.

"I'm watching you," Baldwin called after her.

Mia headed to the table where she'd left her coat and purse. "I'm in a bad made-for-television movie." She caught Christina's gaze and barked at her. "Let's get out of here."

Christina flushed and grabbed her coat, following Mia through the dining room.

When they reached the hallway Trent caught the pair. He put his hand on her arm, stopping her. "Hey, what happened in there? Are you okay?"

Tears stung the back of her eyes, but she wouldn't cry. Not here, not in front of this man. "Your police force is a joke. They think I murdered Adele."

Trent pulled her into an awkward hug and Mia let him. She didn't know why, but she wanted comfort from this man. Someone to whisper in her ear that everything would be all right, even if they both knew it was total bullcrap. Hell, right now she'd take a hug from the devil himself, or Isaac, whichever demon showed up first. She felt her breath slow and the tears back off. She inhaled one last deep breath, stepping away from the extremely hard and comforting chest she'd been leaning on.

"Thanks. I don't know . . ." Mia started.

"It's been a long day." Trent pushed a wayward curl out of her face.

"And it's only noon." Mia smiled. "I'm heading home. I don't want to leave Grans alone more than I already have."

"I'll stop by later." Trent turned back to the dining room, and Christina stepped toward her.

"I'm sorry I said you were gone. I should have lied and said I saw you in the kitchen." Christina looked like a puppy who'd been beaten for chewing a hole in the carpet.

"You told the truth. I'd gone for a walk. If you'd lied, they would have found out." Mia pulled Christina into a hug. "We'll get through this. Honesty is always the right path."

Mia felt Christina's body stiffen under her hug. Maybe she had pushed her too far with the touch. She had a large personal space bubble, especially since her return from Vegas. Not for the first time, Mia wondered what really had happened to send this happy young woman running home and away from her dream of dancing. Mia stepped away, and after seeing the tears flowing off Christina's face, she pulled out a tissue from her purse. "No tears. Seriously, we'll get through this. They can't charge me for something I didn't do."

The two walked out of the hotel and headed to Mia's van. When Mia clicked the doors open she heard Christina mutter, "The cops can do anything they want. They never listen to the truth."

CHAPTER 4

Grans swung open the big wooden door as soon as Mia and Christina started up the walkway. Mia wondered who'd called to let her know they were on their way; probably James. Caring for the town and its residents seemed to be as important to James as feeding their bodies. The guy was all heart. Maybe that was why he'd relocated to a small town where his culinary talents would be overlooked. She was convinced the guy could be head chef at any of the swank California stops, if not running his own restaurant. *Stop analyzing; people find joy in different things*, she reminded herself.

"Get in here, the snow's about to start again," Grans called from the doorway. "I don't know what Mark Baldwin was thinking, keeping you all over at the Lodge for so long. It's not like either one of you killed poor Adele."

Mia paused in the entryway and sat on the wooden

bench she'd bought from a local craftsman. She pulled off her snow boots and parka, uncoiling the cable-knit scarf Grans had given her for Christmas. She slipped on ballet slippers she kept in a basket by the door. Finally free of her outdoor gear, she pulled her grandmother into a hug. "I'm so, so sorry about Adele. I know you loved her."

Mia could hear Grans sniff. She let the hug continue until she felt her grandmother's squeeze and then stood back.

Grans wiped at her eyes with a tissue she pulled out of a sweater pocket. "Adele was my best friend for over sixty years. I know she could be difficult, and most people only saw that side of her. But she never turned her back on me, no matter what mistakes I made, including stealing her date one night after the apple festival." Grans smiled. "When I dumped him the next week we both realized he wasn't worth the fight."

Christina had slipped off her coat and shoes and stood next to her and Grans. "I'm sorry about your friend."

"Thank you, Christina. I've got lunch ready upstairs in the kitchen. The church is holding a gathering later this evening for those wanting to express their condolences. I guess I'm the closest thing Adele had to family."

They started to walk up to the kitchen. Mia stopped. "There's a nephew."

"What are you talking about?" Grans paused on the stairs. "Adele didn't have family."

"But she did. When the two of you stopped by yesterday morning she said her nephew, Will or Bill, was coming to the party with a guest." Mia looked at her grandmother. "You didn't hear her?"

"I must have been in a zone, dear. In all the years I knew Adele, she never once told me about a nephew. Her only sister died in the eighties, somewhere around the same time that space rocket blew up."

"You mean *Challenger*?" Mia asked as the three women continued their walk up the second flight of stairs.

"That was the one. Adele refused to fly to Arizona for the funeral because she didn't trust airplanes after that. She wanted me to drive there with her. Could you see the two of us driving that far? I told her she should just buck it up and take the plane." Grans paused at the top of the stairs, her breathing labored.

"Are you okay?" Mia lowered her voice. No need to upset Christina even more. She looked positively scared to death. Growing up, Christina's family had kept the baby of the family pretty sheltered. This was probably the first time she'd known someone who died. Or at least was murdered with a knife. Not for the first time, she wondered what Baldwin had said to her. She'd have to ask Trent how graphic the cop got during Christina's interview.

"Too many trips up and down these stairs this morning. I know you love your new home, but now you know why I love my ranch. I did stairs as a kid. Your great-grandmother's house was a two-story with all the kids' bedrooms stuck at the top. My brother claimed the attic. Even then, I would rather have slept on the ground floor." They walked into the apartment and the smell of fresh-baked bread surrounded them. "I made a potato and sausage cream soup to go with the bread."

Mia's stomach growled and she realized she hadn't eaten since the half of a muffin before Fredrick found Adele. In the next moment her throat constricted. Poor Adele.

The trio headed to the kitchen, where Grans ladled

soup into bowls and Mia cut the fresh bread. They ate in silence, each one lost in their own thoughts. As soon as Christina had finished, she stood, took her bowl to the sink, and turned to Mia. "Can I go to my room?"

Mia nodded. "You don't have to ask; you're a grown woman."

Christina offered a weak smile. "Old habits. But I did want to make sure you didn't need me for something. I mean, we were supposed to be catering a dinner."

"Go get some rest. I'd like you to come with us to the gathering tonight." Mia offered a warmer smile to the young girl.

"Sure, whatever." Christina left the kitchen after giving Grans a quick buss on the cheek.

As soon as she'd left, Mia felt the call from her kitchen witch, Gloria. The doll's power surrounded her, and Mia felt the tendrils of power easing her grief and pain. Being a kitchen witch had its advantages, especially when you were troubled. Your familiar knew how to make your emotions settle. Kitchen witches had been healers from the early days, using herbs and spells to ease the pain of their neighbors. Until the season when the crops died from lack of rain; then, if the woman didn't disappear, her formerly thankful neighbors would turn and blame nature's flaws on her. No wonder the coven had gone underground, become a secret passed from generation to generation.

"She's worried about you." Grans smiled as she watched the healing. "Gloria doesn't like to see you upset."

Mia stretched, letting the tension flow away from her body. "Thanks, Gloria." Then she opened her eyes and let her mind wander. The power in the room dissipated and the little rag doll on the windowsill became just a doll again.

After Gloria's healing, Mia sat thinking, her soup cooling in the bowl, forgotten. This event should have been the announcement for the new business. Now, not only did she have thirty squab sitting frozen in her freezer, she'd also have thirty porterhouse steaks waiting for a party that wouldn't happen. An idea began to form. She looked at her grandmother.

"What time is the reception at the church?"

"Six thirty, but I wouldn't call it a reception. Most of the town will be there, paying their respects to Adele, I guess. Maybe I'll get to meet this nephew of hers." Grans looked at her, curious. "Why?"

"I have a lot of food that's going to go to waste because of the party. Why don't we cater some appetizers for the gathering? We could cook here and then drive everything over to the church by six." Mia smiled. "It's the least we can do for Adele. Besides, I'm charging her estate for the food."

Her grandmother shook her head, laughing. "Sometimes you need to just stop talking when you're ahead."

"I didn't mean to make light of the situation, but there's always food at wakes, right?" Mia looked at her grandmother. Cooking would help her feel needed and just a bit less lonely.

"I think it's a grand idea. Give James a call and have him deliver all that prep over here. We'll have to work on adjusting your menu from a sit-down dinner to appetizers, but Adele would love the fact that we weren't wasting the food. The woman had a touch of the miser in her."

"You call James, I'll go get Christina. I guess she was right, we do need her." Mia kissed her grandmother on the head as she left the room.

As Mia walked up to Christina's door, she could hear

the girl's muffled voice. Mia knocked on the door before she opened it a crack. Christina sat on the bed, her cell held to her ear. When she saw Mia, she flushed.

"I gotta go," Christina muttered into the phone and, without waiting for a response, hung up.

"You didn't need to end your conversation." Mia stepped into the guest room, which had become Christina central. She'd put up posters all over the wall—musicals, old and new. Mia wondered if Magic Springs still had the summer theater, maybe if Christina was still here in June? She shook her head: unlikely.

"That's okay." Christina bounced off the bed, her blond hair flying around her. "What's up?"

"Grans and I are doing appetizers for the gathering tonight. You want to help?"

Christina's eyes brightened. "Sure. Just let me get changed. I'll be right there."

Mia stepped out of the room and paused. Had Christina been talking to Isaac? Was that why she'd hung up so quickly? *It's not all about you*, Grans's voice echoed in her head. But this time Mia wasn't sure her gut feeling wasn't spot-on.

Four hours later, they were ready, the food stored either in the oven to stay warm, or in warmer trays, or tucked inside the industrial-size refrigerator Mia had ordered as soon as she'd known she'd won the bidding for the old school. Christina had driven Grans back to her house to change, and when they came back the trio would load up the food and carefully drive to the church.

James had corralled serving staff from the Lodge for the event. Once they'd arrived at the destination with the food, Mia, Christina, and Grans had been shooed out of the kitchen and into the multipurpose room behind the chapel. Long tables were set up at the sides for coffee, along with whatever food was brought by the visiting guests. In the middle of the room round tables were set, allowing guests to mingle or sit and watch as mourners entered.

Mia leaned over to her grandmother and whispered, "Too bad Adele couldn't have been here tonight, she would have loved *this* show."

Grans swatted her on the arm, but a grin tickled her lips. Grans left them and walked over to the first table and started greeting old friends. Mia stayed back with Christina. She cleaned up well, she had to admit. Mia had loaned her one of the several little black dresses she'd kept on hand for a variety of occasions. Mia walked with her to the coffee table. "I need some caffeine if I'm going to get through an hour of this, much less three."

Christina laughed, the sound ringing clear over the hushed tones of conversation and the string quartet that played classical music in the corner. She slapped a hand over her mouth, embarrassed. "Sorry."

Mia rubbed her arm. "Never apologize for real laughter. People take themselves way too seriously most of the time."

"Yeah, like Isaac?" Christina poured a cup of coffee from the urn and handed it to Mia. "I never knew what you saw in my stupid brother. You were way too good for him."

"Thanks, I think." Mia sipped the coffee, appraising her sous chef. "You look amazing in that dress, by the way. I may just have to give it to you."

Christina blushed. "You don't have to do that. It's too

much." She smiled as she ran her hand over the taffeta fabric, clearly in love with the way the dress felt.

"The dress looks like it was made for you. I never quite felt right wearing it, so the poor thing stayed in my closet. You know how some pieces just don't feel right? You'd be doing me a favor taking it off my hands. That way I can go shopping for a new dress." Mia pointed to an empty table. "Let's go sit before all the tables are gone. I don't know how long I can stand in these heels."

They wandered over to a table and were soon joined by Grans. She eyed their coffee.

Christina got the hint and stood. "Black?"

"Oh, dear, that would be lovely." Grans smiled at her until she turned away. "Someday I'll learn to wear flats to things like this. My dogs are already barking and I've only been to half the room."

"I can't help you. I wore stilettos myself." Mia nodded to the last table Grans had visited. The man had looked familiar, but Mia couldn't place him. "Who were you talking to over there?"

"Oh, that's Sheriff Cook and his wife, Mary. Nice couple. They've lived in the area going on forty years."

"So they're new to Magic Springs." Mia sipped her coffee. James had mentioned that the sheriff had a lot more power in the small community than he should have. Maybe he would find Adele's killer, getting Mia out from under Baldwin's suspicious gaze. She took a deep, cleansing breath. She wouldn't let herself get worked up over something she had no control over. Time for a little sage cleansing when she got home.

"Don't be snide, Mia, it doesn't suit you." Grans nodded to the table over to the left of theirs. "Now, Charity and Randy Graham, they're new. Just this last year. Another retirement couple. I swear, we're all going to die of heart failure one day because there won't be anyone under sixty to drive the ambulance."

"The town isn't aging that fast, is it?" Mia frowned. Businesses went under when towns died. Especially without an influx of young families to keep the town growing and healthy.

"Maybe it just seems that way. The new doctor and his wife are your age. He just opened his practice here, focusing on sports medicine, and I guess he gets a lot of referrals from the ski lodges, as well as the golf courses in the summer." Grans pointed to a distinguished-looking man standing next to a stunning blonde. She focused her gaze on the bar where a woman stood alone, her black dress tight and her heels just a bit too high for a solemn occasion like Adele's wake "And Angel there is looking for husband number three. Although I don't know why. The last one left her rich enough to live comfortably anywhere."

"Too bad I didn't bring my business cards." Mia glanced around the room, studying the faces. Her prime target market was either sitting in this room or knew the people sitting in this room.

"I already handled that little problem."

A stab of fear entered Mia's thoughts. "Grans, what did you do?"

Christina returned, setting the white china cup in front of Grans. James had brought out the chapel's good china for the event. No Styrofoam cups for Adele's wake. "What are you guys talking about?"

Grans took a long sip before she answered. "I asked Fredrick to make sure that when he set up the flowers he left your card on each table. You are basically sponsoring this by providing most of the food." She glanced at the dessert table, filled with cakes and cookies community members had donated. "Or at least the edible food."

Christina agreed. "I had a cookie from that table. Totally gross."

"You two are awful." Mia reached out and grabbed her business card from the centerpiece. She couldn't believe she hadn't noticed it before. Tacky to advertise at a funeral. Or a wake. Or whatever.

"Mary Alice, you must introduce me to your granddaughter." A woman stood by the table, staring at Mia. Her shocking red hair was obviously a dye job and she wore a tight blue silk dress, the boat-neck collar sporting a too-large strand of pearls.

Grans rolled her eyes before she turned to greet the newcomer. "Oh, Helen, I'm glad you could come tonight. I worried you might still be back East."

"That was last month. We had to close up the Chicago house. You know you have to keep an eye on the help, otherwise they'll walk off with everything." Helen shrugged. "Adele taught me that lesson. She said never trust anyone you haven't completely vetted."

Grans face paled at the mention of her friend. "She was strong-minded."

Helen's hand flew up to her mouth. "Oh, my, I just don't think sometimes. I'm sorry for your loss. I know the two of you were good friends."

"Thank you. That means a lot to me."

Helen patted Grans, looking more like she was dusting off her back than offering a gesture of real condolence. Helen's face brightened. "I know. I can take Adele's place in your doubles tennis team. I'm very good, you know. Maybe we can run the charity auction together next month. It will be such fun."

Mia couldn't believe the nerve of the woman. Grans's friend had just died and this woman wanted to take Adele's spot?

"That won't be necessary," Grans's voice sounded like iron, cold and flat. "But thank you for offering so graciously."

"You poor dear, you're in grief and I'm sitting here talking about tennis." The woman patted Grans's hand again, then seemed to notice my presence. She shoved a hand near me. "Helen Marcum. I tell you, my husband is desperate for you to open. He says my cooking is atrocious. What can I say? I wasn't a Betty Crocker, stay-at-home housewife. I had a real job."

"Nice to know I'll have at least one customer." Mia shook the clammy, soft hand.

"Oh, no, dear. You'll have so many customers you won't know what hit you. Everyone I've talked to loves the idea of not cooking. There's talk that many of the ladies are giving away their cookware, just to make sure their husbands get the hint."

Mia couldn't help it; she grinned.

"I heard you found the body?" Helen's words removed the grin and caused Mia's stomach to clench.

Frowning, she shook her head. "No. Where did you hear that?"

"Oh, you know, gossip. Never can trust it." Helen's attention was diverted as a woman's tinkling laugh floated across the room. Her face hardened as she watched a man brush back blond hair from the shoulder of Angel, the woman Grans had pointed out earlier, calling the shapely woman the next trophy wife. "I'd better go rescue Travis. Nice to meet you."

The woman scurried away toward the couple. When

he looked up and saw Helen barreling toward them, the smile on his face vanished. Mia watched him whisper something to the blonde, then Hurricane Helen was on them and the other woman quickly disappeared.

He's in trouble. The marital disagreements between Helen and her husband seemed to overwhelm the room, black wisps of smoke probably only she and Grans could see.

A noise came from the back of the room. Raised voices broke through the music and the conversation stopped, with everyone listening to the strands of loud words from the hallway. All Mia could hear was phrases like, "my aunt deserved . . ." and then, "I'm just going to talk . . ."

The tone and pitch of the voice made her very glad that whoever was in the hallway, at least they didn't want to talk to her. She looked over at the next table and saw John Louis. He raised his cup like a toast when he saw he had her attention. She noticed a woman dressed in what must have been a Chanel suit standing next to him, her eyes downcast. She guessed there *was* a Mrs. Louis. And as she'd predicted, the wife looked more like a whipped pup than the spouse of a successful real estate broker. Black smoke flowed between the two of them as well. *Not my problem.*

Mia turned her attention to Grans. "How long do you want to stay?" She took a sip of her coffee.

Grans didn't respond. Her eyes were focused on something in the back of the room. Mia turned to see a man walking toward them. Or at least what Mia thought was a man. The way the day had gone, a Greek god coming down from Olympus wouldn't have shocked her any more than what had already happened. "Earth to Grans, how long are we staying?"

"Until I have a few words with you," a male voice from behind her snarled. Mia looked up into the man's face. The chiseled lines, the deep blue, almost purple eyes, and the scowl that made it all seem more attractive, not less.

"I'm sorry, who are you?"

"William Danforth the third. You are Mia Malone?"

She sighed. Getting out of this wake wasn't going to be easy. Then she felt guilty about rushing her grandmother. Putting on a smile, she answered, "Yes. How can I help you?"

"I want to know why you killed my aunt." The man's voice rose louder, and the murmured conversations that had been floating in the large gym stopped. Even the band seemed to be on break at the moment.

"I'm sorry?" Mia felt trapped, confused, and scared all rolled up together. The man continued to stare at her, and now Mia realized he was older than he looked, probably in his sixties, but the dye job on his hair kept the gray just a salting of the color rather than the predominant strain. "I had nothing to do with Adele's death."

"That's not what I'm hearing. John said you didn't like her. And then she comes up dead? What are the chances?" The man tapped his finger on the table, stepping closer. "I didn't much care for the old broad myself, but that doesn't give anyone the right to kill her."

John, of course. Mia's gut twisted as she looked at the now-smiling broker at the next table. He'd said he'd make her regret buying the place. Apparently, he'd gotten the ear of Adele's nephew pretty fast. If this total stranger thought she killed Adele, how many others in the room thought the same thing? How many more people had John's poison words reached? If she became involved in the investigation, she might as well kiss her business goodbye. Small towns had long memories, and even if the police force cleared her, she'd be suspect number one until the real killer was found. She glanced over at Grans, whose face had gone white.

"Look, I don't know what John's been saying, but I didn't kill your aunt." Mia stopped; she'd been about to say she had kind of liked Adele, but lying was lying, either in court or out, and she knew she'd be caught in that one.

"You're not getting away with this." William Danforth stepped closer, towering over Mia. She felt suffocated by his presence and his Brut cologne. Mia hadn't known anyone who wore Brut since her grandfather had died, twenty years ago. But now, instead of inflicting good memories, the scent cloyed, making her thoughts fuzzy.

All of a sudden, she could breathe. She put her head in her hands and leaned toward the floor, taking in deep breaths of clean air. Lifting up her head, she saw Trent looking at her with concern. "You okay," he asked.

When she nodded he turned back to Danforth, who had been pulled away from the table and now stood between two of the waiters, both holding tightly to one of Danford's arms. Trent put up his hand, trying to calm the man. "Look, I know you're upset, but if you can't act like a human, you're going to have to leave."

"You probably helped her kill Aunt Adele," Danforth accused, his eyes wide and one of his hands already balled into a fist. No doubt about it, Mia's first catered event was going to turn into a fight.

"That's enough." Officer Baldwin appeared beside the table. "Trent's right, it's time for you to leave."

The man glared at the men standing in between him

and Mia, catching her eye. "I'll leave, but this isn't over, missy, not at all." He struggled free of his restraints, straightened his shoulders, and ran his fingers over his jacket. Happy with his new, free condition, he glared at Mia. "I'll make you pay."

Officer Baldwin walked with Danforth as he left the room, the man shrugging off the police officer's hand on his arm. He pushed through the door, slamming it against the outside wall. Mia flinched at the bang. Baldwin followed him out of the building, and so did a short, petite redhead. She still wore a fur coat, and a bright red dress peeked out from under the coat, the bottom half of her long legs covered in knee-high hooker boots. Mia watched the procession, dumbfounded.

"What the heck just happened?" Grans asked.

"I think our friend John Louis has been riling him up, telling him stuff that isn't true." Mia stood, ready to give the other man a piece of her mind. Trent grabbed her arm and lowered her back into her chair. She spun toward him. "What?"

He didn't release her arm as he leaned closer, lowering his voice. "You need to stay away from that guy. Him and this William Danforth. He seriously has it in for you."

"Trent, he's telling people I killed Adele." Mia slumped in her chair. "And people are listening to him. This nephew thinks I killed her. Can you believe that?"

Trent pulled a chair up to the table from another grouping. He leaned on the back, watching her face. Concern filled his face when he answered her. "John's not the only one."

CHAPTER 5

Mia turned over again, glancing at the clock. An hour had passed since she'd gone to bed and she wasn't any closer to sleep than she'd been when she'd climbed out of her morning shower. Trent's words kept rolling around in her head. She'd sunk every last dime of her savings into the purchase of the old school. She'd negotiated a business loan with the local bank to complete the restoration, and now everything could be taken away. Especially if she was known as the business owner more likely to kill than provide a warm meal at the end of the day. Sunny yellow walls or not, she'd lose everything.

Sighing, she threw back the covers and reached for her robe. No use just lying there. She padded barefoot to the kitchen. Tonight she'd forgo the sleeping spell and ease her insomnia the old-fashioned way, by cooking. Opening the door to the refrigerator, she reached for peppers, sausage, and mushrooms. She pulled out the loaf of bread she'd bought from the local bakery a few days before. *Just stale enough*, she thought as she squeezed the crusty loaf.

She moved through her prep work—the mise en place, as her culinary school teacher had called it—without thinking. Finishing chopping the peppers, she started chopping an onion to add to the mix. Once everything was prepped, she flipped on the gas stove and sautéed the veggies, slowly crumbling the sausage into the pan. The kitchen smelled wonderful. She flipped on a second burner under the teakettle. Brewing coffee would only keep her awake longer. A nice cup of cinnamon apple tea, however, might slow her racing mind. And she might, just might, get back to sleep tonight.

She sat at the butcher-block table and pulled out the notebook she used to plan recipes. This breakfast strata would be a nice addition to the weekend menu. In fact, she could do it as a welcome gift for first-time clients. Purchase a dinner for four, get breakfast free. And the strata could make use of the day-old bread that always seemed to accumulate in a kitchen. She could make them in batches and freeze them for future sales.

She added the idea to a list for Christina for menu development. She had amazing graphic art skills. Roxanne Adams had been wrong to steer her daughter toward a business degree. Christina might not be able to make it as a dancer, but Mia knew with her artistic ability and marketing savvy, she'd be amazing in advertising or design. Even untrained, Christina was twice as good as the account executive hired by her ex-employer when they redesigned the menus.

Thinking of Christina made her glance toward the direction of the bedrooms and the hidden safe that held her cookbook. Isaac had insisted he owned the recipes she'd developed for the catering section of the hotel's business. Converting recipes to feed a larger group had been a challenge. But soon it had come naturally. Grans always said she still cooked for a large family, even though she'd been living alone for close to thirty years.

As if she'd been called by Mia's thoughts, Christina showed up at the kitchen door. "It smells amazing in here. Want some company?"

Mia smiled at her houseguest turned roommate. "I'd love some." She stood and removed the whistling kettle from the burner. "I hope I didn't wake you."

Christina shrugged. "I couldn't sleep. I feel bad about what I told the police. And then that jerk at the wake. Why would anyone suspect you?"

Mia laughed and poured steaming water over two cups with tea bags already in place. She turned off the stove under the cooked meat and veggies, setting it aside to cool before finishing the strata. "People around here know anyone who worked with Adele for longer than a day would want to kill her. But that also works in my favor, because the list of people who hated her is pretty long. I probably overreacted a bit when Baldwin questioned me. He has to question everyone, right?"

"Still, if I hadn't gotten up and seen you gone last night, they never would have questioned you." Christina took the offered cup and played with the tea bag, pulling it up and down. Isaac used to do the same thing, unwilling to wait for the water's heat to do the magic.

"There's a saying: It's none of my business what others think about me. And because I didn't kill Adele, nothing anyone thinks will convict me. I'll worry about it when there's something to worry about. Right now we need to focus on getting the business up and running before our grand opening. You think you can stay on until then?" Mia glanced at Christina. They hadn't talked about anything past Adele's party. "I'm starting to depend on you. You're amazing with the marketing ideas. I've listed off a few more things for the menu I'd like you to play with."

Christina stood and went to the stove, absently stirring the mixture in the pan. She kept her head turned away from Mia as she spoke. "I'd like to stay. Mom's pushing me to go back to school next semester. She's even talking about summer school."

"You've been talking to Roxanne?" Mia didn't know how she felt about this—betrayed, happy? Something in between?

"Something Grans said a few weeks ago made me call her." Christina turned back from the stove. "You know, when we were talking about family and how they always love you, no matter what?"

Mia remembered the conversation. Christina had told Grans that her mother hated her, especially after she'd left for Vegas. Grans, being the eternal optimist, had told Christina that a mother's love never died, no matter what the child did. Mia hadn't been so sure; she'd met the mother in question. Roxanne Adams could be described as controlling and vicious, but those words would be too gentle for the woman.

"I remember. Grans would be proud to know you took the first step." Mia walked the high road, even though she didn't think a family reunion would be in Christina's best interest. She hoped for the girl's sake her gut feeling was dead wrong.

Christina smiled and sat back at the table. "I was worried you wouldn't like that I called her."

Mia leaned over and fist bumped against Christina's hand to get her attention. "No matter what I think about Isaac and your family, I hope I'll always be a part of your life. I'm here for you, don't forget that."

Christina nodded and sniffed.

"Let's get this strata together and go to bed. Tomorrow we're getting back to renovations and putting this dream of mine in the bag. That way when you leave for summer school, I'll barely miss you." Mia stood and dumped the cooling meat into a colander in the sink. "First we need to drain off the fat from the mixture. Get me one of those large metal bowls."

The next few minutes they worked like they'd been cooking together for years. Mia would miss Christina when she left. And, from what Mia could tell, Christina might just miss the work. She had a knack for creating, and being innovative was a good quality for potential chefs. She put aluminum foil over the baking dish and slipped it into the fridge. By the time they woke up, the strata would be ready to slip into a nice, hot oven and they'd be ready to start a new day.

Mia turned out the lights, slipping downstairs to check the main door locks one more time. With the living quarters on the third floor, a prowler could do a lot of damage downstairs before anyone even noticed. Mr. Darcy silently padded after her, jumping up on the window seat when she went into what would be the kitchen to check the back door.

Certain that the locks were solid, she turned out the downstairs lights and went back to where she'd left Mr.

Darcy. The cat had already abandoned his post. "Here, kitty, kitty," she called. No responding meow.

She checked the downstairs rooms that had their doors open. No cat. Shaking her head, she glanced up the stairs. The feline had probably returned to curl up on Christina's bed. Mia went up the stairs, shut the apartment door, and went straight to her room.

This time when she slipped between the sheets sleep found her and she drifted off into a dreamless state.

The insistent buzz of her alarm clock woke her promptly at seven the next morning. Late, compared to her usual start time, but early for her body, which objected to the lack of her normal eight hours. She slipped on her robe and slippers and headed to the kitchen to put the sausage strata in the oven and start coffee.

As she walked through the living room, a scratch sounded at the apartment door. She unlocked the door and Mr. Darcy ran in, heading to Christina's bedroom.

Mia watched the cat paw open the door. Where had he been? She'd looked through all the downstairs rooms without finding him. She glanced at the apartment door as she gently closed it. Maybe she'd have to put in a pet door. She hated to think of him wandering the downstairs all night.

In the kitchen she turned on the oven. Going through the rote motions of making coffee, Mia's mind puzzled over the cat's whereabouts. He must have found one of the second-story-room doors open. Mia would have to make sure to walk through nightly and close up all the doors. Especially when the construction guys started next week.

Satisfied she'd solved the mystery, she sat at the table

with her cup of coffee and started making out a list. They'd delivered a large dumpster on Friday. Today, she'd finish cleaning up the trash from the first floor, and by the end of the weekend all the painting would be done and dry. She'd added another twenty items to the list before Christina walked through the kitchen, Mr. Darcy in her arms.

"Good morning. You have about thirty minutes before the strata's done." Mia let her voice rise into a happy chirp. "You want some coffee?"

"How can you be happy this early?" Christina plopped in the wooden chair. Then she groaned. "Coffee."

Mia handed her a cup and a spoon, moving the cream pitcher and sugar bowl closer to the girl. "You take out the strata when the buzzer sounds. I'm grabbing a shower."

"Ugh . . ."

Mia hoped that meant, sure, no problem in grumpese. Walking through the living room, she saw the light flash on the wall. Someone had just rung the doorbell. The previous owner had set up the warning light mostly because it was impossible to hear the door chime this far up. She glanced at her pj's and tightened her robe. No time to worry about changing clothes now.

She headed down the stairs, hearing the chime buzz again as she got closer to the door. "Hold on, I'm coming," she called out.

Undoing all the locks took some time, but finally she swung open the door. Trent Majors stood there, a box in his hands. He pushed past her and quickly closed the door.

"It's freezing out there this morning. Waiting on you, I could have been a Popsicle." He glanced around the room. "I like the color. Sunny."

Mia stared at him. "I don't remember inviting you over this morning." She glanced at her wrist at a nonexistent watch. Self-conscious, she pulled the robe tighter around her throat. "So why are you here?"

"Figured after I dropped that bombshell last night I had some explaining to do." He held up the box and grinned. "I brought doughnuts."

People lined up on summer weekends to get Majors bakery doughnuts before they sold out. Mia smelled the grease and sugar combination and her stomach growled. "You bring a maple bar?"

Trent smiled. "Two."

"Then come on up. I've made coffee and the strata is just about ready." She pointed to the stairwell. "I'll follow you."

Trent glanced around the lobby area. "You've been busy. I hated that gray. The school got a deal on the paint and went through the whole place with it."

"Yeah, I know. I'm not totally settled on the yellow, but it will get me started. I haven't even started the upstairs. But the contractors are coming to finish the kitchen, so if I get an all clear from the county, I'll be set up for home delivery and catering maybe late next week." Mia smiled. *Just keep going.* Her grandmother hadn't raised her to be a quitter. Sure, Adele's death had been a shock, but honestly, it had nothing to do with her. *Follow the plan and everything will work out.* She noticed Trent wasn't following her. He just stood in the doorway, looking at her.

"I don't think that's going to happen." Trent almost looked sad.

"Quit messing with me. I'm not in the mood to be

teased." Mia's heart raced. *Please don't give me bad news, please.*

"Not messing with you. George Kennedy is in Alaska fishing for two weeks." Trent shook his head. "I would have thought he would have said something."

"Who's George Kennedy?" Mia's thoughts raced through the names of people she'd met since she'd moved here; no George in the bunch.

"He's the health inspector. The one who has to sign off on your business?" Trent headed to the stairs. "I think I smell that strata now."

Mia watched him bound up the stairs. Two weeks? By her business plan she needed to open no later than May 1 and she wouldn't even have her inspection for two more weeks? She glanced again at her missing wristwatch— too early to call the county to see if this George guy had left someone else in charge. Besides, it was the weekend. Who did she think would answer?

Sighing, she followed Trent up the stairs to the apartment. She might just eat both of those maple bars to drown her sorrow.

She had just reached the entrance to the apartment when she heard a rapping on the door. "Grand Central freaking Station, today. I'll be right back." Mia glanced at Trent. "Christina's in the kitchen. She's pretty mute until she gets a few cups of coffee in her, but she might talk to you if you offer her a doughnut."

"She won't bite my hand if I feed her, will she?" Trent peeked around the open door, apparently looking for a booby trap.

"She's not a wild animal; she's a young woman who likes to sleep in. I don't think she'll bite, but keep your hands out of reach just in case." Mia turned and started down the stairs. Who needed step class? She had a fitness program right here. Two flights of stairs, twenty times a day.

"I'm not feeling safe here," Trent called after her.

"Pull up your big boy pants and go get some coffee. I promise, she won't bite—hard." Mia grinned. She liked Trent. Christina had hit the nail on the head when she'd said Mia and Isaac's relationship had been all business. She'd had more fun with this man in the few days she'd known him than with the boyfriend she'd lived with for the last five years. Trent teased, laughed, and brought doughnuts. Now he could be couple material.

A smile crossed her lips and stayed there right up to the time she opened the door. Isaac Adams, her ex-boyfriend, Christina's brother, and the person voted least likely to cross her doorway leaned against the doorframe. He pushed his dark-brown hair out of his eyes and smiled at her. The smile that had changed her mind so many times in the past, but now all it did was remove the smile from her face.

"Hey." His voice was soft and playful.

Mia crossed her arms. "What do you want, Isaac?"

He raised his eyebrows. "So we're playing *this* game?"

"I'm not playing any game. Why are you here?" Mia glanced at the car sitting by the street, no passenger. "And where's your new catering director? Sleeping in?"

Isaac shook his head. "Jealousy doesn't become you. Tanya stayed in Boise. She's not here."

"But you are. Why?" Mia held the door closed with her foot.

"I come in peace." Isaac held up his hands in mock surrender. When Mia failed to respond he sighed. "Look,

Mia, I told Mom I'd come by to give Christina some money and check in on her. Do you mind? Can I see my sister?"

Mia wanted to say no. She wanted to slam the door on Isaac. She wanted to kick him in the groin. Finally she stepped back and opened the door. "Come on in. She's upstairs in the apartment."

She shut the door after him and marched up the stairs. At least Trent was here. Maybe Isaac would get the wrong idea about her and Trent, so she wouldn't have to worry about him trying anything stupid.

"Smells amazing. You make that strata I love?" Isaac's voice followed her up the stairs. "What, not sleeping?"

Mia groaned. For years, whenever she'd had a problem, she'd gotten up in the middle of the night and cooked. She couldn't count the number of times she'd surprised Isaac with a hot breakfast, usually something new that they would try out with the catering staff.

She opened the door and motioned him into the apartment. Christina could fill him in on all the craziness around them. Mia just wanted coffee. "Things have been hectic."

As they walked into the tiny kitchen, Trent sat at the table drinking coffee. The doughnuts were out of the box on a plate in the middle of the kitchen. Christina stood at the stove, cutting the strata into servings.

"Isaac, this is Trent Majors. Trent, Isaac Adams, Christina's brother." Mia left the rest of the descriptors out of the introductions.

"And you said I moved on fast." Isaac studied her, smirking. He winked and then held out his hand to Trent. "Nice to meet you. You and Mia dating?"

Mia gasped. "Not your business."

Trent smiled and stood to shake Isaac's hand. "Nice to meet you. Your sister is a sweetheart. And starting to be a pretty good sous chef."

Mia smiled at Trent, thankful he'd try to steer the conversation away from their relationship. But Isaac wasn't done.

"I didn't expect Mia to have company this early in the morning." Isaac released Trent's hand and slipped into a chair at the table. "Mia, honey, pour me some coffee."

Mia sighed. This would not be pretty. *He's here to talk to Christina*, she reminded herself.

Before she could move to the coffeepot, Christina put her hand on Mia's arm. "Go sit down; I'll get the coffee."

"Thanks," Mia whispered.

Trent glanced at her as she slipped onto a chair and grabbed a napkin and a maple bar. He leaned back into his chair and refocused his gaze on Isaac. "I brought doughnuts. Why are you here?"

Mia bit her lip to keep from smiling. When Isaac didn't answer Mia swallowed the bite of doughnut and supplied the answer. "Christina's mom worries. Isaac is here to make sure I don't have her chained to the stove."

"Mom wouldn't think that." Christina set a cup of coffee in front of Mia and then one for Isaac. "She liked you."

Mia snorted. "Your mother never thought I was good enough for her little boy."

Christina brought the plates and set them in front of the three. "She likes you a lot more now that he's dating that crazy Tanya."

Isaac's turned toward her. "Who told you that?"

Christina cut off a bite with her fork before she answered. "Mom. She says you burning Mia shows how stupid you really are."

Trent chuckled. "Nothing like family to focus on your faults."

Instead of responding, Isaac stood, his face beet red. He pulled out his wallet and threw a handful of hundred-dollar bills at Christina. "That's from Mom. I'm at the Lodge until tomorrow morning. Come over tonight for dinner and we'll talk."

Mia started to stand. Christina put her hand on her arm, stilling her. "Stay here and enjoy breakfast with Trent. I'll show Isaac out."

As brother and sister left the kitchen, Trent sipped his coffee. When the sound of the front door to the apartment closing echoed through the quiet kitchen, he set down his cup. "You okay?"

"Sorry about all that. I guess you figured out Isaac and I used to . . ." she paused. What had they been to each other? At one time she thought he would be her one and only. Now, she saw him through different, clearer eyes. And she didn't like what she saw. Especially since she'd realized he'd always been this way. She sighed. "Stupid, I know."

"Being in love can make you do stupid things. And there's nothing wrong with following your heart." Trent's voice sounded wistful. He shook his head and took a bite. "The man's a fool if he can walk away from something like this."

Mia wondered if Trent's words meant more than the strata. She ducked her head and smiled. Maybe today would be okay after all.

CHAPTER 6

"I don't have to go." Christina looked at Mia, her gaze pleading for an excuse. Any excuse.

Mia straightened the girl's shawl over her bare shoulders. "It's just dinner with your brother. You've lived through worse. Like Thanksgiving with you mother."

Christina snorted. "Remember the year Grandma decided to cook, but instead we went to that awful buffet?"

"Your mom had steam rolling out of her ears by the time dinner was over. Which, besides the coffee, was the best thing about the dinner." Mia put her arm around her and walked her toward the door. "I'll drop you off, check in with James and get the stuff I left at the Lodge, and, if you want to leave when I do, you can catch a ride back. Otherwise stay and talk to him. He's your brother." Mia didn't add, *Even though I think he's an ass.*

They walked through the empty corridors out to the

main lobby. Tomorrow the place would buzz with workmen finishing up the kitchen and the last touches. Now, just to find the missing health inspector and she'd be in business. Literally.

Mia locked the main door, flipping on the outside lights. The sun had set early, leaving the little town bathed in streetlights, but the glow from the old-fashioned lampposts didn't even start to reach the porch. The previous owners had put the parking lot at the back of the building along with the basketball and small tennis court. Mia imagined summer flowers lining the driveway and leading the customers to the lot. Then she'd put in a stone pathway to direct them to the entrance. She pulled on Christina's arm. "Come on, you were supposed to be there at seven. He's going to think I'm the reason you're late."

"Why do you care what Isaac thinks?" Christina grumbled, but slid into the passenger seat.

Mia grinned. "You're right. Habit, I guess. Want to drive around the Lodge a few times just to keep him waiting?"

"See, that's better. I like having a partner in the I Hate Isaac Club." Christina watched Mia as she drove. "Trent's hot."

Mia didn't take the bait. "He's too old for you."

Christina made a face. "Ugh, gross. I didn't mean for me. I meant for you."

"Don't you think I have enough on my plate without starting to date again?" Mia didn't look over until she stopped at the town's only stoplight, which always seemed to be red for her. No matter how many times she tried to wish it green, the traffic light ignored her attempts at magic. "Besides, who says I'm looking for a new guy?"

"He likes you." Christina grinned. "I thought he was going to freak when he saw Isaac come through the door."

"He didn't even know who Isaac was." Mia drove the van the last few blocks to the Lodge after the light finally turned green.

"So why'd he get all defensive when another man showed up at your doorstep first thing this morning?"

Mia let that comment slide. Had Trent been defensive, or had Christina read the situation wrong? Didn't matter; she needed some Mia time. And it wasn't like she didn't have a building to renovate or a business to build. There would be time later for dating. Now, she needed to focus.

Life doesn't work that way. Mia pulled into the Lodge parking lot and found a spot on the north edge. She hated that little voice sometimes.

As they walked through the slush to the front entrance, Christina seemed as lost in thought as Mia. Finally, as Mia reached out to open the front door, she stilled her hand. Mia smiled at her. "What? I don't think we can stall anymore."

"You know I appreciate everything you've done for me. I'm totally on your side in this thing." Christina's voice choked up.

Mia pulled her into a hug. As she released her, Mia wiped a small tear that had escaped onto Christina's cheek. "Having dinner or visiting with your family doesn't bother me at all. Even when that family member is the man formerly known as Isaac."

Christina smiled. "We need to make up a new name for him. Like Jerk."

"Jerk is good. And it's still short, so he should be able to spell it."

A laugh escaped the young woman's lips. "I need you to know, no matter what, I really appreciate you taking me in."

Mia reached for the door again, but this time Christina let her open it. "Believe me, you saved me a major disaster by helping me with Adele's party. Or at least what was supposed to be Adele's party. I should be thanking you for showing up."

"You don't understand—I'm a train wreck." Christina glanced around the lobby. "Look, I need to tell you something. . . ."

Christina's words were cut off when Isaac came up to them from a hallway behind the reception desk. "I was calling you. Being late isn't polite."

"I'm sorry," Christina blushed. "It was my fault. We were talking."

Isaac stared at his sister. "Seems like you talk too much sometimes."

"Stop it. She's here now; go have dinner and stop harping at her." Mia hugged Christina, glowering at Isaac over the girl's shoulder. She whispered, "You sure you don't want me to wait?"

Christina shook her head. "I'll meet you at home, I mean the school." She glanced at Isaac.

"I'll take her back to your place. Don't wait up. Mom made me promise to find out all about what's happening in my little sister's life. We might take a while." Isaac smiled and stepped closer to Mia. She could smell his cologne. "Unless you want to have dinner with us? Like old times?"

Mia tried not to visibly shudder. "I think our old times are ancient history." She stepped backward away from him, not concerned about how it looked to anyone. "I'm not in the forgiving mood right now and I'd probably say things that shouldn't be said in public."

Christina reached a hand up to her face, covering the grin that Mia had caught. Mia couldn't be sure, but she thought she'd seen her mouth the word *Jerk*. Mia focused her breath, calming herself so she wouldn't bash Isaac with her purse and look like an episode of *Trailer Trash Relationships Gone Wild*. No, she'd be the adult in the situation; she always had been.

"You know I'm going to win here, right?" Isaac's voice was hard, the gaze he had on her menacing.

"We're done, Isaac. You aren't getting anything else out of me, including a reaction to your threats." And then she turned toward the kitchen.

Get stuff, get out of here. She repeated her list to herself three times before she got far enough away from Isaac that she knew he couldn't overhear her words. She let the kitchen door close, then the word exploded out of her like pellets from a shotgun. "What a complete and ultimate dirt bag. I don't know what I ever saw in the guy."

The line cooks glanced over at her, their eyes wide. James came around from the back of the kitchen. "Who's got you wound up tonight? Can't be Trent. He's been out fishing most of the day."

Mia waved her hand like she could just push the idea away. "Sorry, my ex is in town and he can twist me three ways to Sunday in about three-point-two seconds." She brushed cake crumbs off James's jacket. "Baking tonight?"

"My pastry chef has the night off. So it's up to me to wow the masses. You here to help?" James looked at her, clearly confused at her presence.

"Sorry, when they brought over the stuff from Adele's

party, my knife set wasn't in the boxes. I just want to grab it and run." Mia watched the man's face as he glanced to the back of the kitchen. She liked him. He reminded her of a younger Chef Boyardee from the commercials, all smiles. And from what she'd eaten of his food, a talented chef, maybe too talented for such a small lodge, but you never knew what path people would take in life. Maybe he loved the outdoor lifestyle Magic Springs provided as much as the locals. Stranger things had happened. She smiled, thinking of her path to paradise. Would people wonder about her reason for wanting to plant roots here?

James frowned. "I supervised the packing myself yesterday. I don't think we missed anything. Are you sure the knives are missing?"

Mia nodded. "I finished unpacking all the boxes this morning. I've got a full set in a case, and the last time I saw them was here, just before we found out about Adele." The vision of Adele's legs sticking out from under the lily-white tablecloth popped, unwelcome, into her mind. She shook it away. "Do you mind if I check myself? Sometimes I tend to stuff things out of the way."

James glanced at the tray a waiter was carrying out to the dining room. He grabbed the guy's arm and yelled back at the kitchen. "Wait, who plated this salmon? How many times do I have to show you the correct sides?"

"You're busy. I'll come back later." Mia stepped back, knowing the line cooks were about to be lectured.

"Might as well look now. You're here." James started walking to the line. "I've got to handle this, sorry."

Mia watched him carry the tray back to the pass. The good thing about working catering was that everything was the same. You didn't have twenty or a hundred different orders going out at the same time. She didn't miss working a real dining room. She'd done that for years before Isaac hired her for the hotel catering job and she'd found her passion.

She walked back to the area where she and Christina had been prepping for the party. The steel tables gleamed. The area appeared empty. The Lodge's kitchen was huge, allowing for several different areas for prep work. James must use this for the parties that came through the Lodge most weekends. She marveled at his generosity. Most chefs would be frantic if a competitor came into their kitchen. The business could be cutthroat. Maybe that mentality didn't exist in this kitchen. She squatted and searched under the tables. There, shoved in the back, was something black.

Reaching down, she stretched her fingers and grabbed the canvas tote. It must have been knocked under the table in all the commotion. Relief filled her as she pulled out the bag and, dusting it off, placed it on the table. She'd bought the knives with her first paycheck as a chef. Well, her first year of paychecks. She'd put down 10 percent and paid them off in a year. A chef was only as good as her tools of the trade. And if that motto was true, she was an extraordinary cook.

She opened the bag and ran her hand over the handles. One spot was totally empty. Frowning, she squatted again, and this time crawled back under the table to check the shadowy crannies. Nothing.

She stood and stared at the open tote.

Her chef knife was missing.

Chapter 7

An hour later, the entire kitchen having been searched not once, but twice, James gently led Mia to the door, slipping her coat over her arms as she tried to protest.

"Look, I'll do another search of the kitchen as soon as dinner service is over. Right now, you're killing the wait time for the dining room." James stepped outside the kitchen door that led to the back parking lot with her and lit up a cigarette. He took a long drag, then squirmed under her scrutiny. "Don't judge me. My job is more stressful than you realize. Do you know that some of my customers are doing South Beach and some have some raw food fetish? Seriously, are you sure you want to set up a catering business here? The normal world doesn't exist in town."

Mia smiled and put her hand on James's arm. "Sorry

about the look. My dad died of lung cancer. The man smoked like a chimney. The only baby picture I have is him holding me up for the camera, a cigarette hanging from his mouth."

"Now here comes the guilt. Look, I know I'm taking a chance here, playing with fire, so to speak, and I'll stop someday." He sucked another drag and then put out the cigarette on the stone wall that bordered the walk. James slid the half-smoked butt into a pack. "Today's just not that day."

"No judgment. But if you ever want to talk, call. I'm a great listener." Mia leaned against the wall and sighed. "Those knives were the first thing I bought out of culinary school. I know it sounds dumb, but I had hoped I'd have the same set throughout my career. Or at least retire them when I bought a better set."

"Not silly at all. We get attached to some of the strangest things." James gave her a look she couldn't read. "Speaking of attached, I hear the devastatingly handsome man having dinner with Christina is your ex. Nice choice; he's yummy."

"I think the fact he's my ex tells the whole story." Mia tilted her head at the slightly pudgy man in a full white chef's uniform standing in front of her. "You're not married?" *Or something*, she added silently.

"Girl, being tied to one person is like eating only chicken for the rest of your life. I like my plate filled with variety." He smiled, but this time the smile didn't come close to filling his face or his eyes.

"I think you doth protest too much." Mia smiled. "I guess I'll head home. I've got a plate filled with desserts from the wake waiting for me that I'm calling dinner.

After that I'm crawling into a tub filled with hot water and bubbles with the latest Robb book and a glass of wine. I'll read until the water chills."

"Baby, you know how to party." James kicked a rock that had been holding open the door and headed back into the kitchen. She smiled at the memory. The catering staff had used the same method of sneaking a smoke. If they left through the kitchen door and let it shut, the employee would have to reenter the kitchen through the hotel lobby. Management and guests alike frowned on the people cooking their meals taking smoke breaks or anything else when they were supposed to be creating.

She crossed the parking lot and held out her key fob, clicking until her lights flashed.

Yep, dessert, wine, book, and bath desperately on the agenda tonight. She needed time to clear her head of oh, so many things, Isaac being the most recent. She corrected herself—losing the knife was the latest tragedy. As she started the car, letting the air blow on high heat before she even tried to leave, she watched the door to the kitchen. Easy in, easy out. A chill ran up her spine.

Could the door have been left open and Adele's killer just walked into the busy kitchen without anyone seeing or taking notice of them? And, obviously, someone had stolen one of Mia's knives, but why? She shivered as a thought came to her. God, she hoped she was wrong. She needed to be wrong, just this one time.

She put the van in gear and headed home. She'd super-size the wine when she got home, just like at Mickey D's. No use getting up early tomorrow. She still had to find the missing health inspector before any of the contractors would go another step in the remodel. Mia had tried calling three times that afternoon, only getting voice mail.

Tomorrow morning she'd start calling again. Or, better yet, get dressed and go to city hall. The guy couldn't hide forever, could he?

Grans's face came to mind, and she chided herself. Maybe the man needed attention or a work ethic; making fun of him at his expense wasn't the way she had been raised. Mia felt ashamed, even though she hadn't done anything. Not one thing. Grans was good with the guilt. Excellent, even with a long distance between the warring factions.

She pulled the van into her parking spot and frowned. She had to stop frowning at every little thing or her face was going to freeze that way. At this time in her life, Mia realized her mom's idle threats may not be so idle any more.

Mia unpacked the few boxes in the back and carried the load onto her porch. As she struggled in her purse for the keys, she heard a crash inside. Mr. Darcy. Had he gotten into something while they were gone? The cat loved exploring the three floors, finding unusual sleeping spots he quickly claimed as his own. Hopefully the damage was minor. The key slipped into the lock just as another crash sounded, this time louder.

"Mr. Darcy, what are you in to?" Mia opened the door, flipped on the entry lights, and then she felt a pain in the back of her head and everything went black.

When she awoke her arms were at her side and she lay prone on a bed. A warmed blanket had been spread over her body, and she fingered the fabric. Heavy cotton. Voices surrounded her. She kept her eyes closed as she tried to remember something, anything. The sound of Mr. Darcy knocking over a box, or maybe even a table, was the last thing she'd heard. She opened her eyes and saw the unpainted ceiling of her foyer. The voices she'd been hearing belonged to her favorite local police officer, Mark Baldwin, and some tall hunk of awesome she'd never seen before. The cute guy bent and smiled at her.

"Hey, you're awake. I thought you'd sleep through the ambulance ride for sure. That's some bump on the back of your head." He flipped on a small flashlight and studied Mia's eyes. "You know where you are?"

"I'm at the school. I mean, my house." Mia tried to sit up, but straps held her to the gurney. "Why am I strapped down?"

"Safety precautions. I was just getting ready to load you in the ambulance and get you to the hospital. You'll feel better once the doc checks you over. I can't give you anything for the headache. Policy, you know." He reached over and felt her wrist for a pulse.

Mark Baldwin stepped closer. "Do you remember what happened?"

Mia turned her head, straining to see his face. "I think someone was in the house when I got home."

The look on the officer's face told her everything she needed to know. In his eyes, she was at best an idiot, and at worst maybe a killer. He sighed. "Why do you think that?"

"Uh, duh? Do you see me strapped to this gurney?" Mia's face felt hot. She squirmed, but the EMT held her gently.

"Calm down," he said.

Mia closed her eyes as calm floated over her body. She breathed a blessing to the Goddess that she wasn't dead. Now, if she could just keep from killing Officer Baldwin, she'd be peachy.

"Miss Malone, please, just answer my question. Why

do you think someone was in your house when you arrived?" He hadn't even taken out that notepad she'd seen him madly scribbling in while he interviewed people after they'd found Adele.

"I heard a crash—two actually—just before I opened the door."

"And yet you came in, alone?"

Now it was Mia's turn to sigh. "I have a cat. Cats get into things where they don't belong. I thought Mr. Darcy had knocked something off a shelf."

"Who's Mr. Darcy?" Now Baldwin looked confused.

"The cat." Mia glanced at the door. "How long has that been wide open? Mr. Darcy could have gotten out."

A new voice joined the conversation. A familiar new voice. Isaac. "The door was open when I dropped off Christina. I made her wait in the car while I checked the place out, then I saw you crumpled on the floor." He touched her face, concern filling his eyes. And for once, Mia thought it might be a real emotion. "Are you all right?"

Mia closed her eyes, willing the tears to stay away. She bit her lip. When she opened her eyes he'd stepped away from the gurney and lowered his hand to his side. "I'm fine."

Isaac must have heard all the things she didn't say because he studied her face carefully before speaking. "Christina locked Mr. Darcy upstairs in the apartment. She's getting you a change of clothes in case they keep you overnight."

Office Baldwin spoke up. "Glad everyone's on the same page; now, can we get back to the situation? What exactly happened when you opened the door?"

"I reached over, turned on the lights, then the back of

my head exploded. The next thing I remember is hearing your charming voice." Mia stared at the police officer, who must never have taken customer service training in his life.

"Look, you can question her later. I've got to get her to the hospital." The EMT stood and pushed the gurney to the door.

"Wait, what about the house?" Mia glanced around for Christina, who still hadn't appeared. "Who will lock up?"

Isaac came to the side of the bed. "No worries. Christina and I will take care of everything."

He smiled at her and her heart sank. Any positive emotion she'd thought he'd held for her disappeared in that one smile. She'd bet as soon as the building was clear, he'd be looking for her cookbook. That had to be why he had even made the three-hour trip, to con Christina into spying for him. Now, he had full access to everything.

Except the cookbook's in the safe. Confident that he'd never find the hidden safe, she smiled back at him. *Do your best.*

Isaac continued watching as the EMT loaded her into the waiting ambulance. When the doors closed and she couldn't see him anymore, Mia relaxed just a bit while the cute guy settled in beside her.

"My name's Levi. You know my brother." He rapped on the side of the wall separating the back from the driver's area and called out, "We're ready to go."

She felt the ambulance move and her stomach turned queasy. She gripped the blanket tightly in her hand. *Don't pass out, don't pass out.* She focused on the EMT, now known as Levi. "I know your brother? How?"

"Does it help when I say my last name is Majors?" He

smiled, and Mia saw the resemblance. Same green eyes, same dimple in the chin, but Levi had jet-black hair instead of his brother's light brown, almost red mop.

"I didn't know Trent had a brother." Mia frowned, her head pounding. "Wait, maybe he did say something."

"He has two, actually. Will's an attorney in Boise. Trent runs the store. I'm the baby and the underachiever."

"Working as an EMT isn't an underachiever." Mia studied Levi's face; he probably wasn't much older than Christina.

"It is when both your older brothers have graduate degrees and are certifiable geniuses." He adjusted the IV line. "Mom wanted me to be a doctor, I wanted to ski. This is a compromise so we both get what we want."

Mia frowned. She hadn't even noticed the tube he'd hooked up to her; must have happened before she'd woken.

Levi saw her glance. "Just a precaution. We in the medical field believe in hydration. You wouldn't believe how many people pass out just because they are dehydrated."

"I didn't pass out." Was she going to have to explain she was attacked to everyone she met? What, did she look like someone who was so fragile she walked around passing out?

"Yeah, I know. Baldwin can be a tool sometimes. He gets something in his head and bam, you're on his list forever. Before you showed up that focus was all on me." Levi grinned. "I'm glad there's someone new for him to focus on."

Mia felt the ambulance slow for Magic Spring's only stoplight, which, of course, was red. It was always red. She guessed she wasn't dying because the ambulance driver hadn't even turned on his lights or siren. She focused back on Levi, who seemed to be a normal, if highly inked, EMT. "Why would you be on his list?"

Levi stood and walked to the back of the ambulance, grabbing a second blanket for her. As he covered her up, he grinned at her, "Don't you know I'm the town's bad boy warlock?"

Mia studied Levi's face to see if he was just joking with her. She didn't know all the members of Magic Springs's coven.

"I just want you to know we have a small, discreet coven with members from the surrounding area. Nothing too big or demanding; we usually only get together on the holidays, like summer solstice." He grinned. "At least not since the new management took over a few months ago."

"Potlucks?" Mia relaxed. "What, are you the local welcome wagon for new magical folks who move into Magic Springs?"

"Something like that." Levi leaned back on his seat. "I'm the only one in the family who follows the old craft, if you were wondering. Trent and the others seem to think our heritage is better off staying myth and smoke."

Well, so much for her and Trent having anything but a casual fling. The next real relationship she had, there would be no secrets. And if the guy came from a magical family and didn't embrace the life at least a little, he couldn't be the one. The Goddess would bring her a mate. All she had to do was ask. But right now, getting the business up and running was first on her list. Oh, and figuring out who had attacked her. And why.

"It must be hard hiding your true self." Mia warmed to the guy. He felt like he could be a great friend. He was easy to talk to and understood her magical side. A side she'd had to keep hidden while growing up and, if she was honest with herself, most of her life. She'd always tried to keep her relationships normal, which meant she kept them casual—never letting anyone know all of her.

"I think you might just know more about that subject than me. So, you used to date that tool, Isaac." Levi's grin showed the dimple in his chin. "What were you thinking?"

"Blame it on wanting to be normal." She leaned back on the gurney. "Wait, who told you that we dated?"

"He did. He kept explaining to the cop how the two of you were a couple. Baldwin wasn't buying it, especially when that cute blonde piped up and ratted him out. Boy, she doesn't like her brother one bit, does she?" Levi glanced out the window, but Mia thought she saw a tint of pink on his cheeks.

"Christina shouldn't have to take sides. I've told her not to. She's mad at him for the way he dumped me. Of course, if I'd listened to my intuition, I would have expected something like that." Mia blew out a long breath. "Honestly, I knew we were over for years. I just didn't want to be the one to bury a body in case there was a breath left. When I caught him with his new girl, I was shocked."

"Love gets in the way of power. It can make us blind. Believe me, I've dated a few disasters in my life who I should have run away from screaming. Women. And they call witches scary? Some normal women are the true horror stories." Levi patted her hand. "Sorry you got hurt."

"I'll survive. I've moved on. Figurative and literally. Beside, now I get to meet surprising new friends." She felt the ambulance turn into Magic Spring's Memorial Hospital parking lot.

Levi stood. "We'll do coffee one day and compare love war stories. You should come to a circle. You might like the coven."

"I've been invited before; it's just that we're not those type of witches." Mia's words slurred. She leaned her head back on the pillow. All of a sudden she felt tired, beat tired. She didn't hear his answer before she'd fallen asleep.

CHAPTER 8

Mia heard her grandmother's knitting needles clacking together before her eyes focused on the one person who'd always been there for her. Mary Alice had her head down, her gaze on the soft fluff of what was beginning to look like a scarf. Mia could watch her grandmother knit for hours.

"How's your head feel?" Grans didn't look up from her work. Her needles changed the balls of yarn and transformed them into cloth so soft, Mia wanted to sink her face into the uncompleted project.

Mia closed her eyes and checked out her injuries. "Like I lost the bet and had to go into the bear cave alone."

Grans chuckled. "Could be you're not that far away from the truth."

Mia sat upright in bed even though the swift movement made her head pound even more. "What do you mean? Did they find out who was in the building?"

"I think they have their suspicions, but the good news is, Officer Baldwin almost believes you didn't kill Adele." Grans patted her forearm. "Lay back down, child. The doctor will want to check you out before you go all avenging angel on someone."

"I feel so relieved," Mia said, leaning back into the crisp pillow. "Not. What makes you think he doesn't suspect me anymore?"

"You couldn't have hit yourself over the head at the angle of your attack." Grans smiled. "You never know what blessings an action will bring."

"Yeah, like a splitting headache." Mia reached up, gently touching the bandage on the back of her head and winced. "Who would do this?"

"I have one theory. Isaac." Grans put her knitting aside and pushed Mia's call button. "We'll get a nurse in here with some juju juice to make you feel better. They wanted you awake to check your responses before they gave you anything."

Mia thought about her grandmother's words. Isaac? Why would Isaac hit her over the head? "Grans, that can't be right. Isaac was at dinner with Christina. I saw him."

Grans sniffed. "Doesn't mean he didn't send someone to do the dirty work. I never thought he had the gumption God gave a snail."

Despite herself, Mia chuckled. "Don't make me laugh; it hurts."

"Where is that nurse?" Grans glanced at the closed door. "Maybe I should . . ."

Mia held up her hand, stilling her grandmother's movement. "Stop. I'm not the only patient on the floor."

The room fell quiet for a second and Mia could hear the whoosh of the oxygen machine from a nearby room. Mia lowered her voice, just in case. Her grans had told her it was better to be discreet when discussing this type of information.

"The EMT guy, Levi Majors, is part of the coven. Did you know?" Mia watched her grandmother as she had returned to her knitting, the metal needles clacking in rhythm with the flowing oxygen.

"Did I know what, dear? That Levi is a witch? Of course." Grans didn't even look up from her knitting. "Not everyone in the family practices, if that's got you worried. Just Levi."

"Why would that worry me? And why is everyone making sure I understand that Trent isn't practicing?" Mia frowned, then rubbed her face and the frown away. She pushed the question aside with a wave of her hand, like she was trying to get rid of a gnat buzzing her face. "Did you attend the coven here?"

"No. Adele and I both felt the coven membership was more for the younger set. What are we going to do, dance around naked in front of a bunch of twenty-year-olds?" Grans shook her head. "She would have turned them into stone if they'd even looked cross at her. No, sending Adele into the local coven would be letting the fox loose in the chicken coop."

Mia played with the remote for the television that hung on the opposite wall, looking for the music stations. She found a country video station and stopped, processing what Grans had said. "Wait, Adele had power?"

"More than you'd know. She was quite the witch in her day." Grans nodded at the door; someone was coming. Mia thought about all the times she'd seen Adele.

Never once had the woman let on that she had an ounce of power. In fact, she tended to mock Mary Alice whenever she'd mention the craft. This didn't make any sense at all.

"You're awake. Good. Let's check how you're doing." The nurse bustled into the room and then slipped a blood pressure cuff on Mia's arm and stuck a thermometer in her mouth. Grans stood.

"I'll be right back. I'm out of coffee." Grans patted Mia's foot under the cotton blankets. She focused her attention on the nurse. "She's in pain."

The nurse nodded. "I called up the doctor before I came into the room. I had a feeling she'd be awake."

Mia frowned, wondering what her grandmother wasn't telling her. Isaac couldn't have done this. He'd been at dinner with Christina. But if not Isaac, who?

She closed her eyes and let the nurse do her job, but the image of Isaac's face when she left Christina at the Lodge wouldn't leave her mind. Could the elation she'd seen on his features been more than just seeing his long-lost sister? Or were they going after Mia's recipe book? And now she'd left her home unguarded and unprotected. She should have spelled the book the day Christina arrived at her door. That would have kept the book safe, even if it wouldn't have stopped the attack.

Mia watched as the nurse pushed a drug into the IV, and then her eyes drooped and she stopped worrying.

Night had fallen outside by the time she awoke. Grans was gone, a note on her table explaining that she would return in the morning to take her home. Mia sipped her water and felt hunger roll through her. She hadn't eaten for hours, maybe days. She grabbed the food menu and called the number on the phone next to her bed. A cup of soup, a sandwich, coffee, and a cup of milk and she was done. Thirty minutes to wait. She turned on the television.

"She's right, you know; your grandmother, that is. The two of them wouldn't have been welcome in the coven. The young ones like their pleasures of the flesh." The voice sounded old, shaky.

Mia turned off the television and pulled back the curtain separating the two beds in the small room. "I'm sorry if I woke you. I didn't know anyone was there."

"No worries, child. Back at the home, I share a room with Gertie, who's so deaf she keeps the television on full blast, even when she's asleep. I'd ask for a change in rooms, but beggars can't be choosers, as the social worker tells me when I complain. I know I should be grateful they have to take on a few Medicaid patients, I just wish they didn't have to remind me about their sacrifice on a daily basis." The woman in the bed next to her waved a shriveled and gnarled hand. "If you want to watch television, you go right ahead."

Mia smiled and gently rolled over to her side to see the woman clearer. She couldn't decide on an age; the woman looked ancient with her long, gray hair splayed out on the pillow. The face lined from years of life. "I'm Mia Malone. I'm Mary Alice's . . ."

"Granddaughter. I know, child. I'm old, not senile. I hear you bought the old schoolhouse. I attended St. Catherine's Prep there back in the day. I loved the way the windows showcased the Magics, no matter what classroom you were stuck in."

"The Magics? Oh, you mean the mountain range." For

a minute Mia thought the woman had been talking about the local coven. This conversation was going off the rails, mostly because Mia was so tired.

The woman rolled over on her side to mirror Mia. "Dorothy Purcell. I'm the oldest woman in Magic Springs."

Mia thought back to what she'd said originally, then whispered, "Were you part of the coven?"

A short bark of a laugh came from the woman. "Heavens no. I haven't got a drop of power. My husband did, bless his soul, but it didn't keep him from being killed in a mining accident. Power can only go so far; you have to have the brains God bestowed on an earthworm, and unfortunately my Harry should have been further down the evolutionary scale."

Mia bit back a smile. "Then how do you know about the covens?"

"Don't you listen? My husband told me. He'd go to meetings, then come home, reeking of liquor and perfume, and blab all about how much I missed because I was just a human." She shook her head. "Harry swore he never fully participated, but a woman knows."

Mia could hear the sadness in the woman's voice after all these years. Love twisted you up, especially when the one you loved wasn't worthy. Isaac's face popped into her mind. She wondered if he'd resorted to tearing up her warm, cozy apartment yet, looking for the cookbook. *Please, Christina, keep him in line*.

"Actually, we're not the same type of witches who attend covens. We practice a kitchen witchcraft, focused on healing. Usually covens use cooperative magic. Ours is more individual." Mia heard herself chattering; Grans would be furious. She wondered if the painkillers were lowering her natural resistance to talking about her power. "I have a kitchen doll that's my familiar. Gloria. I've had her since I was five and turned Thanksgiving dinner into a table filled with all types of candy. And I have Mr. Darcy, but he's having some issues lately, so I just leave him be."

Dorothy chuckled. "Sounds like you're Glinda the Good Witch."

"Or just someone who loves candy." Mia sighed. "Mom was furious, Dad, scared. I went to stay with Grans for a year before I started school. She trained me not to talk about this to anyone who wasn't in the family. To be normal."

"Sometimes normal isn't what it's cracked up to be." Dorothy adjusted her blanket. "I was normal and my Harry still strayed."

"I'm sorry." Mia tried to focus on the woman next to her. The room was getting warm and her eyelids heavy. No way she'd be able to stay awake to eat and she really had wanted that soup.

"No worries. When the accident happened the mine paid me a hefty settlement and monthly checks. I'm pretty sure they were wishing I'd pass myself, or at least remarry after the first fifty years of payments." The woman's voice seemed farther away now. "Adele's father tried to hitch me up several times so he could stop the checks."

Mia felt fuzzy, but something sounded off. "Adele's father?"

"He owned the mine where Harry was killed."

Mia felt Dorothy's gaze more than saw the blue eyes watching her as she drifted off to sleep. As sleep overtook her, the thought of connections as live wires to people turned into her dreams where people floated in and out of her subconscious, not speaking, but attached with a mess of wires. Wires Mia couldn't untangle, no matter how hard she tried.

Sun streamed in the window when she woke. She glanced over at the other bed to say good morning to her roommate and gasped. There, where the other bed had been last night, was a recliner where Grans sat, knitting. She glanced up when she heard Mia's outburst.

"Wondered when you were going to get up. Dr. Mike says I can take you home as soon as he checks your bandages." Grans stood and came closer, taking Mia's hand. "What's wrong, dear?"

"Where's Dorothy?" Mia sat up, looking out the door. "Did they send her home already?"

Grans put her hand on Mia's chest, gently restraining her and pushing her back to the mattress. "What are you talking about? Who's Dorothy?"

"My roommate. We talked last night after you left. She said she knew Adele's father. That her husband worked in his mine." Mia sipped water from the straw of the jug Grans had handed her while she talked.

"You've never had a roommate." Grans's tone sounded flat, like she was trying to convince not only Mia but herself. "How did you know about the mines?"

"She was in the second bed." Mia caught Grans's gaze and something flickered in her eyes; a recognition, maybe?

"Mia, the only other piece of furniture in this place for the last day has been that recliner where I sat, waiting for you to wake up. No second bed. You must have dreamed it." Grans pushed the call button. "Let's get that nurse in here so we can get you home where you belong."

Mia leaned back and closed her eyes. Dorothy had seemed real, but now that she thought about yesterday, she remembered seeing Grans in that same recliner. There wasn't any way there had been a second bed in this tiny room; it wouldn't have fit. "Dorothy Purcell. And her husband's name was Harry. Did you and Adele know them? The husband was killed in a mining accident?"

Mia heard the hitch in Grans's voice when she spoke. "I don't know a Dorothy or a Harry Purcell."

And for the first time ever, Mia knew her grandmother had just lied to her. Before Mia could press the button, the nurse came in and checked her vitals one last time. As soon as the nurse wrapped a blood pressure cuff around Mia's arm and stuck a temperature gauge in Mia's mouth, Grans stood.

"I'll be right out in the hallway. I need to make a call." And with that the conversation was over.

"I bet you're glad to get out of here," the nurse chatted. Twenty-four at the oldest, the woman had short, black hair and the hint of a tattoo on the exposed skin of her chest. A bracelet of roses tattoo circled her wrist. Following Mia's gaze, she laughed. "My boyfriend bought me the tattoo for my birthday last year. The chief nurse hates it. Wants me to wear long sleeves all the time, but I've checked the policies and procedures handbook, and it doesn't say anything about tats."

Mia liked the young woman, who reminded her of Christina. Always trying to find her way in the world, trying to color just outside the lines.

"For a woman who was attacked yesterday, you seem to be doing great." The nurse, Kat from her name tag, keyed some information into her computer and what Mia assumed was her electronic chart. Even in a small town like Magic Springs, medical records had gone high-tech.

Probably because the hospital wasn't locally owned, but part of a statewide medical group. Which was another reason Kat got away with her personal decorations.

After Kat removed the thermometer Mia spoke. Now or never, she thought. "Have you worked here long?"

"Since I got out of nursing school. I love being able to ski right after work. If I hadn't torn my ACL in high school, I would have gone professional, you know." Kat kept typing as she talked.

"Did you ever meet a woman named Dorothy Purcell?"

Kat's reaction surprised Mia. The nurse laughed.

Frowning, Mia watched as Kat finished her note and closed the small laptop. Then she sat on the bed next to Mia. Kat checked the doorway before she spoke in a low tone. "So, you met our resident ghost?"

"I don't understand."

"I'll tell you the story I heard when I started working here. Dorothy Purcell was the oldest woman in town. She lived out at that nursing facility near the lake, before the company that owns it now bought it and made it a luxury retirement community. Like that's possible. It just allows them to charge more." Kat shook her head. "I tried to get a job there because they pay awesome, but the manager only hires locals. I've lived here six years now and I'm still an outsider."

"You were telling me about Dorothy?" Mia tried to focus the conversation, afraid the nurse would get called out or Grans would return.

"Oh, yeah, sorry. Back to the story. She lived out there with the upper crust because they had to keep her; it's a law or something. They didn't like it because she cost them money, but the woman just kept on living, even when she was over one hundred. When she got sick they rushed her to the hospital, thinking this was her last hurrah, and she bounced back." Kat's pager buzzed. "Crap, Mr. Evans. The man thinks getting a sponge bath is an erotic opportunity."

Mia bit back a smile. "So one day she didn't bounce back?"

"One day they walked into her room and she was just gone. No fanfare, no preceding illness. She seemed fine when the night nurse checked on her and when the morning aide came in to get her up for breakfast, she was gone." Kat snapped her fingers. "Just like that. I guess when her body gave out, her soul didn't want to leave. For the last ten years, we've had sightings here and out at Lakeview."

"You really believe in ghosts?" Mia asked as the young woman started to leave the room.

Kat paused at the doorway. "You tell me. You were the one she came to visit. I've worked here day and night and never even felt a chill. You're here one night and you see our ghost. You think that's a coincidence?"

Mia watched the young woman wave goodbye to Grans as she reentered the room. "You ready to get out of here?"

"Definitely."

Grans handed Mia a stack of clean clothes. While Mia changed in the bathroom Grans must have bundled up all her personal items because when she exited the bathroom, Grans grasped her arm and led her out the door. Mia stopped in the doorway and glanced back in the room. For a second she thought she saw an elderly, gray-haired woman standing near the window, looking out, but then the sun wavered and the dust danced in the air, and Dorothy was gone. Again.

"You all right, dear?" Grans's voice seemed far away. When Mia turned her grandmother stood right in front of her, and her hand reached up, pushing a lock of Mia's hair out of her eyes.

"I'm fine. I just want to get home before Isaac destroys my apartment." She put her arm through her grandmother's and they started toward the entrance.

"No worries there. Trent went over last night and escorted him and Christina out. He dropped Christina off at my house to watch Muffy because I would be here at the hospital." Grans's blue eyes twinkled.

"And so Isaac couldn't strong-arm her into letting him back in once Trent left." Mia shook her head. "You guys take pretty good care of me."

"Of course, dear. That's what family does." They were at the front door now, and Grans's car stood at the entry, the door open, waiting for them.

"What if Isaac just went back?" Mia froze at the thought. At least with Christina there someone was watching the place.

"Trent would have called me." Grans gently tugged on Mia's arm to get her walking again.

"But how . . ." Then she got it. Trent had dropped off Christina, then returned to the school to stand guard. Like a Knight of the Round Table. Perfect. Okay, maybe a bit too perfect, but right now Mia didn't care. She slid into the front seat. When her grandmother climbed in next to her Mia smiled. "Any way we could stop by Majors for some doughnuts? I'm starving and don't feel like cooking."

Grans nodded. "That could be arranged. But, dear, maybe I should drop you off at the house and go back myself."

Mia frowned. "Why? It's on the way to the school."

Grans pulled the car out of the parking lot and onto the recently plowed street. "Do you really want Trent to see you like this?"

"Why does it matter? We're not dating or anything."

Grans slowly angled the car on the slick roads. "Just keep telling yourself that."

CHAPTER 9

They made a quick stop to pick up Christina, then to Majors for junk food and other supplies, including a bottle of Tylenol. Grans ushered them quickly in and out, and the women actually sighed when they returned to the car, sans a Trent sighting. Mia dry swallowed three pills to cure a headache that had started just about the third time Grans mentioned the way Trent's hair curled over his ears.

Mia glanced at Christina, who sat in the back seat. She had a mile-wide grin. "Stop it, both of you."

Christina shrugged, "I don't know what you mean."

"I'm not dating anyone. I've got a business to build. And an inspector to track down." Mia eyed the bag of chips in the grocery bags next to Christina. "The only thing I'm doing for the next two days is sleeping and reading."

"I thought the kitchen guys were coming."

"Crap, did someone call the contractor?" She glanced at her grandmother. "Let me guess: Trent handled it. Okay, I'll get them going, then collapse on the couch." She reached for the potato chips and Grans slapped her hand. "What?"

The woman didn't even take her eyes off the road. "No eating in my car. New rule."

Mia slipped back into her seat, thankful the ride was almost over. She glanced back at Christina. "You didn't say how your dinner with Isaac went. Everything okay between the two of you?"

Christina sighed and pulled out her earbuds, shutting off her MP3 player. "I'd say normal. I got lecture number 534, in which he explained how important college is and how I'm breaking Mom's heart by not going."

"I thought you said you were going in the summer." Mia watched the front of the house as Grans pulled the car into the driveway.

"That's what I told him. But he was so far into the speech he couldn't stop. The guy never listens. How did you put up with him for so long?" Christina jumped out of the car as soon as Grans parked, grabbing the grocery bags. Apparently she didn't expect an answer to her question.

Grans patted Mia's hand. "She has a point."

"I'm not there now. That's all that matters." Mia groaned as she pulled herself out of the front seat. "Time for a long soak in that amazing tub of mine."

"I'll make us some lunch, and by the time you get out we'll eat in front of the television. I brought over *Sleepless in Seattle*." Grans moved next to her and the two women walked up the steps.

Mia couldn't help thinking the last time she'd seen Adele, she and Grans had been walking away from the house. Would she always have that memory when she thought of Adele?

Christina stood in the doorway, holding open the door. Now a new memory hit Mia and almost knocked her to her knees. She'd walked in, expecting to see Mr. Darcy next to some overturned furniture, and then blackness. She paused in the doorway.

Grans gently pulled at her arm. "It's your home; don't let the troubles win."

Mia smiled, nodded, and stepped into the hallway. When she didn't black out she let loose a breath she hadn't realized she'd been holding. She barked a short laugh and Grans frowned. "I've made it into the building. That's a good sign."

The trio made their way upstairs to the apartment. Christina, even carrying all the bags, made it there twice as quickly as Mia and Grans. For the first time Mia questioned buying the enormous school building. What happened if she got hurt? Or if she couldn't work? How would she get up and down two flights of stairs?

"Don't bring tomorrow's worries out for today." Grans paused on the landing. "I think I'm doing pretty good for an old broad."

"You shouldn't read my mind. You never know what you'll find." Mia took her grandmother's arm and helped her up the remaining stairs.

"Like that weekend you were supposed to sleep over at Marsha's, but really you were meeting Kevin at the lake?"

Mia laughed. "I always wondered how you knew."

"Until you found out I had magic." Grans smiled as they reached the apartment. "Of course it didn't hurt that I saw you sneak out the sleeping bag with your overnight bag. I knew that boy was trouble and wasn't supposed to be in your life. It just took you a little longer to see his true colors."

"Grans." Mia felt the heat on her face. Her bad boy stage hadn't lasted long, but she'd been convinced that Kevin was her future. Until she'd found out that because she hadn't gone to the lake that weekend, he'd found someone else to warm his sleeping bag.

"That's the seedy underside of reading minds. You don't always hear what you want to hear." Her grandmother paused at the top of the stairs, and Mia could see the tiredness on her face.

Christina reappeared in the apartment doorway. "I put the bags in the kitchen. You need help making lunch?"

Grans walked over to the doorway and patted Christina's shoulder. "Don't worry about it. I said I was making lunch. I'm fine. A couple of flights of stairs aren't going to take me out for the day."

"Then I'm going to my room to check my email before we do the movie day thing." Christina took Grans at her word. Mia, on the other hand, knew the toll the last few days had taken on her grandmother. Christina paused before she left the kitchen. "I don't think I've seen *Sleepless*."

"Deprived child, I will educate you in the magic that is Meg Ryan and Tom Hanks." Mia swept a hair out of Christina's eyes. "Thanks for helping out yesterday."

Mia could have sworn she saw a look of pain cross her face.

"No problem." Christina headed down the hall.

Mia bit her lip and watched her disappear. Blood or love, who knew what would win out? She just hoped Christina knew what she really wanted.

"You think she's working for Isaac?" Grans's voice went low.

"I think it's a possibility." Mia should have known her grandmother was thinking the same thing. "If you're sure you're okay to make lunch, I'm going to my room for a minute. I'm beat. And a long, hot shower might just help. I'll see you after I get cleaned up. If I don't show up in an hour, send submarines in to find me."

"Thirty minutes. I'm making chicken tortellini soup and rolls." Grans hugged Mia, then pushed her away. "You stink."

"Love you too." Mia disappeared into her bedroom, locking the door behind her. The first thing she did was move the vanity mirror over to uncover the small wall safe she'd found when she moved in. The Realtor had given her the combination with the closing papers. She clicked off the numbers, then pulled the door open. Her cookbook and the copy were still there. She touched the cover and sighed in relief. She'd known Isaac and Christina wouldn't have been able to find the safe—not without a little help—but it felt good to know her book was safe. A knock sounded at her door.

"Just a minute." Quickly she closed the safe, spun the lock, and checked the door. She moved the mirror back to cover the wall and stepped over to open the door. Christina stood there, tears flowing down her face. "What's wrong?"

"Do you think Isaac did this? I mean sent someone to hurt you? Would he?" Christina glanced toward the kitchen, "I heard what Grans said."

"She's just worried, that's all." Mia wiped a tear from Christina's face. "Your brother wouldn't hurt me. He doesn't like me right now, but he wouldn't intentionally hurt me."

"That's just the thing. I'm not sure that's true." Christina's head dropped. Then she spun around and sprinted to her bedroom, leaving a dazed Mia standing in the hall-way watching her go.

When Grans announced that lunch was ready the three huddled on the couch eating soup and watching Meg Ryan try to assure herself she had magic with the man she was about to marry. Christina didn't speak. No chatter, no groaning at the sappy parts, only a thank-you for the soup and then she was silent.

Grans glanced over at Mia after an hour of the silent treatment and Mia shrugged her shoulders. Christina needed the time to work out whatever was bothering her. Eventually she'd talk, but even then, Mia knew Isaac's part in the break-in would be questionable. She didn't like the guy, but she'd lived with him for long enough to know he wouldn't do this type of crap; not to her, not to anyone. He was more of a liar and a cheat rather than someone who would take on criminal activities.

After the movie Christina carried their bowls into the kitchen. Mia heard the water running as Christina rinsed the dishes, then Mia saw her slip on her jacket. "You going out?"

Christina turned. "Just for a while. I want to walk around the square."

And with that, she disappeared out of the apartment. Mia looked at Grans. "You think I should go with her?"

"She needs some time. You said it yourself. Her brother is a jerk; she knows that. Now she has to deal with the fact that he might have also orchestrated this whole attack on you." Grans shushed her. "Even if he didn't plan the attack, he was more than willing to use the situation in his favor. And that she knows."

"I hate Isaac. Hurting me is one thing; hurting his sister, that's just cruel." Mia thought about calling the hotel and giving him a piece of her mind. But what would be the use? As if she thought it into being, the phone rang. She picked up the cordless receiver. "Mia Malone."

Dead silence on the other end of the line, but Mia thought she could hear someone breathing. "Who is this?"

"Wrong number," a familiar male voice responded. Then she heard a click.

Grans glanced up from her knitting. "Isaac?"

"Not Isaac. It's just, I mean, I thought I knew that voice." Mia frowned, trying to remember. As she tried to focus, the phone chirped again. Mia answered it curtly. "Who is this?"

"Carrie Jones? We met at the lovely wake you catered? I mean, the wake wasn't lovely, but the food was amazing. I'm sorry, did I wake you? I heard you had some issues."

Mia remembered the petite blonde who'd stopped by their table after the chaos with Adele's nephew. "I'm sorry, I've been a little stressed." She put a smile on her face, hoping the action would show up in her tone of voice. "What can I help you with?"

"I need a caterer for my husband's work event. Nothing big like you were planning for Adele's birthday, poor thing." Carrie Jones went on to explain the details as Mia grabbed a notebook from the coffee table and started making notes. When she hung up Mia had an event in two weeks and a real smile on her face.

"I told you putting out your business cards at the event was a smart move." Grans smirked. "I've gotten you two of two events you've booked."

"And look how well the last event turned out."

Grans gasped and threw a couch pillow at her. "You ungrateful child."

"Just kidding. The business cards were brilliant, if a tad tacky." She held up her hands in surrender, "Of course I think most advertising borders on tacky, so who am I to judge?"

"Exactly."

Mia pulled out the list of contractors to get a phone number. She stood and walked into the kitchen to sit at her desk and start planning. "Brent? Mia Malone. I'm just checking in on the status of the main kitchen. You still think we can be operational by mid next week?"

Mia scribbled on a yellow pad while she talked. When she hung up she felt fairly confident she could pull off this job without borrowing the Lodge kitchen from James. The Joneses were hosting at their home, and from what Carrie described, their kitchen would be adequate for the job if she could prep here. The kitchen downstairs would be perfect, but it hadn't been inspected and approved yet. Doing catering from her home apartment, she could risk any fall out because the majority of the cooking would be at Carrie's. She glanced around the small kitchen in the apartment. Not the best prep kitchen, but in a pinch she'd be fine.

Things were finally looking up. Especially because Carrie loved the idea of roast squab. When the phone rang a third time Mia smiled before answering. *Good things come in threes*, she thought.

"Mia Malone," she almost singsonged into the receiver.

"You should get out of town before the next hit on the head takes you out permanently."

CHAPTER 10

Mia was still reeling from the call. Her mind kept replaying the threatening message. But somehow she'd done all the things she was supposed to do. Call the police, gather up Grans and Christina so she knew where everyone was, and then wait for Baldwin to show up. He'd come faster than she'd expected and she'd had to go downstairs to let him in to the school while she was still chopping veggies.

He'd come into the kitchen and asked her question after question about the call. Most of them she couldn't answer. But she could make a beef vegetable soup while he grilled her. So she did.

The questioning was over before the soup was ready. Baldwin assured her that he would get to the bottom of this. Now, with the soup simmering, she needed a new project to keep her mind off the fact that someone had threatened to kill her. Or at least scare her. He'd been successful in doing that. How she reacted now was up to her. Go screaming into the night and away from Magic Springs? Or stay and fight?

Right now she had a catering job to work on. The running away would have to be postponed for another day.

Mia found her clipboard and went to the living room to find her grandmother. "Grans, what do you think about setting up a picnic lunch theme. With a buffet of salads? Squab instead of fried chicken? People are health conscious today. You think I can pull it off as upscale?" She froze in the doorway when she finally looked up from her list and saw the visitor with Grans. She'd thought he'd left an hour ago after drilling her about the phone call.

Grans sat in one of the wingback chairs and Christina sat on the floor nearby. Officer Baldwin sat on the couch with a cup of coffee and a plate of cookies in front of him. He wiped cookie crumbs from his mustache and picked up his pen, aiming it toward Mia. "I had a few more questions for you after interviewing your grandmother and roommate. You didn't tell me about the hang-up call. Were the hang-up and the threatening calls from the same guy?"

"I don't think so. Something about the first guy sounded vaguely familiar, but I only heard one word." Mia's head had started pounding again a few minutes before. Now she just wanted to be alone to sleep this headache off.

"I thought he said 'wrong number?'" Baldwin checked his notes.

"He did." Mia rubbed her temples.

"That's two words." He tapped his pen against the table. "It's important that you stay consistent and accu-

rate in your statement. Cases are lost at trial and murder-
ers go free just because of errors like this."

Mia bit her lip, willing the words to stay in her head
and not fly out to bite off this guy's head. She took a
breath and started to respond, but Grans interrupted her.

"Mark, I have some questions about what happened to
Adele. The world has gone a little crazy the last week or
so, don't you think?"

"Mrs. Carpenter, I can't speak to an open investigation, you know that." He sat up straighter and straightened his tie on his blue uniform shirt. "And, please, either
call me 'Officer' or 'Officer Baldwin,' not Mark."

"Pshaw, I've called you Mark since I babysat you
when your folks used to attend all the Lodge events. You
think just because you're grown up I don't remember the
trouble you used to get into?" Grans patted his leg. "Remember the day you got locked in the cellar because you
were playing Twister? We've never even seen a tornado
up here in the Magics."

"Mrs. Carpenter, please. I need to talk to Mia." Officer
Baldwin glanced over at the door. "Do you mind?"

"There's nothing Mia can tell you about poor Adele.
She had nothing to do with this. Tell me about your
mother and her new husband's place in Florida. How do
they like Tampa?" Grans leaned back and watched the
police officer expectantly.

"Grans, we'll be in the kitchen." Mia walked out of the
living room, waiting for the officer to follow her. When
he did she sat at the table.

Mia nodded toward the room they'd just left and her
grandmother. "She's a bit overprotective."

"Believe me, I know. Once a neighbor kid tried to steal
my quarters at the arcade. I thought she was going to go

all Rambo on the guy. I really liked her as a babysitter. Never boring when she came over to the house." He glanced at the door. "Just make sure you don't tell her I said so."

Mia grinned; the guy may not be as bad as she thought. "Our secret." She scooted toward the front of the chair. "What can I help you with?"

"Just a few more questions." Office Baldwin pulled out his notebook. He looked up at her from the page, his eyebrows bunching together into one Muppet brow.

Why did men think that waxing was only a female option for overabundant body hair? Mia tried to look away, but the brow kept drawing her in. He'd already asked the question when Mia heard the question mark. "Sorry," she almost blurted out, "woolgathering," but thought better of it.

"Again, where were you the night Adele was murdered?" Now he tapped his pencil on the table.

Mia leaned back. So much for kindred souls. "I told you the last time we talked. I was here."

"Except for the time you went for a walk." He glanced at his notes. "Around the square because you were nervous?"

Mia sighed. "Yes, except for that walk, I was here."

The man stared for a full second, then nodded. "And you were hired by Adele to cater her birthday? Didn't you think that strange because you weren't even open for business yet?"

"Officer Baldwin, you obviously grew up here and know my grandmother. She and Adele were friends. Do I have to spell it out for you? It was a pity job. Grans made her ask me." Mia rubbed her temple; the headache wasn't going away easily. "Do you have any new questions?"

Office Baldwin scribbled in his pad. He nodded. "Just one. Tell me what happened to your missing knife."

"Hold on a second." Mia stood and poured herself a cup of coffee and took a sip before she answered, hoping the caffeine would help cut the edge off the headache. "The day before the party I took my knives to the hotel with my prep. I should have brought them back home—I never leave my knives anywhere—but I was distracted. By the time I realized I'd left them at the Lodge, I figured the kitchen would be closed."

"When did you realize a knife was missing from the set?"

"Yesterday—well, not yesterday but Saturday, when I dropped off Christina at the Lodge. Spending a couple of days in the hospital messes with your sense of time. Anyway, I went back to the kitchen and found my case stuffed under a shelf. One of the knives was missing then. We searched the kitchen."

"We?" Baldwin had filled a cup with coffee and now stirred sugar into the cup, the deep roast smell comforting Mia in an odd way. He glanced around the table for creamer but didn't ask. Mia didn't offer either. Baldwin could drink his coffee black.

"James, the Lodge chef. He helped me look; then, when we couldn't find anything, he kicked me out of the kitchen. He said he'd find it." Mia paused, "Wait, how did you know my knife was missing? James told you, didn't he?"

Grans bustled into the room and didn't give Baldwin a chance to respond.

"My granddaughter is very fatigued. It's been a long week. Can we continue this later?" Grans's voice was soft yet firm.

"No worries, Mrs. Carpenter, I'm done anyway. We'll check with the phone company and see if we can trace the calls. I'll let you know what we come up with." He stood and brushed crumbs from his lap onto the floor.

He put his notebook in his pocket, then clicked his pen, glancing up at Mia. "One more question before I leave."

"Of course." Mia tried to keep the sarcasm out of her tone.

"Do you know anyone who would want to kill you?"

Sleep proved elusive and Baldwin's question kept bouncing around her head. Or at least want her out of town. That really was the question. She knew someone who wanted her out of town, and he'd even pay her the fair market price for her building. If he had wanted her dead, she would have been killed the night she was attacked. Unless the two events weren't connected. And of course someone being a jerk didn't mean they were a killer. It had been a crazy week. First Adele showed up with a knife in her chest. Now Mia was being attacked and threatened. She felt like she should be living in Los Angeles rather than tiny Magic Springs.

She sat up, put on her robe and slippers, and headed out to the tiny kitchen. If her insomnia kept up, she'd gain twenty pounds just from all the baking she'd be doing. She'd think about dieting later; tonight she wanted brownies. Cheesecake brownies.

As she passed by Christina's door, she saw light bleeding out from the bottom into the hallway. Reaching up her hand to knock, she heard Christina's voice from inside the room.

"I really don't care what you want. She's been good to me. A lot better than any of you. I'm not betraying her." Christina must have been almost shouting into the phone for her voice to be heard through the closed doorway.

Mia slowly dropped her arm. She'd been right about Christina's loyalty. But how long would it last? Her heart sank as she slowly shuffled to the kitchen. She'd wanted to be wrong about Isaac. Just for once, why couldn't he have been that sweet boy she'd seen trying to juggle the grill at the hotel the first day they'd met. He'd been all thumbs that day, and later he'd admitted she had been the cause of his distraction.

The betrayal she'd felt during this whole breakup came back. Tears filled her eyes as she pulled out the flour and sugar, along with some baker's chocolate from the upper cabinets. She knew she had fallen out of love with Isaac many years ago. Yet she still grieved. As she grabbed the butter, cream cheese, and eggs from the fridge, she realized she wasn't grieving the man. She cried for the loss of what could have been. Wiping her eyes with a cotton kitchen towel, she shook her head. Their relationship had never been the fairy tale she'd wanted or believed in. The next time she fell in love, she'd do it with her eyes wide open. And he'd have to walk on hot coals for her before she'd give in. A high standard, but she was worth the pain.

"Isn't that right, Gloria?" She focused on her kitchen witch perched on the windowsill. The doll seemed to grin back at her. "The next man better be worth the future tears. This one definitely wasn't worth a drop."

The air around the doll shimmered, and Mia felt the comforting blanket of air envelope her. She hadn't felt this kind of attention from the doll in years. Not since she'd left for college. Mia had spent hours as a teenager talking about her problems in the kitchen, either with her grandmother or just alone, the doll in the window, listening. She'd named her Gloria as a child when the doll used to live in her room. Gloria had been the replacement of her imaginary playmate, only Mia hadn't outgrown her attachment to the ancient doll. As it happened to all kitchen witches, the attachment grew over time, until the witch felt strong enough to perform healing spells on their own.

She felt the gentle laughter shimmer over the room.

"Sure, laugh at me now. But just wait, you'll see how strong I am when the next man comes calling. He's going to have to be special for me to even notice him." Mia broke the eggs into a bowl and then, before she whisked them with a fork, she turned on the small radio she kept in the kitchen. "We need some music."

Humming, she focused on making the brownies. Creaming the sugar into the butter, she thought about using her Cuisinart, sitting on the counter, but discarded the idea of using the mixer. The machine was fine when she was in a hurry or making large batches, but tonight was less about the result and more about the process. She wanted to feel the sugar cream into the butter and know she created that new concoction. Baking felt better than any of the money she'd spent on therapy over the years. Mostly because in therapy, she still held back. How could she explain to anyone that part of her angst was carrying the secret of the witchcraft she practiced? Although being a hearth witch was less about the action and more about the being. She could no more not be one of the ancient coven as she could change her DNA sequencing.

Thinking about covens brought Levi to mind. His

dancing eyes making her smile in spite of herself. The
guy had magic all right, mostly in the flirting department.
So different from his serious brother. Sure, Trent flirted
with her, but it was on a different level. More substantial.
With Levi, you knew it was a game. Trent's interaction
felt more serious. Maybe he was like this with everyone.
He seemed to know everyone in town. Probably a side effect of running the store.

And why do you care? Gloria's thought burst through
her mental wanderings.

Mia glanced at the doll. "You're right, I don't care."

"You don't care about what?" Christina's voice came
from the doorway. "Who are you talking to?"

Mia spun around, spoon in hand. "You scared me.
Why are you up?" Telling Christina she'd heard her on
the phone would make her look like a stalker, or nosy.

"I heard the music." Christina filled the teakettle with
water and put it on the stove to heat. "We really have to
stop meeting like this."

Mia smiled. "I couldn't sleep. Being accused of murder and being told you're a possible victim in the same
breath kind of does that to a person."

"Baldwin's a jerk. He hates you because he doubly
hates me. I'm just trouble." Christina made the air quotes
with her hands.

"You're not trouble." Mia pushed a lock of hair out of
Christina's face. "Even when you are at your worst, you're
just confused. People need to get to know you."

"Mia, you are naïve. You wouldn't say that if you
knew what happened in Vegas." Christina sighed. "Maybe
the cops would stop hassling you if I left. I know a guy in
Boise who said I could crash on his couch for a few
days."

Mia sat in a chair and pulled Christina's hands toward her. She squeezed them together. Christina had been like a sister to her all during her relationship with Isaac. She wasn't giving up on her now, just because they weren't actually going to be related in the future. "Look, you're not a problem and you aren't leaving to sleep on some guy's couch. I need you here. If you want to go back to school, or home," Mia paused to let the word sink in, "that's fine. But you aren't leaving because Baldwin's giving me trouble."

"But he wouldn't . . ."

Mia put up her hand. "He would. I'm the new kid here too. Even with Grans's family being descended from one of the town's founding fathers, the guy looks at me as an outsider. We have to stand together and show him he's not going to push us out. Besides, I didn't kill Adele. You didn't kill Adele, did you?"

"No." A small smile started to play on Christina's lips.

Mia stood. "Then we're not going to run. If we have to find out who killed Adele by ourselves, we will."

Mia walked back and removed the melted chocolate from the microwave. She folded the chocolate into the batter. "You want to learn how to make the cheesecake topping?"

"I guess. What kind of kitchen sidekick would say no?" Christina went to the sink and washed her hands. Setting aside the towel, she picked up the kitchen witch and settled it farther on the windowsill. "Seriously, who were you talking to when I came in?"

CHAPTER 11

The door actually creaked as Grans pushed the large front door open and they stepped into the foyer. The stone house looked more like a castle than a house. According to Grans, Adele's family had lived in the place since her great-grandfather moved to oversee his cattle ranch a few miles out of town. "As Adele told it, Great-Grandmother made one request of her groom before she'd say 'I do.' And that was to build this house."

The foyer was more grand entry than mudroom. The wooden surfaces shone as cherry or some other dark wood, Mia couldn't tell. But she was sure the wood wasn't the more locally available pine, which would have been cheaper to use. Adele's great-grandmother must have been some catch for a man to build this home for her. Mia reached out to touch the glossy banister. "It's amazing."

"What are you doing? Don't touch anything. Just because I have the key doesn't mean we're not trespassing in the eyes of the law. I should have told folks about that time I caught him shoplifting. That would have kept him from thinking he's high and mighty." Grans nodded to the back of the house. "Adele's office is back there, in the old servants' quarters. She turned it into a library ten years ago."

Mia followed Grans to the back of the house, her hands now shoved into the pockets of the wool peacoat she'd picked up at the army/navy surplus store last winter in Boise. The house felt warm and welcoming, not like Adele at all. Maybe she'd misjudged Grans's friend. The woman had to have something nice inside for Grans to put up with her.

When they reached the office Grans pushed open the door. Files were strewn on the desk, the couch, even on the floor.

"I didn't think she'd be this messy." Mia glanced over the files on the desk. Mostly old clippings from the local paper about births and obituaries.

"Adele was ultra organized. This isn't her doing. The office has been ransacked." Grans glanced around the room. "I don't know what they were after. Adele didn't keep any money at the house. She believed in using her debit card for every transaction. She never carried a dime's worth of cash. I don't know how many times I had to give her a dollar for a soda or a candy bar. The woman must owe me a few thousand dollars from the change I've given her over the years."

"The door was locked, right?" The back of Mia's neck had started to tingle. Someone had been looking for something, and recently, unless Adele's maid hadn't come in since her death.

"I heard the click when it opened. Yes, it was locked. And the front door is the only entrance. She kept getting warnings from the fire department that she had to have at least two exits, but Adele said that her grandfather had built one door and that was the way the house would stay. She thought the old guy had been afraid of his wife sneaking out and running away. One door was easier to watch than two." Grans frowned. "I didn't realize Adele was doing genealogy."

"What do you mean?" Mia removed a pen from her pocket and poked at the clippings.

"This family tree. She was tracing back something." Grans picked up the paper, glancing at the writing.

"Hey, I thought you said not to touch anything."

Grans didn't even look at her. "I told you not to touch anything. I've been over here more times in my lifetime than I can count. No one will question my fingerprints showing up. You, on the other hand, are a suspect."

"Ouch." Mia faked taking a shot to her midsection.

"It's the truth, dear girl." Grans frowned. "Didn't she tell you that Danforth was her nephew?"

"I think so. She said the guy probably ran through the money her sister had given him. I guess I just assumed. Why?"

"It may have been an omission, but her sister doesn't have any children listed on this family tree. There's a cousin with a 'Billy' listed, but nothing under Barbara."

"So you think William is Billy?" Mia stepped closer to the desk. Maybe they'd found the killer. The so-called nephew who'd called her out at the wake. That would tie everything up nice and tidy. Hope filled her as she tried to read Adele's handwriting.

"I don't know. And if he was, why would she call him

her nephew? It's probably just a mistake. Adele's eyesight wasn't the best lately. Maybe she just wrote the name in the wrong spot."

"Maybe."

A footstep echoed overhead. Mia's eyes widened. Grans had heard it too. "Come on; someone is in the house."

Mia pushed Grans out of the office and into the lobby, but then voices sounded from the top of the stairs. They retreated into a coat closet next to the office door. She put her finger to her lips, seeing Grans in the dim light. Adele's furs had been stored in the closet and Mia tried not to sneeze, the fur tickling her nose. Grans, instead of being scared, looked like she was about to laugh. Mia leaned closer to the barely opened closet door.

"So when do you think probate will close and you can sign over the deed?" A male voice boomed in the empty foyer.

"A month or two. As soon as I get permission, I'll clean out all of Adele's junk and you guys can move in. We can set up a presale lease contract." A different male voice answered, one that Mia recognized. She tried to remember if it was the same voice as the guy who'd threatened her.

"Don't get rid of too much. Adele had such great taste, I'd like to keep her furnishings." A woman's voice was added to the mix.

Grans frowned and leaned closer to the door.

"No worries, we'll just add that to the price of the contract. I'll clean out the closets and take out her personal stuff. I'm sure I'll have to take it all to Goodwill. The woman had no taste at all." The man hesitated, then added, "In clothing, I meant."

Even in the dim light in the closet, Mia could see

Grans's face tense. She reached out and touched her grandmother's arm in warning. She didn't know who was in the house, but she knew barging out of the closet wouldn't make the situation any better.

"Have your attorney draw up an agreement and we'll look it over. I hope we can have this completed in the next month or so?" the older male voice asked.

"No worries. The sooner I get out of here and back home to Arizona, the better." The voice Mia now knew as William Danforth the Third's drifted out of hearing range, and then she heard a door shut.

Grans reached for the closet door. "I am so mad. I can't believe he said all those things about Adele. The poor woman's body isn't even cold. The lawyer better speed up the reading of the will or that nephew of hers will have this place sold off before he even officially owns the house. Poor Adele."

"Hold on a second; let's make sure they're gone." Mia thought about her van parked across the street. Good thing she drove an older vehicle. Most people around here didn't even notice what type of car you drove unless it was a Range Rover or a Hummer. Anything else was for the servants or townies. People like the couple who'd just made a deal with Danforth weren't interested in the lower classes. Mia thought about them. "Any clue who the other two were?"

Grans opened the door a crack so they could watch the front entry. She glanced back at Mia. "I know both of them. I recognized her whine. Helen Marcum and her husband. The people from Chicago."

After five minutes Mia couldn't stand the smell of mink or rabbit or whatever other fur Adele had stuffed in the closet anymore. She slowly opened the closet door.

When they reached the front hallway she glanced out the side window by the door. Not seeing any car parked in the driveway or any neighbor out in their yard, the two of them slipped out of the house. Instead of running directly to the van to keep from being seen, they walked around the side away from the driveway. Then Mia pushed through a break in the hedge and returned to the street, using the side yard of the summer home of a famous actor and his equally famous wife. Or ex-wife, Mia mentally corrected. The celebrity faces changed fast, with the happy couple together one summer, and the next season just the wife or just the husband would return. Usually with a new lover in tow. She'd seen a couple of the Sun Valley elite milling around at Majors the last few weeks. Grans called them "wannabes." The Hollywood and New York celebrities never showed before June or after the Christmas ski season ended. Now, the Lodge was filled with die-hard ski fanatics. Rich or poor, they all came for the powder.

When they reached the safety of the van Mia glanced at her grandmother. "What now? Do we take this to the police?"

"And tell them what? That her nephew is showing the house to prospective buyers?" Grans pulled out the piece of paper with the family tree. "Mark would laugh us out of the station, if he didn't arrest us for trespassing."

"Well, me, not you." Mia corrected. She had no doubt Magic Springs's finest would waste no time in charging her with a crime if she freely admitted her guilt.

Grans's smile brightened her face. "You have got his panties twisted, haven't you?" When Mia protested, Grans put up her hand. "I'm just teasing. But you're right. He would throw you in a cell."

"In a heartbeat." Mia started the engine and steered the van away from the curb.

Grans tapped the paper. "The answer is here, I know it."

"In the family tree?"

She nodded. "You always find skeletons when you start to do this kind of research. I just wonder what Adele was looking for."

"Don't all old people do genealogy?" Mia headed the car toward Grans's house a few blocks over.

"Don't age profile us. Just because our hair's gray doesn't mean we are all the same. Adele wasn't the sentimental type. About her family or her age." Grans swatted Mia's arm.

"Yes, ma'am. You need some help?" Mia eased the car down the snow-covered street.

Grans put the paper that she'd been studying on her lap. She turned to Mia and cocked her head. "Now you think I'm too old to do research?"

Mia twisted to check for oncoming traffic as she made a right on to Grans's street. She didn't answer until she'd pulled the car into the driveway and turned off the engine. "I was just going to offer to hold out the paper farther so you could read the words."

"Smart aleck." Grans sniffed and tucked the paper into her purse. "Thank you for the ride. I'll let you know when I find something."

Mia leaned over the seat. "I'm here for you."

"You're here to tease me." Grans slammed the door, then wiggled her fingers at Mia. Their secret symbol. Grans had taught Mia the sign when she'd first said good-bye and left the Boise house to return to Magic Springs. Be good, be loved, be everything. Grans had explained the symbolism behind the action. Mia had never forgotten.

She waved back and considered following her grans into the house. Instead she waited for her to find her keys and unlock the door before Mia put the car into reverse. As soon as she touched the gearshift, her phone rang.

"Mia Malone." She smiled as Grans curtsied in the doorway, then shut the large wooden door. The woman could still surprise her.

"Where are you?" a male voice asked.

"Where am I supposed to be?" Dropping her hand, she decided to finish the call before leaving the driveway. She still hadn't invested in a Bluetooth, and Officer Baldwin could be just around the corner. The man was just looking for an excuse to write her a ticket or, at worst, throw her in jail. The voice registered finally and she asked, "Trent?"

"You should be here talking to your contractors. They are ready for the building inspector." Trent's voice held a touch of humor. "And I brought you a present."

"I'm dropping off Grans, I'll be there in a sec." She glanced behind her, trying to gauge the chances the town's police cruiser was even out in the more residential areas. Baldwin tended to man the town's speed trap out on the main highway toward Sun Valley. Reaching up to put the car in gear, she watched out the window for any sign of the cruiser. "What's my present?"

"If I told you, you wouldn't be surprised." Trent added, "Just drive safe and get over here."

"Who said I like surprises?" Mia realized she was talking to dead air. She tossed the phone into the passenger seat. "Seriously, that man is . . ."

She paused. What had she been going to say? Infuriating? Bothersome? Hot and sexy as hell? Her hormones must be flying for her to be in lust at ten in the morning. Seeing Isaac had brought back a lot of emotions, a lot of pain.

Now, less than six months later, she was considering a relationship with a new guy? Okay, to be honest she really was only considering having sex with the guy. Maybe several sessions, just to make sure she truly was over Isaac. Mia smiled at her reflection in the rearview mirror as she pulled out of the driveway. Finally arriving home, she slid her van into the principal's old parking spot and sprinted into the building. When she entered the front door she ducked involuntarily. She hoped she'd be able to stop doing that someday.

Voices sounded from back in the kitchen area. When Mia stepped into the room she gasped. All the work she and the general contractor had planned was done. Well, the floor still needed to be replaced and the window treatment had totally disappeared, but the appliances were in, and, heaven help her, the subzero freezer looked cuter than it had in the store. The kitchen reminded her of a mini version of the Lodge's kitchen. But totally big enough for Mia's Morsels. Now she just had to find the missing inspector.

Trent gestured her over when he saw she'd arrived. "Hey, what do you think?" He waved his arms around the room.

"I didn't think we'd be done until late next week at the earliest." Mia glanced around, looking for the general contractor. He tipped his hat when their eyes met. "What happened?"

The man stepped closer. "Mr. Majors can be very persuasive. Especially when he's explaining how much opening this place means to you."

Trent stepped between the two, blocking Mia's attempt at more conversation. "I didn't bring you here to chitchat. Meet George Kennedy."

Mia gasped. "Mr. Kennedy? I'm so glad you made time for us out of your busy schedule." A little butt kissing may work better than vinegar on the elusive Mr. Kennedy.

"Trent told me about your little predicament. I'm glad to help out." The inspector glanced around the room. "I'm sure with a few upgrades you'll be code ready in about a week. How does that sound?"

"Like heaven." Mia signed in relief. She'd be able to cook and prep for the ritzier party next week, once the kitchen was complete. She'd be a real caterer then. And between her and Christina, they'd make a kick-ass menu for the first drop-off dinner clients and the word-of-mouth advertisements happy customers brought. She'd be doing a brisk business in less than a month. The thought excited her. Her own business.

"Mia? What do you think?" The men were looking at her like she'd missed a button on her blouse.

"What?" Mia smoothed the front of her T-shirt.

"George wants to know what you are doing about the gas lines. Are you going to return to the original kitchen configuration?"

"I don't understand." Mia glanced around the room. "Isn't this the original setup?"

George barked a chuckle. "Heavens no. The school did some unapproved remodeling to allow them to bring in a larger refrigerator, one with a lock." He walked over near the window. "The stove and hood were over here, which lowers the stress on the gas lines and assures a better distribution. Over there, you're looking at running all new lines and wires. And probably adding a week or two to your initial proposal."

"No delays. I can't afford them. Let's just move the stove back." She tried to imagine the updated kitchen. The room flowed better with the change George suggested. She'd expected a long list of corrections before she opened, but this guy was nice, sweet even. She just must have been used to the Boise inspectors, who took glee in writing up even the tiniest infraction.

George handed her a clipboard. "Just sign here and I'll give a copy to your contractor, giving him the go ahead to continue working with the caveat that these items will be corrected."

Mia glanced at the list. Twenty-two items. "I don't understand. All these things have to be fixed? Or are these just suggestions?" She gave the inspector what she hoped was a somewhat friendly smile.

"Either fix them or don't open. We take building safety seriously in Magic Springs." He nodded to the clipboard. "Now, if you'll just sign that you got the list, I'll be out of your hair."

Mia glanced at the list. "You want us to install earthquake straps to the large appliances. Earthquakes?"

"The Stanley Basin is a hotbed of tremors. I'm surprised no one told you." George pointed out the window to the distant Magic range. "A fault runs directly through this valley. Those tectonic plates are shifty little devils."

"When was the last earthquake that did any damage, 1910?"

"It was 1983—the Borah Peak quake basically destroyed the town of Challis, just down the road." He pulled on his coat. "I'm not here to argue with you. Either do the work or don't open. Pretty simple."

Mia watched as he walked out of the kitchen and toward the front door.

"I'll calm him down." Trent squeezed her arm then turned to follow the inspector. "Doesn't do any good to have George mad."

"Calm him down?" Mia glanced at the clipboard still in her hand. Sighing, she signed the paper, ripped off her copy, and shoved the rest at Trent. "Take this with you. I don't have an option here."

Dollar signs danced around in her head as she tried to estimate the additional costs. Thank the Goddess she'd taken Grans up on her offer of a loan. The kitchen remodel budget had just doubled. She glanced around the room again, watching the dust dance in the sunlight beams forcing their way through the dirty panes of glass. It didn't matter the cost. In a week she would be putting on her first real event since she left Boise. A chance to start over. All wrapped up in a cocktail party for the Magic Springs elite.

CHAPTER 12

The music flowed out of the speakers in the Joneses' kitchen. Bach, if Mia's classical music training at the one private high school in the Boise area held true. Mia had wanted to attend the local high school where all her friends from elementary and junior high had gone, but her parents had insisted on the Catholic school run by Bishop Kelly. Four years of excruciating hell from being the misfit. Those kids had been born into their cliques. Mia hadn't had a chance even before she opened her mouth.

Music, singing, or just listening to a violin solo along with an unhealthy attachment to the library and a goal to read through all the books in the collection had kept Mia sane for those years when she didn't have a single friend.

When she graduated and escaped to college, then cooking school, Mia knew she'd never return to the campus. Not for homecoming, or career day, or even to bring her kids to the school. She was done with the place. She'd never been invited to any reunion and she'd never attended. The process worked well for both parties. Mia didn't have to shoot anyone and the pompous jerks didn't have to die.

No wonder she'd taken Christina under her wing when she'd arrived at the house Isaac and Mia had shared. Mia saw herself in Christina, even if her upbringing was a lot more privileged and refined than Mia's own.

Mia glanced at the door, hoping her thoughts would bring her wayward sous chef back home. Christina had been disappearing for days now. Isaac had returned to Boise on Monday, just like he'd promised, but Mia could hear him playing on her sympathies at night, when he called to harass his sister.

Now that she was out of the relationship, she didn't know what she'd seen in Isaac in the first place. They hadn't really talked for years, not about what mattered: their relationship, their future. No, their conversations had been all about work and remodeling and Isaac's family. The problem with denial was that when you really opened your eyes you were standing on the edge of the world, waiting for a push over the brink.

She set out the Green Goddess dressing she'd prepared earlier and emptied the rest of the items from her tote bag. She looked at her list. She had to get going or the food wouldn't be ready in time. She couldn't fail.

Mia had finished chopping the onions when Christina finally showed.

"Sorry I was late. We didn't have a clock." Christina pulled on an apron and turned to the sink, washing her hands.

"*We*?" Mia smiled. Maybe there was something to

keep Christina hanging around besides the job. She liked having company around the house.

Christina blushed, grabbing a towel from the rack. She pulled out the cutting board and glanced at Mia's prep list. "Where do you want me to start?"

"You're lucky we're running late or you'd never get away with dodging my question like that." Mia glanced at the list. "We need to get the squab started."

Christina bit back a smile, but Mia saw it anyway. She'd have to ask Grans about the young men in town. Mia just hoped it wasn't one of the spoiled rich kids from Sun Valley, slumming it with a Magic Springs girl. Many a heart had been broken when the *real* girlfriend showed up for the weekend to stake her claim. Even though Mia had been a summer resident for most of her teenage years, she'd never fallen for the prep boys. Give her a bad boy to the core, and if he had a little grease under his fingernails, more the better.

The two women worked side by side for the next hour. The only conversation centered around preparing the salad bar Mia had imagined. Chicken Green Goddess, Ahi Tuna Surprise, How Green Is My Valley, Not Your Mama's Potato Salad, oven-roasted squab, and a selection of cheeses. Not the most gourmet of meals, but all the salads were spot-on delicious. The hostess needed a spread that wouldn't offend the more down-to-earth business sponsors her husband's firm were courting. As Mia put the last bowl on the buffet table, Carrie Jones came by to see her.

"I love it. I can't believe you pulled this together so quickly." Carrie used a fork and speared a potato from the salad. She swallowed, then squealed. "The food is amazing. Jacob is so going to love me."

"I'm glad you like it. Everything's out and displayed, so my assistant and I will leave now. What time do you want us back to clean up?"

"How about ten? My husband plans on taking the group out to the Lodge for a nightcap." Carrie pressed a key into Mia's hand. "Just lock up when you're done. Leave the invoice in the kitchen, I'll have a check waiting for you when you come back for your things. Thank you again. I'm sure we'll be seeing a lot of each other."

"Satisfied customers always bring me repeat work." Mia put on a hostess smile. Especially because the phrase seemed forced, Marketing 101 level. She didn't have to worry because Carrie had already disappeared back into the living room. Mia heard her call out that dinner would be served in the dining room and took that as her clue to duck back into the kitchen.

Before she could escape John Louis blocked the door. His smile looked more like a crocodile opening his mouth. "Well, if it isn't Mia Malone. Have you considered my offer? Ready to get out of here and start your new life?"

"This *is* my new life, so no, I'm not ready." She stepped around the jerk. "Thanks for the offer, though."

His hand reached out and squeezed her arm hard enough to bring tears to her eyes. If they had been any-where else, Mia would have used her ten years of martial arts training to put the waste of space on his butt. "Look, sister, I need that property. And if you haven't figured out yet, I get what I need around here. I would have thought what happened to Adele would have spooked you enough. I don't like it when I'm ignored."

Mia set her jaw. "Now you're trying to tell me that you killed Adele?" She laughed, the sound harsh and tinny. "I don't think you have the balls to actually kill someone.

Sure, beat around a defenseless woman or two, but not kill."

"You don't know what I'm capable of." John leered at her. "Maybe you need to find out?"

She shrugged out of his grip. "In your dreams, buddy. I think, though, that Mark Baldwin will be very interested in this conversation, and the fact that you sound so much like the man who called and threatened me over the phone the other night. Do you like pushing around girls?"

Now his face was beet red. "You don't know who you're messing with. You should have left when I told you to. Now you'll just be collateral damage."

A polite cough sounded in the doorway of the dining room.

John spun away and almost ran over a portly man who was obviously looking for the food. Mia greeted the man with a quick smile, then pushed on the door to the kitchen. She had to get out of there.

As she stepped away, she felt a hand on her arm. She looked up into a pair of deep-brown eyes in a face she didn't recognize. "Can I help you?"

The man blushed and pulled away his hand. "I'm sorry to bother you, I just wanted to see that you were okay. You're Mia Malone, right?"

"Since I was born." She let out a breath. "Sorry. My conversation with John has me a little on edge. Thanks for showing up; he's intense."

"No one deserves to be talked to in that manner. Not even his wife, who has taken his crap for years." The guy eyed the buffet table as he continued. "I'm Barney Mann."

"Nice to meet you, Mr. Mann." Mia waited for her breathing to slow. The man in front of her stood five-foot-two, maybe three. Mia saw the heels on the shoes under the cheap suit. From what she could tell by the girth of the man, he might have been five-foot wide as well. His eyes now peered at her from a puffy face. "Are you enjoying the party?"

"Normal chitchat crap. You'd think these people would learn how to get a life. It's always the same thing: who they saw, who they know, what they paid for their new car. I get tired of talking within the first fifteen minutes of one of these things." Barney grabbed a plate and filled it with potato salad. He took a bite, "This is actually good. Too bad it's just picnic food."

"Mrs. Jones wanted a more casual presentation." No way would he get her to talk bad about the only client she had who was alive to give a reference.

"Carrie. That girl may have married well, but her husband would have been better off sending her to a finishing school rather than the plastic surgeon to enhance her assets. You know she's from Alabama, right? And not the good part either. If there is such a thing."

Mia bit her lip to keep herself from smiling. The guy may not like gossip, but he sure had his own to spread around. She nodded and stepped to the left to the kitchen door. "I'd better go. Enjoy your meal."

"Wait, I need to talk to you." Barney shoved another spoonful of potato salad in his mouth and chewed with his mouth open. He set down his plate and held up a finger, holding her in the dining room.

Mia waited, more out of curiosity to see if the man would choke before he asked his question.

Finally he swallowed and wiped his mouth with the sleeve of his suit. "I'm Adele's attorney."

Mia waited. When he didn't continue she prodded. "And?"

"I understand her nephew has been spreading some gossip of his own. Like telling people you killed Adele." The man's eyes went sharp as he watched her for a reaction.

"I can't control what other people say, but I didn't kill Adele. Why would I?" Mia refolded a linen napkin that had been lying on the table.

"I believe you. I'm sure there were many others with actual motive to kill my client. I just thought you might like to know what he was saying." He glanced at the doorway. "John has been egging him on, at least in my opinion. You must have gotten on his bad side quick. You've only lived here, what, two months?"

"My grandmother told me years ago that it didn't matter what people said about you, the only opinion that mattered was your own." Mia glanced at the kitchen door. She wanted to rush through it, run home, put up her feet, and forget about tonight.

"True." Barney Mann leaned closer to Mia, and she could smell the cologne covering an odor of sweat and decay. The man would be following Adele into the next life sooner than he knew. "Honestly, I think Mr. Danforth has a secret. A secret that could affect your grandmother."

"I don't understand. What does this have to do with Grans?" A chill hit the back of Mia's neck under the collar of her chef jacket. Laughter sounded in the hallway; the rest of the guests from the party were arriving for their meal.

"I'll keep you informed." Barney glanced at the people coming into the room. "Just keep your grandmother safe."

Mia reached for his arm to ask him more, but he shook her off and went to the hostess. "What an amazing spread. Did you spend all afternoon in the kitchen your-self?"

Mia heard Carrie's laughter as she slipped into the kitchen, Barney's words still ringing in her ears. *Keep your grandmother safe.*

Christina leaned against the counter, talking in a whis-per into her cell. She froze when she saw Mia.

"You can go. I'll need you back here at ten to help me clean up." Mia pushed Christina's coat into her arms. "Who am I to stand in the way of young love?"

Christina blushed, mouthed the words *thank you*, then exited the house through the back door. Mia watched as she climbed into a two-seater sports car, probably worth more than most houses in good neighborhoods in Boise. So much for hoping she wasn't seeing one of the Sun Val-ley elite. "Lord help us if he dumps her," she muttered to the empty kitchen.

Mia grabbed her purse and coat. As she dug in her purse for the envelope with the invoice for the Joneses, she pulled out the letter to Christina. The one she'd never given to her. She'd put it on Christina's bed as soon as she arrived home.

When she arrived at the school she groaned. She'd for-gotten to turn on the downstairs lights again. The build-ing's windows gaped black at her, reminding her of the haunted houses she used to draw in Mrs. Stewart's second-grade class.

Fear trembled through her for a second and she gripped the steering wheel, considering her options. She could go to Grans for a few hours, she could go grocery shopping, she could . . . She could get her butt up out of this car and go into her house. She knew the feeling was a natural result of the attack. But there was no way a criminal would get away with breaking and entering, hitting her on the head, *and* make her afraid of her shadow. That was not going to happen.

Mia, determined to fight the fear, grabbed her bag and left the warmth and safety of her car. She slowly made her way up the walk, telling herself the lack of speed had more to do with the slight chance of an ice patch and less to do with the fact that she knew she'd be hit as soon as the door opened. And once again she'd be in the back of the ambulance, talking to Trent's very charming brother.

Now why couldn't Christina date Levi? The guy seemed nice enough. Maybe a bit of a player, with all the coven stuff. So many witches used the coven roster as their personal little black book. The thrill of the hunt, along with the risk of being turned into a frog, or a snake, or even a garden gnome.

Not for the first time, she wished her magic worked like normal witchcraft. She would have loved to be able to turn Isaac into the slimy, stomach-dragging creature he'd become. But as a hearth witch, her spells and charms seemed to be limited to mostly three things: healing, cooking, and world peace. She'd tried cleaning spells, but had had limited success. The world didn't seem to be taking on the daily peace charms she chanted in her kitchen after Christina went to bed. Kitchen witches in history had been the village healers. Not the most scary or powerful image. Mia thought about Gloria's smile as she pictured the kitchen witch doll in her kitchen. She knew more than Grans had explained. Mia wondered what secrets the doll carried.

She stood at her door, key in hand. Stalling; she was stalling. Glancing around, Mia didn't see anyone lurking in the shadows. She slipped the key in the door and tried to push it open. It hit something on the other side. Mia's stomach clenched.

"Who's there?" she called out. Instantly her face flushed heat. Did she really think her attacker would introduce himself before bopping her on the head again? She slipped her hand in her pocket and felt for her phone, just in case. Then she pushed the door again.

This time it slowly creaked open, and Mia realized a box blocked the doorway. She flipped on the light switch, and bright shop lights gleamed around the hallway. The electricians had been in today when she met with the contractors and had stripped out the old lighting fixtures, but apparently hadn't gotten the new recessed lighting installed yet. So they'd left her with standing lights that made the entry look like an airport runway.

Satisfied no one hid in any dark corners—mostly because there weren't any dark corners to be found, at least in the foyer—Mia slipped in the door, closing and locking it behind her. She needed to get in control of this fear. Maybe Grans had a safety spell she could wear until she felt more in control. Glancing at the object that blocked the door, Mia was surprised to see the box was wrapped in silver paper and ribbons. She picked up the gift and headed up the stairs to her apartment, leaving on the hallway lights for the moment. She'd be meeting Christina over at the Joneses' in a couple of hours. She had just time enough to grab some dinner herself and maybe kick back with the mystery she'd been trying to read for the last month. Not like her life hadn't been mystery enough.

After slipping into her apartment she set the box on the table and turned on the lights in the living room. Again she locked the door to her sanctuary. *Better safe than sorry*. She walked down the hall, turning on lights as she walked. The brightly lit apartment might be glowing from a casual glance from a townsperson, but the glow helped ease the chill Mia felt. She moved into the bedroom and went right to the bathroom. Slipping out of her chef jacket, Mia turned on the shower, letting the water heat.

She pulled her hair out of the clip that held it up and stared longingly at the bed. She'd been up since five, running from one fire to the next. Sleep would be nice, but she knew if she laid down her head, she'd sleep right through the cleanup. Regretfully, she turned away from the bed and walked to the shower, every muscle in her body screaming.

Ten minutes later she emerged from the bathroom and slipped on a black T-shirt and jeans. She sat on the bed and pulled on her leather boots. She leaned back and closed her eyes for just a second. Then she remembered the gift she'd left in the kitchen. She glanced at the clock as she walked through the hallway. Seven thirty; lots of time. She put the teakettle on to boil and grabbed a piece of bread, slathering on peanut butter. Putting the bread on a paper towel, she sat at the table. She watched the box as she ate her sandwich.

Couldn't be Isaac. In the five years they'd been together, the man had never given her a gift. Trent? But why would a man she barely knew leave her a present?

She finished her dinner and brushed the crumbs from her hands, excited to find out. She unwrapped the box and pulled off the lid.

There, in a bed of red tissue paper, was her knife.

The whistle from the teakettle screamed.

CHAPTER 13

Even though Mia was almost twenty minutes late arriving back at the Joneses' house, Christina hadn't returned yet. The house, although empty, had been ablaze with light, a stark contrast to the way she'd found her house when she'd arrived home what seemed to be days ago.

After she found the knife she sat at the kitchen table and tried to think this through. Why would someone go to the trouble of stealing her knife just to wrap it up and send it to her as some kind of practical joke? Did someone really kill Adele with one of her knives? Or was this John's idea of a sick little joke? The guy was getting on her nerves.

Finally she picked up her cell and called Officer Baldwin. She'd reached his voice mail and left a message, and when she hung up she heated up a bowl of the soup she'd made earlier that week and turned on the television.

When the news came on she realized it was time to return to Carrie's. She needed to clean up from the catering job. She may be arrested for a crime she didn't commit, but she wouldn't go without finishing her job.

As she moved the empty serving containers from the dining room into the kitchen, she tried to think through the last week. Adele's nephew had come in as a surprise for her birthday. Then, the next day, Adele showed up dead. Stabbed. And who had a missing knife? Mia Malone, a new, thereby suspicious member of the community. Now the knife in question had been returned, so the evidence that had damned her before was irrelevant. Mia smiled. Even a bad made-for-TV movie would have better motivation.

She glanced around the kitchen for her tote baskets. She glanced at the door to the basement. Crap; she'd told Christina to take them down and out of their way. She hated basements. Mia glanced out the window, but the only car in the driveway was her van. She sighed and opened the door. The wooden stairs looked new, not like the ones in her grandmother's basement. Mia still shuddered, thinking about the cobwebs she might touch.

Just do it. God, she hated that shoe commercial. She glanced out at the empty driveway one more time for the sports car that had whisked Christina away. Nothing. Christina was going to get a royal lecture on the importance of being dependable first thing in the morning. Even if Mia had to drag her out of bed to do it.

She strained her neck around and could see the blue plastic totes just around the corner on the bottom of the stairs. Two quick trips and she'd be in and out. Taking a deep breath, she took one stair at a time. As she reached the bottom, she heard a door open upstairs. "Christina?"

No one answered. Mia called out again. "I'm in the basement. Come and help me with these containers."

Mia heard footsteps, and then the lights to the basement went out.

"Not funny," Mia called up the stairs. She had her hand on the banister. "Turn the light back on."

Then the door slammed shut. Any light that had been streaming into the basement from the open door vanished, and Mia felt the darkness surrounding her. Her arm tingled and she felt little feet crawling up toward her face. She dropped the plastic container she held and sprinted up the stairs, pushing on the door. Nothing. She tried to turn the knob. Nothing. She kept turning and, with her other hand, banged on the door.

"Let me out of here. This isn't funny." Mia's breath came fast and through her mouth. She felt her heart trying to beat out of her chest. *Slow down, breathe. This is just some bad practical joke.*

She banged on the door again. "Seriously, let me out. I'm freaking out here."

She heard a door open in the kitchen, or at least she hoped it was opening and not closing. Who knew how long the Joneses would stay out partying with their guests? She'd rather not be locked in their basement until they wandered into the kitchen for coffee the next morning. Forcing tears out of her voice, she called again, "Hey, open the door."

Visions of spiders dropping from the ceiling filled her mind and she banged harder on the door.

All of a sudden the light flashed on and the door swung open, almost pushing Mia down the stairs. She regained her footing and pushed through until she was back in the kitchen. Breathing hard, she turned to face her savior and/or the practical joker. "Christina?"

"Why were you in the basement?" Christina's face scrunched up. "Are you okay? You look a little jacked."

"Someone turned off the lights and locked the door on me." Mia sat on one of the black kitchen chairs. She focused on Christina, "Tell me you weren't just pulling a prank."

Christina put her hands in the air in mock surrender. "Not me, man. I know I'm late, but we kind of lost track of time. I just got here." Christina knelt by Mia and put her hand on her shoulder. "Besides, do you really think I could be that mean?"

Mia shook her head, unable to speak. Her thoughts raced. If not Christina, who? And if it was Christina, why? Things were spiraling out of control and Mia didn't like that, not one bit. She closed her eyes, let her mind focus on the kitchen witch back in her apartment, and breathed. *One, two, three, time to let things be.*

She repeated the chant three more times. Calmed, she opened her eyes. Christina still watched her, concern filling her face.

"Someone shut and locked that door on me. But the sooner we get all this cleaned up and packed in my van, the sooner we can get out of here. Can you go get the totes? I'm . . ." Mia paused, not willing to admit the fear that crept in just thinking about going down the steps again.

"No worries. I'll be right back." Christina stepped toward the basement door. "I'm sorry. I should have been here."

"Then we'd both be there in the dark together," *Or*

worse, Mia thought as she waved her away. "Go get the totes and let's get this packed up."

Mia stood and started gathering her tools. When she came to her knife case she ran a finger over the slot where her chef knife should be, instead of being back home in a gift-wrapped box. Maybe she was looking at this the wrong way. She felt Christina more than heard her approach. Turning, she pasted on a smile. "So, how was your date?"

Christina turned beet red from the roots of her blond hair to where her neck met her collar. "Good." Then she turned back to the basement. "One more trip and all the boxes will be upstairs."

Mia tried to let a smile curve her lips as her helper disappeared into the basement, but she just felt cold. Christina had it bad. She grabbed one of the boxes and started stacking plates into the tote. She'd developed this system when she catered for the hotel. The lid of each tote listed what should be packed into the box. Implementing the organizational system had saved the hotel over $10,000 in lost or misplaced kitchen tools and supplies the first year after she started the process. Another feather in Isaac's cap, not her own, as she'd found out later.

Ten minutes later she'd put the lid on the next-to-last tote. All that was left was the one Christina was working on. "You about done?"

"There's one thing missing from the list, and I know it should be here because I used it today." Christina glanced around the now-bare kitchen counters.

Mia's heart sank. Not again. She carried the tote she'd finished packing over to the door where the rest were stacked. "What's missing?"

"The corkscrew wine opener." Christina glanced at the closed door to the dining room. "You think someone borrowed it to open another bottle after we left?"

Mia considered the idea. "Possibly." She walked over to the table where Carrie Jones had left a check for the catering with a big thank-you written on the receipt. "I'll just leave a note for Mrs. Jones. Maybe it will turn back up."

She wrote out the note on a slip of paper from her notepad, slipped the check into her purse after verifying the amount, and started helping Christina to load the totes. The profits from this one catering job would go a long way to paying back the costs of the Adele party. She thought of the man she'd met that night. Maybe Barney Mann could cut her a check for her costs out of the estate. It wouldn't hurt to ask. Maybe it was tacky, but the dead woman had ordered the party, as well as the two different proteins. She'd call the guy first thing in the morning and get a fax number so she could send the bill for the party that never was.

As she climbed into the driver's seat of the minivan, she looked over at Christina.

"What? Why do you look like the Cheshire cat?" Christina set her purse on the floor of the van and pulled out a bottle of water. Cracking open the lid, she offered a sip to Mia.

Mia accepted the bottle, then, handing it back, asked her sous chef in training, "Ever hear of a kill fee?"

The next morning, Christina still tucked away in her bed, Mia paced in the kitchen. Baldwin had yet to call her back. She glanced at the box holding the kitchen knife and her blood chilled. Glancing at the clock, she decided to call the lawyer. Earlier, she'd completed her invoice, cringing a bit when she added in the thirty steaks and additional supplies from Adele's request, but she had bought the stuff. It wasn't her fault the birthday girl had been murdered. Her gaze dropped to the still-boxed knife.

"Mann Law Offices, this is Sheila. How can I help you today?" a bright, cheery voice bubbled in Mia's ear.

"My name is Mia Malone. I understand your office is handling the estate for Adele Simpson. I have a bill I need to submit for payment. May I get your fax number?" Mia held the pen over her scratch pad.

"Honey, that thing hasn't worked since the last snow-fall. We always lose fax and, before we switched up to this other provider, sometimes phone service too. I wish Barney would just bite the bullet and add the fax line to the new guys." Sheila had a touch of drawl in her voice. Mia wondered if she was more than receptionist to the portly lawyer. Sheila's voice broke through her vision, bringing her back to reality. "Can you just drop it in the mail? Or come by? I'll be here until five."

Mia wrote down the street address and told Sheila she'd be right over. Too much energy ran through her body to sit there and do nothing. She didn't have another catering job lined up, the renovations were still in full force on the first level, and writing up a marketing plan just didn't seem like fun. Besides, she needed to drop the Joneses' check into the bank. She jotted a note for Christina, promising to bring back supplies for breakfast, maybe for a cinnamon roll French toast recipe she wanted to try out. A lot of people loved having breakfast for dinner. Especially families with kids. It might turn out to be a popular menu choice if she could make it more special.

Pulling on her boots and down parka, she tucked the bank deposit along with the envelope with the invoice into an inside pocket with her wallet. *Keep busy and the*

work will come, Grans's voice filled her mind as she quietly shut the door and headed outside. Mia hoped that
Grans's country wisdom wasn't off track. She needed this
business to thrive sooner rather than later or she'd be
forced to return to Boise to find a new job.

The sunlight twinkled on the snow-lined streets. Mia
loved the way the ice crystals made the snow glimmer in
the bright sunlight. According to the local weatherman,
they'd be snowed in by the weekend, and she made a
mental note to stock up on some new romances and mys-
teries when she hit Majors. Maybe a few magazines too.
Christina might be too old for *Seventeen* or *Teen Beat*, but
she'd seen the way she'd latched on to the celebrity rags
that seemed to breed on the newsstand, a new one every
week or so.

Thanks to Adele's canceled party and the leftovers
from the Joneses' event, food wouldn't be an issue. But
buying a generator might need to be on this year's must-
do list rather than next, just in case they lost power during
this storm. And now that she wasn't going to eat Adele's
supply costs, she felt comfortable spending a bit of her
savings.

She arrived at the bank and the teller handled her deposit quickly. She glanced around the deserted lobby.
"Quiet today."

"Everyone's getting ready for the storm. We've had
plenty of people at the drive-through and ATM, but I
think you're my first walk-in of the day." The girl smiled
as she handed Mia her deposit slip. "Anything else I can
help you with?"

"That's it." Mia waved as she left. Yep, maybe a generator wouldn't be a bad thing. And maybe a few more sup-

plies than just reading material. When the hard-to-rattle townspeople started preparing for a storm, you better listen. She pulled her cell out of her pocket. Letting the phone ring, she kept walking toward the law office. The cold air chilled her cheeks.

"Good morning." Grans's voice, sweet and positive as ever, filled her ear.

"Hey, you want to come over and stay with Christina and me for the weekend? I'd feel better if you weren't alone during the storm."

"This wouldn't be the first time I'd weathered a snowfall," Grans chided her.

"I know, but maybe we can make a girls' night out of it. It will be Christina's first big storm. I'm sure she'll be worried about you." Mia bit her lip and waited.

"Sure, pull out the big guns about upsetting that sweet child." Grans sighed. "Honestly, I'd love to come over. But I'm not sleeping on that couch."

"You can have my room. I'll take the couch." Mia saw the brick building that housed the law offices of Barney Mann along with the Laundromat. Mia wondered if Barney owned that small business as well. "I'll pick you up late tomorrow afternoon."

"I'll be ready. You know I'm bringing Muffy too."

Mia smiled. Mr. Darcy would have a cow; he hated the little dog. "I figured. He'll have lots of room to run around. See you tomorrow."

She clicked off the phone and opened the door with the law office's name painted on the window. The foyer opened onto a stairway.

She climbed the old oak staircase that shone with what seemed to be a recent oiling. The stairs had black skid strips on the rungs, keeping people safe on the trip up. *A lawyer thinks of everything.*

When she reached the top of the stairs two doors greeted her. One said "Private," the other "Barney Mann, Esquire," painted in black on the frosted glass. She turned the antique brass doorknob and pushed open the door. A gray-haired woman with wire-rimmed glasses and her hair in a bun smiled at her. "You must be Mia Malone." The woman stepped forward to greet her, hand outstretched. "I'm Sheila. I've been friends with Mary Alice for decades. Oh, that sounds like we're old. Let's just say I know your grandmother."

Mia smiled. Of course she knew Grans. She couldn't go anywhere in town without someone bringing up her grandmother and their connection to her. "So nice to meet you." She pulled the envelope out of her pocket but held on to it rather than shove it at the woman. "You must have known Adele too?"

"Adele Simpson was a mean, self-centered old bat. I don't know how your grandmother put up with her. I don't like to speak ill of the dead, but I would say the same thing if Adele herself stood before me." Shelia motioned to the couch. "Can I get you some tea or cocoa? The weather's got your cheeks all bright and rosy."

"Actually, I'm heading over to the grocery store to stock up, and then I've got more errands. I'd better get going." Mia held out the invoice. "I just charged for the agreed-upon costs and extra supplies. I think you'll find the bill very conservative."

Sheila grabbed the envelope and threw it on the top of her desk. "You should have charged double. That old prune is, well, *was* the richest woman in the Magic Springs area.

And, I imagine, most of Sun Valley too." Sheila shook her head. "A lot of good her scrimping and saving did her. I don't think she bought a new coat in the last ten years. Life is for the living, Mia. Remember that."

Mia smiled. Sheila tended to speak her mind. "I'll see you around. Stay warm during the storm."

"Oh, don't worry. We're closing the office tomorrow, so I'll be snug in my cabin, reading a book and simmering a batch of my famous clam chowder. I'll make sure this gets filed and paid as soon as we start to close the estate. You should hear something by the end of the month." Sheila shuffled back to her desk and Mia noticed for the first time that the woman had a tendency to favor her left hip. Shelia slipped back into her desk chair and rolled over to the coffee maker to fill up her cup. She held up the coffeepot. "I could pour some of this in a to-go cup if you'd like."

"Really, I'm okay. I'll talk to you soon." Mia started to open the door. Then a thought hit her. "Sheila, can you tell me if Mr. Mann's looking into the nephew? I mean, his family connection with Adele?"

Sheila glanced at the closed door and dropping her voice to a whisper. "Where did you hear that? Mr. Mann's been keeping that piece quiet. Adele's will is very clear, and there's no mention of this guy. You would think if she had a nephew she would have mentioned him."

"Just a nagging thought. I've never heard of the guy before." Mia assessed Sheila's willingness to spill the dirt, then drove through anyway. "Who would have inherited, if this nephew hadn't shown up?"

Sheila's head tilted to the side. "I would have thought you already knew. It's your grandmother. And even with the substantial amount she'll receive, I still don't think it's enough to have put up with that woman all those years. I swear."

Now Barney Mann's words made chilling sense. He thought Danforth might do something to Grans if he thought it would help his chances at the inheritance he obviously thought was coming to him.

As she left the lawyer's office and headed to Majors Grocery, she felt comforted that her grandmother hadn't argued about coming over this weekend. Mia'd be able to keep an eye out for her without letting her know why she wanted her close. "Thank the Goddess for storms," she said as she pushed through the swinging door of the grocery store.

"I always say that, but being a store owner, I have a different viewpoint. We always sell out just before the weather hits. Why are you happy for the storm?" Trent fell into step next to her as she grabbed a cart and headed to the bakery department.

"Let's just say I get to spend some quality time with my grandmother." Mia grabbed two loaves of fresh Italian bread. "So, how'd it go with George Kennedy? Everything okay with my inspection?"

"He's still not sure about some of the supports, but I've got him to agree to another walk-through once the contractor's done, so you're good to go. When I talked to Brent he thought he'd have the downstairs ready for you to open in a week or two." Trent put a bag of doughnut holes in her cart. "He's pretty happy for the work. The winter months are usually pretty brutal for the construction guys."

"I would think that they'd get a lot of remodel work." Mia thought about Helen's comments about Adele's house. "Don't the rich change their homes like they change clothes?"

Trent grinned. "Not quite that often, but when they do they bring in out-of-town crews and Brent's company gets the leftover, grunt jobs. And they always want a winter discount."

As they walked through the small grocery, Mia picking up items like butternut squash for a soup and some more fresh veggies, she realized how comfortable she felt with Trent. Isaac had never wanted to shop with her. That was why they hired sous chefs to do the shopping. Mia loved visiting the local farmers markets, talking with the vendors, looking for the fresh and new from their farms or greenhouses. She tried to tell him that was what real chefs did, but, as always, he was right and she was wrong.

Walking through Trent's store, listening to him talk about his connections with his vendors and suppliers, she felt a kindred spirit. His arms were muscled and toned, like he spent his day in a gym rather than managing a store. Most likely he spent some time tossing the daily delivery of boxes. Mia ignored the blush of warmth in her stomach as she thought about those arms holding her.

They were stopped in front of the small book and magazine section. Trent held a book toward her and broke into her thoughts. Feeling the heat in her face, Mia took the book. "Sorry, thinking about the storm."

"I said, I love this cookbook. The author was on that celebrity cooking show where they try to be the best chef or something. She focuses on using fresh ingredients and local and seasonal food." He tapped the picture on the cover. "She did some tour when this first came out. Did you see her in Boise?"

Mia glanced at the book. She'd wanted to attend the gala, but Isaac had scheduled a competing catering assignment and she'd been put in charge. Funny, now that she thought about it, Isaac had attended the gala and she'd worked. Like so many other times. *Idiot.*

"I didn't get to see her, but yes, I love her philosophy." Mia tried to hand back the book to Trent.

"Keep it. My treat." He smiled, and Mia could see that he and Levi had the same lady-killer smile. "Besides, maybe you'll make me one of the recipes to thank me."

"I could probably do that." Oh my Goddess, she was flirting. She pointed at the cart. "Are the doughnut holes your treat as well?"

"Those are road trip food."

Mia grabbed a few novels and the celebrity rags for Christina. Frowning, she glanced up at Trent. "Road trip? There's a major storm coming and you're planning a road trip? Need something for the store?"

"No, Brent mentioned you needed a generator. And the hardware store is already sold out; I checked this morning." Trent walked with her to the checkout lane, where an older woman started ringing up Mia's purchases. "Sally, don't charge Miss Malone for the doughnuts or the cookbook. Ring those up to me."

The woman nodded, but Mia saw the smile on Sally's face. *Another girlfriend*, must be what the checker was thinking. Mia wondered how many other women Trent had bought cookbooks and donuts for.

"I don't understand. Why are you taking me to buy a generator?" Mia watched as Trent helped her unload the cart onto the conveyer belt. Just like a normal couple. A small smile curved her lips. This might be all in her imagination, but it felt good to be with someone who actually wanted to be with her. For once.

"You want to be in that big school without one? In the dark? Without heat? I hear the place is haunted," Trent teased as he bagged the groceries.

Mia held out three twenties to Sally. "Take that back. I don't even want to know if someone was murdered there, or a ghost haunts the school grounds. That's my home now."

"Thought I'd get a rise out of you." Trent nodded to Sally. "I'm going to be gone the rest of the day. You can reach me on my cell if there's an emergency." He held the two bags and nodded to the third, still on the counter. "You think you can carry that one?"

"I can carry all three." Mia frowned. "What, you going to carry my groceries home for me? I have to say, that's customer service gone extreme."

"Yep. Then we're heading to Twin Falls for that generator." Trent nodded at the bag. "You ready, or do you have other plans for the day?"

Mia shrugged her shoulders. "I give up. I guess I'm ready." She grabbed the bag that held the magazines, the bread, and the doughnut holes. "But I'm driving."

"Good, because my truck's in the shop getting an oil change." The two headed out onto the street and the day. Just like a normal couple.

CHAPTER 14

The roads out of Magic Springs heading down the Magics to the freeway were free of snow. The county must have had their road crews out plowing this morning. Snow piled on each side of the road narrowed the lanes and looked like concrete walls rather than dirt and ice. It wouldn't take long for Mia to drive out of the higher altitude and onto the plains that surrounded the edge of the Magic range.

Mia had brought several country music CDs along and, currently, Sugarland was singing about being just a little late and coming into work with the walk of shame. She sang along quietly to the music. Trent appeared to be asleep through most of the trip. Mia loved the way the light highlighted the red in his hair when it poked through the trees and into the window. She watched as he brushed away the sunbeam like it was a bug trying to awaken him.

Mia smiled and returned her focus to the road. Deer liked to jump out onto the road without notice. Really, she shouldn't have agreed to the trip. What if something happened to Grans while she was gone? Christina had agreed to check in, but she'd been less than dependable lately. If she forgot and someone tried to hurt Grans, Mia would never forgive herself.

"Get in town, get the generator, and get back." Mia said from her town to-do list.

"And get lunch," a gruff voice added. "You forgot the best part of going into town. They have fast-food joints. All the grease you can stomach. And probably more."

"You want to stop at a drive-in?" Mia smiled over at Trent, who now stretched in his seat.

Trent rolled his neck and Mia could hear the cracking. "Why else would I agree to this road trip you pushed on me? I deserve a treat."

"I didn't push," Mia argued, stopping when she saw Trent's grin. She shrugged and turned back toward the road. "Sorry. I'm worried about Grans."

"How come?" Trent turned down the volume on the stereo.

Mia filled Trent in on the conversations with Barney Mann and Sheila. When she got to the part where someone had locked her in the basement, Trent held up a hand to stop her.

"You didn't think to call Baldwin?" Trent's voice sounded hard.

"I did call Baldwin when I found the gift-wrapped knife. He still hasn't bothered calling me back." Mia shook her head. "Besides, he'd probably act like I did it to myself. I'm not one of his favorite Magic Springs residents right now. I'm pretty sure he thinks I killed Adele, and probably shot JFK too, even though I wasn't even born at the time."

Trent watched her as they came up on a stoplight by the truck stop that lined the road next to the freeway exit ramps. "You need to give Baldwin a break. He's trying to do his job."

"By arresting me for killing Adele? You can't be serious. You don't believe I had anything to do with her death, do you?"

"Of course not. But he can't make assumptions. You know how investigations go; you've got to weed out the unlikely suspects to get to the guilty ones. You're just getting weeded. Sheriff Cook makes him feel like an idiot most days, so he tends to follow the book just to prove himself to that old blowhard." Trent put his hand on her arm and Mia felt the heat shoot through her. Not good. She didn't need to be bonding with anyone right now, even Trent. She shrugged him off before the old magic could take effect. She needed her head on straight before she let magic choose a mate for her. And she wasn't sure she'd let that happen anyway.

Confused, he pulled his hand back from her arm and stared at it. "I'll be," he murmured.

Mia drove through the intersection, under the freeway, and headed to the bridge over the Snake. Looking over the left of Perrine Bridge, you could see the ramps where Evel Knievel failed to jump even with a rocket-powered cycle. Since then, his son had tried and failed to set up a re-creation jump across the canyon gorge. The gorge was said to be over five hundred feet deep in places. Mia's heart pounded every time she drove over the bridge. Stupid, she knew. It wasn't like the bridge would collapse and crumble into the river, sending her van plummeting down the steep canyon walls to finally land in the water.

Yet every time she crossed the bridge, she released a breath she hadn't realized she'd been holding. This time was no exception.

"The canyon's a little scary, even when you're on a steel and asphalt bridge." Trent's words soothed her ruffled nerves.

Mia barked a short laugh. "That's for sure. Driving over the bridge always gives me the creeps." She turned into the parking lot of the home improvement big-box store. "You ever go to the Grand Canyon? I hear the Indian tribe built a glass walkway out over the canyon. Not confident I could step out onto the platform. My stomach clenches just thinking about walking on air."

"We might have to make another road trip just to see that." Trent opened the door as Mia turned off the engine after finding a relatively close parking spot. For a midmorning Thursday, the store seemed pretty busy. "Everyone must be stocking up for the storm. Come on; the manager said he would put one aside for us at the customer service center."

Mia followed Trent into the large, orange-painted store. She wondered what he'd meant by the road trip comment. She'd never understand men. She'd thought she'd learned everything when she dated Isaac. But what she'd come to realize was that she'd only learned everything about Isaac. Or everything he wanted her to know. Trent was completely different from her ex-boyfriend. Sensitive, funny, attentive. All qualities Isaac didn't possess or wouldn't even strive for.

This isn't a date, Mia. The man's just trying to help you

out. Mia's logical side tried to calm her runaway day-dreams. She'd felt the power surge between them when he'd touched her arm. Power like that only happened between two magical creatures. Two witches.

Even being a kitchen witch, she could feel the power that being next to him brought out in her. She wasn't supposed to have strong powers. Not like this. Her specialty was more in the healing arts. Charms and potions to make the ill feel better. Prayers and chants to focus powerful positive energy into the world. So why was her magical side throbbing like a tightly wound guitar string?

The manager had the box with the generator on a cart waiting for Trent. While he chatted, it was apparent the man was excited at the prospect of the storm. "I tell you, Trent, if you hadn't called, you'd be walking out of here empty-handed. I've already sold out all my snow shovels as well. And the sidewalk salt supply is almost depleted. Seriously, two or three more storms like this and this will be my best year on record with this store. It's making me rethink the ten percent discount I gave you on that beauty."

A clerk rang up the generator and looked at Trent. "Six hundred forty-seven." She popped her gum.

Mia swiped her debit card through the reader. *Just another cost of home ownership,* she thought. Renting never looked so good. Keying in her pin, she smiled at the young woman when she handed Mia the receipt.

"Thanks for shopping Home Heaven," the clerk chirped and focused on the next customer without waiting for a response.

Mia moved out of the line and went to stand by Trent, who now stood by the cart with his friend. He put his hand on the small of her back and drew her closer. "Thanks for helping us out, Corey. Mia's new place will be amazing once it's done, but right now it's mostly a construction nightmare."

Mia pursed her lips, trying to keep the response from bubbling out. Instead, she looked up at Trent and smiled. "You said you'd buy me lunch. Are we ready? I'm starving."

Trent leaned closer, bending over to meet Mia's gaze. He was going to kiss her. Right here in Home Heaven, in front of his friend and everything. She closed her eyes. It was only a kiss. She could play the role of Trent's girlfriend if it meant she got a discount on the generator. When no kiss happened she opened her eyes to see Trent and the manager watching her.

"I tell you, those seizures are coming faster now." Trent reached out his arm and shook hands with his friend. "Better get some food in her before I have to rush her off to the hospital."

"Nice to meet you," Corey called after them as Trent pushed the cart through the large automatic doors.

When they reached the van Trent lifted the generator into the back and then settled into the passenger seat next to Mia. "What? Corey is kind of picky who he does favors for. I told him we were dating."

"And apparently that I have hunger seizures. Is that even a real disease?"

Trent shrugged. "It looked like you expected me to kiss you."

"I just wanted to thank you for the discount. I wasn't expecting to need to shell out money for this before next year, when we were up and running. I'm going to have to get up faster than I'd planned or I won't have any savings left." Mia started the engine and let the car idle. "So, where to now?"

"I'll buy you lunch because you're pleading poverty. Technically, you should be buying to thank me for helping you with the generator, but I can be generous. Go back over the bridge and take the first left. We'll hit the clubhouse." Trent leaned back in his seat. "I guess if we're dating, I should at least treat you to one meal before we get back to Magic Springs and break up."

"Wouldn't be my shortest relationship." Mia turned the car back on the road and toward home.

"That sounds promising." Trent turned up the stereo. "I love this song. Tell me your dating horror stories at lunch and I'll tell you mine."

They drove to the turn off the highway, then followed the narrow road as it wound the canyon toward the river. There didn't seem to be any businesses in this direction. She glanced at Trent and started to ask if she'd turned down the wrong road, but all of a sudden she saw the building, built off a ledge in the cliff. She parked near the door. The place looked like a shack. "Hot dogs?"

Trent shook his head. "You're a food snob. I knew it. I guess you can't help it, being a chef and all. But seriously, how have you never heard about this place?" He climbed out of the van and walked around to the door of the restaurant. He paused, smiling at Mia, who'd hurried to catch up. "Believe me, you'll love it."

Trent opened the door and they stepped into a large dining room with a fireplace to the right. On the left was a wall of windows, showing off the canyon walls. An eagle floated into view, soared to the left, then dived, apparently after his lunch, floating below him in the river. A hostess seated them and Mia opened the menu.

The listing of items surprised her, and she spent several minutes lost in the restaurant's offerings. When the waitress came for their order she questioned her on how the chef prepared a dish or two, then ordered a pan-fried trout with wild rice and a small salad with house-made blue cheese dressing. Trent ordered a rib-eye steak, a baked potato, and a large order of Italian nachos for an appetizer. She raised her eyebrows at his choice. Thank the Goddess he'd offered to pay.

"Don't look at me that way, I didn't have breakfast." Trent handed the waitress his menu.

"Unless you count the bag of doughnut holes you consumed before we even got down the Magic?" Mia watched as a deer walked out onto the tenth hole and started nibbling on the grass. "This place is amazing. People actually golf here?"

"They pay good money for a membership. Most of the members actually live in Sun Valley and drive down." Trent sipped his water as he watched Mia watch the deer. "I'm a member, more for the business connections. You'd be surprised at how many deals get worked out over a round of golf."

Mia sighed, then played with her fork.

"What did I say?" Trent leaned closer and put his hand over hers.

"I think Mia's Morsels is doomed." Mia set the fork by her plate and leaned into him. "I can't play golf, I don't know the townsfolk, and most of them think I killed Adele anyway."

"Which should give you the sympathy business."

Trent smiled. "I know, not funny. You do have one secret weapon, though."

"I do?" Mia couldn't think of one advantage she had that might help the business stay open in the first week, let alone the first year.

"Your grandmother. She could talk a farmer into buying rubber boots for his cows."

Mia smiled at the thought. "You're right. She's amazing."

The waitress brought the platter of nachos and two plates. She glanced at Mia. "I could bring your salad out now if you'd rather."

Mia laughed, the sound tinkling through the empty dining room. "No worries. I think I'll help Trent get rid of a few of these before I go all healthy."

After the waitress had disappeared from their table Trent pointed a chip at her. "You don't have to worry about Baldwin or the town. I'm sure no one really believes you could kill Adele." He thought for a moment, then added, "Now Christina, that's a different story."

Mia sighed. She wished Baldwin wouldn't single out Christina so much. She'd been through so much already. "Please don't tell me Baldwin's looking at her. She's barely out of high school."

Trent shook his head. "All I know are the rumors that flow through the store. Baldwin and I haven't been buddies since I threw him into the log pond during senior sneak. The creep was hiding and watching the girls change into their swimsuits."

Mia choked on her nacho. "The guy's a Peeping Tom?"

Trent cocked his head. "*Was* a Peeping Tom. I think I cured him of that bad habit. Besides, he married Sarah right out of college. If anyone can keep someone in line, it's Sarah. The woman scares me. She ran the senior class like it was her own small business. You didn't show for an event you were supposed to work, she'd track you down. I think the class still has money in their account, almost twenty years later."

"I thought he had a girlfriend named Tilly." Mia frowned, trying to remember the story she'd heard from Grans.

"Tilly was his first girlfriend. She left town when he was in Boise for the police academy. He was planning on proposing when he came back." Trent sipped his water. "He was heartbroken. But Sarah, she'd had her eye on Mark since kindergarten. So she swooped in for the win. I don't think he even knew what hit him."

"Sometimes people meet their soul mates young." Mia leaned back and watched the canyon as the midday light filtered through the slow-moving clouds played on the walls.

"And for some of us it takes a little longer." Trent's words brought her attention back to him. He stared at her, his light-green eyes seeming to search her face for a reaction. Mia noticed the laugh lines on his face and thought about the touch in the car. Oh, yes, she felt the attraction, the deep, gut-searing need to take this man to her bed and do bad things with him. And then try them all over again.

She decided to change the subject, and quick. "Tell me what you know about John Louis. The man seems to have a serious anger problem."

Trent considered her words as he consumed a fully loaded nacho chip. "He used to live in Sun Valley. His mom's place, I believe. He grew up on the right side of the tracks, but when she was duped by husband number five and lost all the family wealth, John moved to Magic

Springs. He's been married to Carol for ten, maybe more years. From what Levi tells me, she's had more than her share of 'accidents' where the EMTs have been called."

"Kind of what I figured when I saw them at Adele's wake." Mia folded her napkin. "I guess he was the other bidder on the school?"

"Yeah. He told everyone who would listen how this was his big deal. He had an investor lined up to turn the property into a strip mall. Franchise heaven. Rumor had it he was in league with one of the big grocery chains, which was trying to get into the area cheap." Trent considered her. "Is he giving you problems?"

"Yes and no. I mean, he made me an offer on the school. Told me he'd give me asking plus a nice profit. When I turned him down he got mean." Mia glanced around the empty dining room, before continuing. She had to tell someone. "He insinuated that Adele's death should have convinced me to sell out. And I'm pretty sure he's the one who made a threatening phone call to me. Although I haven't shared my suspicions with anyone but you."

"You need to talk to Baldwin. You're acting like you're the Lone Ranger in all this. People don't have the right to scare you into selling." Trent sipped his water. "Tell me you aren't hiding back anything else?"

"What makes you think I haven't told Baldwin? Okay, so maybe I haven't told him this specifically, but he didn't believe me when I called before." Mia held up her hand in what she thought was a Girl Scout salute. She'd only been a Brownie, so maybe it didn't hold her accountable for her next words. "But I get your point. I swear I won't try to solve this problem all on my own."

The moment broke when the waitress came with their

entrées. Neither Trent nor Mia spoke for several minutes after she'd left. Finally Mia chose the easy way out, an old first date trick she'd learned. When in doubt talk about the food.

"The trout is fantastic." She didn't look up to see his response.

"Really? That's all you have to say?" Trent's words were playful, but she knew he expected something more.

"The view is amazing."

Trent held up his hands in mock surrender. "Fine, we won't talk about it more here or now. But Mia, you need to talk to Baldwin. I could call him if you want."

"Well, maybe you *should* call because apparently he'll call you back. He's not getting to back to me." As she heard a hawk cry as he floated over the river, Mia knew Trent was only trying to help. There was a chance at something new with him, something good. But right now he just needed to back off. She didn't need anyone taking care of her. Not now, not ever. "Sorry if that sounded harsh. I just need some space on this."

Trent picked up his fork. "My fault. I can be a little over the top. But if you want to talk, I'll try to be a better listener."

Mia nodded, then focused on enjoying the food in front of her. She tried to quiet the river of thoughts running through her mind. She reached for the knife to cut her trout and the metal caught a stream of sunlight and sparkled.

The knife; she'd forgotten about the knife.

As they finished their lunch in silence, the door to the small dining room opened and two men walked in. The waitress seated William Danforth at a table near the fireplace, and his companion looked a lot like Barney Mann, cheap 42 short suit and all.

"Of all the low-down," Mia whispered. "What are those two doing together?"

Trent jerked his head to follow Mia's gaze. He flipped some bills on the table next to the check and whispered, "Do you want to leave?"

Mia nodded. If she stayed any longer, she'd march over to the table and demand to know what they were discussing. Not a wise move against the man who'd all but branded her a murderer at their last meeting. Besides, Danforth could just be courting Mann to weasel information from him about the will. Barney could just be in the meeting for a good meal. And although his doctor might disagree, she couldn't fault the man for taking a free lunch. Even from a creep like Danforth.

She whispered a quick wish for health for the portly lawyer, the feeling his days were numbered almost overwhelming her as she sprinted out of the dining room. Trent walked close by, blocking her face from view in case the men looked up from their menus. As the door closed behind them, Mia burst into laughter. "I've never snuck out of a restaurant before."

"Not even in college, when you had no money to pay for your meal?" Trent walked her to the van and held the driver's-side door open for her.

"Especially not then." She paused and rubbed her eyes. "Can you do me a favor?"

"Sure, what? Do we need to make another stop in town?"

Mia shook her head. "Actually, can you drive back?

All of a sudden I'm beat. Maybe it was the food, but I can hardly keep my eyes open."

"I can do that." He closed the driver's door and followed her to the passenger side, where he opened that door for her.

The guy was nothing if not polite. Mia handed him her keys. Her eyes burned. Having Trent drive gave her time to power nap before she returned home to the intrigue and danger. *Being a bit overdramatic, aren't we?* Mia bit her lip, trying to keep from laughing. It was bad enough she occasionally talked to herself. If she told anyone that her invisible friend told her jokes, she'd be locked away until a room opened up at the state school or a private hospital.

She slipped into the passenger seat and let Trent shut the door. She watched as he pulled on the handle, making sure the door had completely sealed, a habit she watched her friends with kids do, making sure the door wasn't ajar and could pop open. Trent didn't have kids, did he? One more thing she didn't know about the mysterious grocery store owner, and she had no way of asking without looking like she was prying into his personal life. The pictures in his wallet screamed at her to peek, but she ignored the feeling even when Trent gently tossed the wallet into the console next to her, shrugging.

"I don't like driving with it stuffed in my pants." He shrugged and put the keys into the ignition.

"There are so many responses to that statement that I can't choose one." Mia smiled, her urge to snoop settled.

"You're bad." Trent turned on to the narrow road to head up the canyon. "Must be why I like you."

Those words hung in the air for miles without a response. Mia's eyelids drooped, and soon she succumbed to the sunshine and rocking of the car. She felt it jerk and her eyes flew open.

"What's happening?" She glanced around, confused. Instead of the brown prairies outside Twin Falls, she saw the snow-covered Magic road.

"Hit a patch of ice. Sorry I woke you." Trent turned down the radio. "I've been listening to the weather report. I think the storm's coming in tonight rather than late tomorrow."

"Are we going to make it back?" Mia craned her neck, trying to find a road sign to get her bearings.

"We're only a few miles out. We should be fine."

Mia glanced at her phone. Three bars. She dialed her grandmother's number. When Grans answered she spoke quickly, hoping she wouldn't lose the call. "Hey, pack your stuff and get over to the school. The storm's coming now."

She paused as she listened. "Oh, well, we'll be in town soon. I'll see you then."

She clicked off the phone and watched the road.

"Problem?" Trent swore quietly under his breath as the van hit another ice patch.

Mia frowned; the road had gotten dangerous in the hours they'd been gone. No way Barney and Danforth would make it back to town tonight. Somehow their inconvenience made her happy. She didn't wish harm to them, but delay—that she could handle.

She started to tell Trent about her conversation when a deer jumped in front of them. Trent hit the brakes and the car skidded into the Magic side of the road and crashed into the rocks.

Mia swore as she watched the deer bound away, the

doe looking back at them like they had been in her way, rather than the other way around.

"Are you all right?" Trent pushed her hair out of her eyes and searched her face for signs of pain or injury.

"Fine." Mia blew out a breath. "Glad you went right instead of left. I'm not sure the van would have made it down the mountainside in one piece."

"Never would have happened. I've driven these roads too many times to make a rookie mistake." He glanced at the darkening sky. "Stay here and I'll check out the damage. Keep your fingers crossed that we didn't hurt the car."

Mia watched as he got out, then looked around the car. She dropped her eyes and glanced at her phone. No service. Less than a mile from where she'd just used the darn thing and now nothing. At least she'd taken care of Grans before she'd lost the connection. She was heading over to the school to be with Christina. One less worry. A tap on the window focused her gaze on a worried Trent. Opening the window, she sighed. "Bad news?"

"Both right side tires are flat. I suppose you only have one spare?"

"I've never needed the one." Mia slumped in her seat. "How far is town?"

He glanced up the road and shook his head. "Too far to walk before either the storm hits or night falls. We don't want to be out in the open when either happens. We probably could hike out tomorrow morning."

"So we're staying in the van tonight?" Mia hoped she'd put the emergency kit back into the car after the last event. She couldn't remember.

Trent shook his head and jerked open her door. "Come on. We have another, better option."

"I thought you said we couldn't make town?" Mia grabbed her cable-knit hat and pulled it over her head. She fished in her pockets for her gloves and grabbed her purse.

"We can't. But there's a fishing cabin just over that ridge. One of the summer people built it last year, I worked on the crew part-time. It has a woodstove and plenty of firewood. The pantry's probably filled as well." Trent glanced around the van. "Anything else you need out of here?"

"I don't think so. Let's lock it. I'd hate to lose my new generator. Although there probably won't be anyone on the road before we get back tomorrow." Mia looked at her boots. Thank the Goddess she had listened to her gut when she got dressed this morning. The sexy, high-heel fashion boots she'd considered still sat in her closet. She'd chosen the warmer, uglier snow boots, even though they were heading to town.

She followed Trent down the hill to where a road sign stood, half buried in snow pushed to the side by the daily snow plow runs. "Trout Lane?"

"I tell you, the guy's a big fisherman. He's one who comes to the area for recreation, not just to hang out at the Lodge and be seen. He's some big shot in the movie industry in Los Angeles, but I'd never heard of him." Trent walked in front of her, making footprints in the calf-deep snow for her to follow. "The cabin's not far off the road."

"I'll have to send him a thank-you note when we get back." She followed Trent up the gently climbing hill, her breath catching now and then. What would have been a pretty walk in the summer now reminded her of the opening to a horror movie.

Drama queen. The niggle in her brain told her the

Goddess was laughing at her. Mia ignored the link. Let the Goddess walk a mile, literally, in her shoes; then she could laugh. Mia didn't think the Goddess had inhabited a body for years, maybe centuries.

Not watching, she ran into Trent, who'd stopped at the top of the hill to wait for her to catch up. "Whoa."

She caught his coat with her gloved hand, hoping she wouldn't face-plant into the snow. It might look pretty, but with the sheen on the top, Mia knew there was a layer of ice that would make the landing painful. Trent gripped her arm and she felt herself being righted. She settled herself and peered down the road.

The cabin sat in front of them. All three-thousand-square-feet, if Mia had to guess, of log cabin gone modern, aka Frank Lloyd Wright style. The place rivaled the mini mansions closer to Sun Valley. Trent glanced at her. "Wow, right?"

"You said it was a fishing cabin." Mia slapped his arm.

Trent headed to the front door. "For the owner, it is. He comes up once a month as soon as the snow clears. This fall he's doing some sort of company retreat here. He's already ordered the supplies. I'll give you his number; maybe you can land a catering gig."

"If he doesn't throw us in jail for breaking and entering." Mia followed Trent up on the wide, wraparound porch. She could just see rocking chairs gracing the wooden planks and fishing poles propped up against the cabin wall.

"We're taking shelter in a storm. It's Magic law. He won't mind." Trent reached up to the top of the door-frame and pulled out a key. "Besides, can't be breaking and entering if the owner told me where he hid the key."

As they entered the foyer, the remaining sunlight lit up

the polished pine walls and floors. The cabin had been decorated in country casual à la Ralph Lauren. No day-care colors here. All the furniture was wood or leather, with deep, primary-colored pillows and throws tossed strategically over the couch and side chairs, facing a stone fireplace. She kicked off her snow-covered boots and pulled off her hat.

"I'd better get some wood in here before the storm hits." Trent nodded to the back of the cabin. "The kitchen's back there. See if you can find some lanterns and matches and let's get settled in the living room for the night. No use trying to heat up the entire house."

He went back outside, and Mia moved her boots over to the bench. The decorator had thought of everything, including a box of what looked like never-worn slippers next to the coat closet. She found a pair in her size and, after searching, pulled out three more pair, hoping one would fit Trent's feet.

Then she headed back to the kitchen, the sunlight from the floor-to-ceiling windows bouncing off the natural pine. No wonder this was just a summer cabin. Too many windows to keep the place livable during the freezing temperatures of winter, even if you could keep the road open from all the snow. Mia smiled as she entered the kitchen. She slipped off her glove and reflexively slid her hand over the cool granite countertops. The owner hadn't spared a dime in designing the kitchen. She'd seen pictures of places like this—stainless-steel appliances and oak cabinets—but this one just screamed "cook in me" to her. She headed to the gas stove. Maybe, just maybe, they hadn't turned off the propane lines.

Sure enough, a flame flickered on, and Mia glanced around to find a teakettle and bottled water from the well-stocked pantry. As long as the propane held out, she might be able to make a decent clam rotini soup from what she'd seen on the shelves. She let the water heat while she searched the utility room, finding several lanterns and a handful of emergency candles.

Returning to the living room, she saw Trent had already stacked a pile of firewood on the large tile hearth. She set the lanterns on the end tables around the room and left matches and candles next to them, just in case.

Trent worked on lighting the fire, his broad shoulders framing the hearth. She leaned against the fireplace and watched him. "You want instant coffee or cinnamon tea? I think I saw a box of cocoa too."

"The stove works?" Trent frowned.

Mia shrugged, "For now. I'm going to cook up a batch of soup before we run out of propane."

Trent glanced over his shoulder. "I doubt the furnace will light, but do you want me to try?"

"The fireplace is fine. You know he had someone winterize the cabin. I'm surprised I got the stove to work." She frowned at the decreasing light from the windows. "I think the storm's close."

"Then I'd better finish bringing in the wood. I'll clear a path to the outhouse in the back too." He smiled. "No indoor plumbing, right?"

Mia blushed. "Not that works anyway."

"Check around in the kitchen for some flashlights. I don't want you getting lost if you have to use the facilities in the middle of the night. We've had quite a few bear sightings this year."

"If I go out, you're coming with me to stand guard," Mia joked.

"I guess because this is our first sleepover, I should

warn you, I sleep hard. Not easy to wake me." Trent leaned against the fireplace, looking all cool, and for some reason the look in his eyes made Mia shiver. Quickly she spun the conversation.

"I take it that's code for the fact you snore?" Mia walked toward the kitchen, hoping Trent wouldn't follow.

"I don't snore." Trent pulled on his coat and followed her. "Wow. I've never been in this room since he finished it. Classy."

"It's amazing." Mia opened the pantry door. "You didn't tell me what you wanted to drink."

"When I come in, coffee. But nothing now." Trent glanced out the windowed door. "The snow is starting. We'll be in the dark in less than twenty minutes. I want to clear that path before we settle in."

Mia watched him slip out the door, the cold air flowing inside making the room feel even colder. She grabbed an old tan cardigan sweater from a hook in the mudroom and went to work on the soup. By the time she had it together, Trent had returned.

She grabbed her coat and shoes and made her way to the wooden outhouse. Even though it had been newly built out of the same pine as the interior of the house, Mia felt uncomfortable using the facilities. The only time she envied men was camping. Being a woman made her feel vulnerable in the great outdoors, especially while she was peeing.

Walking back to the cabin, she saw Trent standing on the porch, watching the storm clouds envelop the forest around them. She almost sprinted to the house, only slowing when she slipped on a patch of ice and had to juggle to right herself.

Trent pressed his lips together, trying not to smile. "Better?"

She nodded and went into the house. She replaced her boots and coat with the slippers and oversize sweater and then rubbed sanitizer on her hands. She nodded to the soup. "That's going to take a while. Want coffee now?"

"Perfect." Trent watched as she poured steaming hot water into two mugs, one with a tea bag for her, the other with the instant coffee. Trent carried both cups and walked into the living room. He glanced at the roaring fire and nodded. "We need to light up a few of those lanterns. We'll lose the sunlight sooner than you think."

"It feels like late evening. What time is it?" Mia lit three of the lamps, watching the flame flicker around the room.

Trent glanced at his watch. "Four."

As she settled onto the couch, she threw one of the flannel blankets over the legs curled under her. "So, Trent Majors, what's the most unusual thing about you?"

For a moment she thought from the look on his face that he might lie. But then he expelled a breath and sighed. "From the way you reacted when we first touched, I think you know I'm a witch."

CHAPTER 15

Mia studied Trent's reaction to his announcement carefully before she spoke. He hadn't wanted to tell her. "I met Levi."

"My brother has a big mouth." Trent shook his head. "He loves all this stuff. He runs around that coven like it's his personal harem. And the women let him. I've never been active in the family business, so to speak. I'm the normal one who the townspeople trust. Levi and my mom, they were all about the craft." Trent squatted by the fire, using a poker to adjust the logs before he added a heavier log to the mix. "How'd the subject even come up?"

"He was my EMT when I was attacked. Maybe he felt sorry for me." Mia was glad she hadn't told him more about her. Trent didn't like his heritage; maybe he really wouldn't like it if she explained her and Grans's practices.

Trent left the fireplace and sat on the other end of the couch. "There's something there you're not saying." He laughed as Mia felt her eyes widen and a pit the size of an orange started to grow in her stomach.

"I don't know what you mean," Mia stammered.

He shook his head and focused on his coffee. "For instant, it's almost bearable." He set the cup on the rustic wooden coffee table and put his arm over the back end of the leather couch and watched Mia.

She couldn't help it; she squirmed first. "Okay, so what do you want me to say?"

Trent tapped his fingers on the leather. "We could start with the truth."

Mia set down her tea. "I talked with your brother on the way to the hospital. He told me he knew my grandmother and Adele from coven business."

His eyebrows furrowed. "I don't understand. Why would your grandmother be involved . . ." Then he stopped. "Your grandmother? I mean, I felt your power, but I didn't think your grandmother and Adele . . . Of course, it all makes sense now."

"And there's the answer." Mia smiled. "Although we're not the same, you and I."

"Because I don't practice and you do?" Trent's voice was hard, angry.

Mia shook her head. "No, because we're not the same type of witch."

"I don't understand. There are different types?" Trent leaned forward, the anger leaving his face.

She nodded. "We practice kitchen witchcraft. Mostly healing and throwing spells for happiness and world peace."

Trent laughed. "You spell for world peace? Seriously?

I bet you were a shoo-in during the beauty contest interviews."

"Don't joke, Grans had a pretty successful track record going until the whole oil thing got in the way." Mia leaned back in her chair, waiting for the judgment.

Trent studied her closely. "You're not joking, are you?"

"You've seen the kitchen witch in my window." When he nodded she continued, "Gloria is my familiar. My contact with the Goddess. She allows me to focus on the spell. Mr. Darcy used to be my familiar, but he's got other issues right now."

"I thought the doll was some sort of weird decoration." Trent smiled. "So you're a kitchen witch. Who else knows?"

"The coven, your brother, and my grandmother. Christina knows, but she thinks it's kind of cool. I don't have brothers or sisters, and my parents don't like to talk about this whole thing. But that's it. Or at least I hope no one else knows. It could ruin my business." Mia picked up her tea and took a sip. "I'd hate to be run out of town or burned at the stake. Idahoans are pretty conservative in some ways."

Trent laughed. "In Magic Springs you'd more likely be named to the city council. Our little town has a long history of welcoming the different. Why do you think my family started the coven here? For the amazing skiing?"

"No, that's your brother's thing, isn't it?" Mia pulled on the string of her tea bag, gently swirling it through the water. "Still, I'd rather we keep my little secret. Besides, you don't even practice."

"I don't claim my family heritage. Once my oldest brother went off to law school, I told Dad I'd run the store and Mom could train Levi in the craft. He's been happy as a clam. Gives him lots of slope time." Trent shook his head. "Honestly, not to offend you, but I think it's all a big sham."

"I believe my spells and potions can heal the sick and help the world keep its balance of positive energy." Mia cocked her head. "According to some philosophers, we can both be right."

"In a parallel universe." Trent shook his head. "Let's just agree to disagree. You a football fan? How about those Broncos?"

"Denver or BSU?"

"The girl knows a bit more than she lets on." Trent smiled. "Maybe we can spend a quiet evening in pleasant conversation."

"Just don't bring up politics. I'm pretty liberal using Idaho standards."

"And there we go down the rabbit hole again." Trent stood and poked at the fire.

Mia watched him as he squatted next to the hearth, his powerful legs tight against his jeans. She hadn't noticed when, but he'd traded his hunting boots for a pair of the slippers from the box near the front bench. Just a couple of old homebodies, she thought. What would it be like to make love to Trent in front of the fire, the flickering lights from the lanterns playing with the shadows on their bodies?

A knock at the door burst her fantasy. Her eyes widened as she stared at the door.

"Stay there." Trent walked to the door, the fireplace poker still in his hand. "Maybe it was a branch on the porch."

"Someone's out there," Mia whispered.

Trent ignored her warning and continued walking to the door. He looked out the side window, then opened the door. Mia held her breath as William Danforth entered the foyer. "I saw your lights. I was on my way to Magic Springs when I hit a van someone had left in the middle of the road."

Mia stood from the couch. "You hit my car?"

William pointed at her. "You! I should have known. What exactly do you have against my family that you're trying to kill all of us?"

"I didn't kill Adele. Besides, you ran into my car, not the other way around." Mia felt heat rise to her face, even though the cabin still felt chilly.

William sniffed. "We'll let the law settle this." He pulled off his coat and dumped it on the floor. "Is there any food in this place? I'm starving."

Mia shook her head. If he thought she was going to share the soup she'd made with someone who'd not only accused her of killing his aunt, but now hit her van . . . ? Well, it would be a cold day in hell.

Trent came and stood next to her. A show of solidarity. His next words ruined the thought. "We've got some hot soup. You want some coffee or tea?"

Mia burned at his words. Trent put an arm tightly around her. Then he squeezed. His message was clear, be good. Finally she got hold of her anger. "Why don't I see if the soup's ready?" She shrugged off Trent's arm, and headed to the kitchen. She stopped and glanced back at William. "Hey, where's Barney?"

William looked like she'd caught him naked in the Lodge's ladies' locker room. He swallowed, "Who?"

"Barney Mann, the attorney handling your aunt's estate and the guy you had lunch with about," she glanced at her wrist at a watch that wasn't there, "four hours ago?"

William turned a deeper shade of purple. "How did you know we had lunch today?"

Trent had crossed the room to stand next to Mia again. This time he didn't pull her into a protective hug but edged in front of her. "We ate at the same restaurant. Not very observant for someone who is supposed to be a journalist."

William flashed the fingers on his hand. "Details. I never was good at the detail stuff. That's probably why I'm an *ex*-journalist. Hard to admit that I was here for Aunt Adele's birthday to beg for part of my inheritance early."

"That's why you were in town?" Mia stepped closer, but Trent grabbed her arm, keeping her next to him.

"Sad but true. You said there's coffee?" William sniffed the air. "And soup?"

"Have a seat in the living room. Mia will bring it out." Trent nodded to the fireplace. "You can slip off your shoes and warm up your feet."

"Sounds divine." William pulled off his boots, left them in the middle of the hallway, then went and landed loudly on the couch. "Sugar, no cream."

Mia glanced at Trent. Quietly, she asked, "What?"

Trent leaned toward her ear and whispered, "I don't want to let him out of our sight until we find out what happened to Mr. Mann."

A chill ran down Mia's back and she shivered. "I'll get the soup. You want coffee too?"

Trent nodded, his gaze not leaving their guest's back. "I'll be right here."

Mia walked into the kitchen. As she dug through the

drawers for spoons, she found a knife small enough to fit into the pocket of her sweater. She patted the outside of the bulky cardigan, just to make sure it didn't show.

Filling three bowls with soup and adding spoons to the bowls, she put a sleeve of crackers she'd found in the pantry that didn't seem too stale on a tray. She carried the tray into the living room and set it on the coffee table. The men were silent and watched her as she entered. Even with the crackling fire Mia felt the chill in a room that a few minutes ago had been warm and cozy enough for her to consider throwing caution to the wind and bedding Trent. Just for fun. Now the room felt like a deep freeze, even with the third body.

"Soup's on." Mia tried to sound perky, to break the ice.

"Smells great." Trent smiled at her, and for a second she wondered if he had picked up on her thoughts about throwing him on the bear rug and tearing off his clothes. When his smile widened her eyebrows raised. She definitely was going to have to find out what kind of power Trent had been keeping under wraps. Grans had told her that some families with long roots in the world of witchcraft passed on talents to their offspring, like reading thoughts. On the other hand, the reaction could be her imagination or his ability to read body language. Either explanation was perfectly normal and not supernatural at all.

When Trent chuckled Mia shook her head. *Or not.*

William grabbed a bowl and spoon, crunching crackers into the soup and shaking a ton of salt and pepper over the mixture without even tasting the broth. Mia groaned inwardly. She hated people who never tried the true taste a chef gave food without trying to mask the flavor with seasonings. The worse offender in her mind had been the dishwasher who worked at the hotel. Dusty carried an individual bottle of hot sauce to work. When he ate his employer-provided meal, no matter what they'd cooked that day, he poured hot sauce over the plate. Mia shuddered at the memory. The man was crass and creepy. Just like William.

She picked up her bowl and slipped into one of the wing chairs next to the couch. She tucked her feet under her and focused on eating. Who knew when they'd be able to leave the cabin, and the walk back to the road, and then maybe to town, would be long. They would all need food. She wondered if the pantry held any energy bars they could borrow. Watching the men eat, she wondered who would be the first to break the silence. Her money was on William.

He didn't disappoint. As soon as he finished his soup, he belched, and then pointed at Trent. "You're the grocery store guy, right?"

Trent nodded, still eating.

"The lawyer said he's still waiting for your bill to come in to close out Adele's estate. You need to send that so I can get out of this freezer and back to Arizona." William pounded his finger on the coffee table, making the empty bowl jiggle.

"I send bills to my customers at the end of the month, dead or alive." Trent didn't even look up from his soup.

"That's two weeks away. What am I supposed to do for two weeks? The worthless piece of man this town calls a lawyer won't even release me money for living expenses. The Lodge isn't cheap, you know."

Mia bit her lip. So that was why William had taken

Barney to lunch, trying to get estate money released. The lawyer had stood his ground and got a free meal. He'd played the game well.

"Not my problem." Trent set his bowl on the coffee table and focused his gaze on Mia. "Amazing soup. I can't believe you got so much flavoring out of cans."

"You supplied the owner with some fantastic product. I made a list of what I used so we can restock." Mia bit into the last bite in her bowl. "I'm definitely buying some of this dried pasta. Who makes it?"

"Actually, a local producer. They run a small organic farm in the summer, selling to me and out at the farmers market in Sun Valley. In the winter they produce pasta. You should try their goat cheese ravioli. Heaven." Trent leaned back in his chair, but Mia noticed he'd turned the chair to face the couch, where he could keep a watch on William.

"Food? We're talking food?" William snorted. "I've got a major problem here and all everyone I meet wants to talk about is freaking food."

"What do you expect when you're sitting with a caterer and someone who runs a grocery store?" Mia laughed. "We aren't going to be chatting about auto repair."

William waved his hand, dismissing her comments. "Even the lawyer wanted to talk about how great the food they serve was at that dump of a golf course where he agreed to meet me. You would have thought it was his last meal."

A chill ran up Mia's back at his words. She glanced at Trent and, setting her bowl on the table, moved her hand closer to her pocket. "Where is Mr. Mann now?"

William grimaced. "Still in Twin Falls. He said he had

some business to complete. I think he wanted to hit the all-you-can-eat buffet before going back into isolation. You'd think he'd lose some of that weight while he hibernated during the winter. It's not like you can get a decent meal in town."

Mia focused on Trent, wondering if his mind reading worked on important things, like whether the portly lawyer really was working his way through The Fall's Buffet or lying dead somewhere in an alley. When he shook his head slightly Mia interpreted that as good news for Barney and released her grip on the sweater pocket.

William pulled out his cell. "Crap, still no service. Don't you guys have cell towers here at all?"

"Depends on the provider. Most cell towers are closer to town. People build houses here to get away from all the techie gadgets that run their normal world. Downtime." Trent stood and stretched. He picked up the tray. "Coffee?"

"More instant," William whined.

"Definitely. You still want some?" Trent waited.

"Better than nothing, I guess," William leaned forward, his leer focused on Mia. "Maybe I can get to know you a little better while we wait."

Mia popped up and out of her chair. "Sorry, have to help Trent."

As they walked out of the living room, Mia heard William mutter, "Your loss."

When they reached the safety of the kitchen Trent turned to her. "You okay?"

"Fine. That man is a total pig. First he accuses me of killing Adele in front of the entire community, then he wants to," she added air quotes to her words, "'get to know me.' What a creep."

Trent filled the teakettle with bottled water. "Remind me not to tick you off."

"Funny." Mia searched through the cabinets for fresh cups. "I'm tired and cold and worried about Grans and Christina."

"Christina seems to have a good head on her shoulders. And your grandmother could hunt and skin a bear in the middle of a snowstorm if she needed to, so I think one night without you watching over her won't hurt." The kettle started screaming and Trent moved it off the stove, pouring the hot water into the cups. "Unless there's something you're not telling me."

Mia pursed her lips. Should she mention her fears about her cookbook and the real reason Christina was in town? Could Trent ease her mind about Christina or, worse, confirm that she did have something to worry about. She decided this wasn't the best time to discuss ex-boyfriends and Isaac's schemes. "Not really. Well, there is, but this isn't the . . ."

Her words were cut short by a loud knocking on the front door.

Trent smiled. "For a deserted cabin in the snow, this place is quite the way station."

They joined William, who had reached the door and just stood there, watching the shadowed figure on the other side of the frosted window.

"You going to open it?" Trent asked William. He looked, in Mia's opinion, even paler than he had a few minutes before. For someone who lived in Arizona, the man must not get outside much; he looked whiter than an Alaskan accountant.

Not for the first time that night, Mia wondered about

the whereabouts of the portly lawyer. Had he stayed in Twin Falls, like the smug William had said, or was there something more sinister to his absence?

"Get out of the way." Trent shoved William aside and reached for the door handle. "If we'd acted this way when you showed up, you'd be frozen on the porch, instead of blocking the door."

"But . . ."

Mia didn't hear the rest of what William Danforth the Third planned on saying because just then, Trent swung open the door. Her breath hitched involuntarily as she watched the figure enter the room.

Levi walked through the door, brushing snow from his coat and stamping his feet.

William shrank back and let out a deep breath, like the Ghost of Christmas Future had just passed him by.

"Dude, you know how hard it was to find you in this storm?" Levi nodded to Mia. "Hey, girl. How are you feeling? Your Grans is worried sick. You aren't having the best month now, are you?"

"How did you know we were here?" Mia asked.

Levi flashed a glance at his brother. "Let's just say I got an emergency transmission when you went off the road."

"Took you long enough to get out here." Trent slapped his brother on the back. "I hope I'm not interrupting your storm party."

"As a matter of fact you are. When I left the girls had just opened the tequila and were making margaritas. I hope they save one for me." Levi's face broke into a grin. "Get your stuff, kids. I've got a snowcat out there to take us back to town."

"Seriously? That's great." William sat on the bench and started pulling on his shoes. "Hey, wait. What's a snowcat?"

Levi grinned. "You're about to find out." He glanced at his brother. "You need to lock up?"

"I'll walk through and make sure everything's good. The fire's burned down, so we should be good there if I douse it with some water." Trent winked at Mia. "Wouldn't do for the cabin to burn down. Not sure I could pay the replacement cost."

Mia followed Trent back into the living room, where she cleaned up the plates and bowls they'd used. She rinsed them and set them in the dishwasher. "Hopefully they'll be fine there until the owner reopens the cabin. I feel bad, leaving a mess."

Trent helped her put away the last of the pantry items they'd used. "We need to get going before we don't have any light at all. The road up the mountain can be pretty dangerous at night in the best of times."

As they redressed for the trip into town, Mia felt the knife in the pocket of the sweater. When she slipped off the sweater and put on her coat, she kept the knife close. "Just in case," she whispered. When Trent came to check on her, she pasted on a smile she didn't feel. "Let's get out of here."

The three stood on the porch while Trent locked the door and replaced the key. Mia saw him whisper what she assumed was a protection spell for the cabin and then he turned back.

When their eyes met he had the good sense to look abashed at her seeing him perform magic. The man hadn't told her the entire truth when they had told their secrets, now had he?

"Lowly grocery store owner, my butt," she muttered as they followed Levi and William to the snowcat.

"I know enough to get myself out of trouble, that's all," Trent protested.

"And monkeys fly." Mia climbed into the back seat of the cat next to William, leaving the shotgun seat for Trent. His brother might need his "help" as they inched their way back to town.

She gazed out the window at the quickly darkening sky. And that was the trouble with dating a witch, she thought. They never were completely honest with you. Mia thought about Isaac and his deception and betrayal, not only as her boss but as her lover. Maybe honesty just wasn't a characteristic any man had.

Human or witch, it didn't seem to make a difference.

CHAPTER 16

Mia kept her hand on the knife the entire trip up the Magic to town. Knowing she could protect herself made her feel powerful. Knowing she may have to because someone had already killed Adele and she might be sitting next to the killer made her want to throw up. When they reached the Lodge and William left the snowcat Mia's body sagged in relief.

Levi glanced back at her using the rearview mirror. "You okay back there?"

"Yeah, just wanting to get home." Mia leaned back in her seat and relaxed her shoulders. She had been sitting straight as a board for the entire trip back into town. Every time the snowcat shifted she tensed, until she'd become so stiff, she couldn't imagine relaxing.

"No worries. Next stop, Mia's school for wandering children and orphans." Levi grinned at his brother. "Where do you want to be dropped off, dude?"

"I'll go with Mia. I want to check out that building. You could help me hook up the generator before you take off for your party." They had stopped at the van on the way up to grab the piece of machinery and check on the condition of Mia's car.

"My continued absence will be mourned by one and all, but I can do that." Levi turned the snowcat back onto the road. Snow had been falling for hours in town, making the roads almost impassable.

"An hour. You can miss your snow bunnies for an hour." Trent shook his head. "Little brother, you are a horndog."

"I came to rescue you, so just hush. You're making me look bad in front of the little woman back there." Levi's eyes twinkled as he gazed at her in the mirror.

"You keep calling me the 'little woman,' you're the one who's going to need to be rescued." Mia watched the snow fall as they drove. "And how exactly did that rescue work? I know we were out of cell range."

"Brothers have a special connection. That's all I can say." Levi grinned. Trent didn't even turn his head to look at her.

"Whatever. As long as you and your specially connected brother get my generator set up, I guess I don't care how you communicate." Although deep down inside, she did. Had Trent cast a spell, did they have telepathic abilities? Had the owner of the house installed a shortwave radio? She focused back on the street and watched the snow pile up. The town looked deserted. Shops on Main Street were closed and dark. Even the fake gaslight streetlights had been turned off or lost power from the storm. City Hall blazed bright at the end of the street and several officers bundled in parkas worked on cleaning off the steps, sidewalks, and police cars, only keeping in front of the falling snow for a few minutes. Emergency response would be slow tonight, even with their diligence.

Curving around the square, Mia caught her first glance at her building. The school still had lights. The front walk looked recently shoveled and the entry looked inviting. She really needed to start bringing in some cash before the house ate up all her savings in utility costs alone.

As they pulled into the parking lot, three figures emerged from the front door and headed out to meet them. When she slipped out of the cat Grans grabbed her in a hug. "I was so worried. When Levi called to let us know you were stranded I knew something was wrong. Are you okay?"

"I'm fine." She glanced at Levi. "Thanks for getting hold of her."

"No problem. I figured you'd want her to know you were being rescued." Levi smiled. "And, of course, I wanted the credit."

"Brat."

Grans slapped her on the arm. "Don't be spiteful. Levi didn't have to go out of his way to save you two. But then we found out that Barney and Mr. Danforth had been stranded as well."

"Wait, Barney was with William?" Trent stood by Mia now, questioning her grandmother.

"Right after Levi left we got a call from Officer Baldwin saying Barney had called from the road, and he was stuck too. And he told Baldwin that Mr. Danforth was also on the road to Magic Springs. Did you find them?"

Levi and Trent passed a long look between them. "Help me take the generator in, then head back to City Hall. Tell them what we know. Then give them the keys to the cat and get back here. You're not going back down. Now it's police business."

"But—" Levi started, and Trent shook his head.

"Help me with the generator, then do what I said." He put his hand on his brother's back and led him toward the cat.

Mia did the same to Grans, but gently aimed her toward the door. "Let's get inside where we can talk."

Another arm went around her grandmother, and Mia looked up, expecting to see Christina. Instead, James caught her eye. Reading her expression, he quickly explained. "I found your grandmother's car stuck in the snow a mile from here. After we got here the roads got too bad for me to leave. I guess you're stuck with me."

"And he's teaching me how to make clam chowder," Christina added.

"As long as you're being helpful, you're more than welcome." She smiled at him. "Thanks for bringing her here. I should have had her come earlier."

"I may be old, but I'm not deaf, you know." Grans slipped a little on the ice. "Although if you two don't walk faster, I might freeze solid out here."

"James," Trent called over the whipping wind. "We need you over here."

Mia watched as the man hesitated, then turned to Christina. "I guess our clam chowder lesson will have to wait." He waited for Christina to take his spot next to Grans, then made his way back to the snowcat.

As soon as the three got into the foyer, they slipped off their boots and coats. The school did keep heat well, and the solar panels on the roof helped when there was sun. But as Mia shut the door, she shivered. "Let's get upstairs and finish off that chowder. Maybe we can throw some biscuits in the oven too? It looks like we'll have a full house for the snowstorm."

Grans nodded. "I was lucky James arrived when he did. I don't think Muffy could have walked very far in this storm."

Mia followed the women up the stairs. James did always seem to be in the right place all the time. He'd been at the Lodge when Adele was killed; now he just happened to find Grans in a snowstorm. Mia shook off the thought. She was tired and worried and seeing ghosts where there weren't any. Barney popped into her mind. William had to have lied to them when he said the lawyer stayed in Twin Falls.

Too many questions and no answers. Right now she just wanted to get into a hot shower, some fresh clothes, and cook in her kitchen. Mr. Darcy stood at the top of the stairs watching her ascent. She scooped him up in her arms and rubbed the top of his gray head. The cat purred his welcome home, warming her as she entered the apartment.

"I'll be back out in a second. Tell me we still have hot water." Mia frowned; would the pipes have frozen? "Water, even?"

"This isn't my first storm, missy," Grans shook her head. "We left water dripping through all the pipes here, and at my house as well. But honestly, I think the plumbing is pretty well insulated here. The board put a lot of money into the school to make sure the building would be weatherproofed. That's one of the reasons Adele decided to vote with me in selling the building to you rather than the developer. She hated the idea that they wanted to tear down a perfectly solid building."

"Thank the Goddess for Adele." Mia sat Mr. Darcy on the couch and walked the hall to her bedroom. Thirty minutes later, her hair still wet but the kinks from stress easing out of her shoulders, Mia followed the chatter of voices to the kitchen.

Trent sat at the table with Grans and Christina, but James and Levi were gone. He glanced up and smiled as she entered the room. "Feel better?"

"Much." She headed to the cabinet to grab a cup, but Grans shooed her to a chair.

"I'll get your tea. You relax."

Mia slipped into a chair across from Trent. "The generator up?"

"All set. I'll take you there in a few and show you how it works." Trent glanced at the clock. "I'm waiting for a call from Levi."

"I thought he was coming back here." Mia accepted the cup of hot tea from her grandmother.

Trent nodded. "I told him to call once he got to the police station."

Barney's face surfaced in Mia's thoughts again. "You don't think William could have . . ." She let the words trail off.

"No use worrying about what we don't know." Grans tapped the table. "I did find something interesting in Adele's genealogy files, however."

Any thought of sleep vanished from Mia's body. "What?"

"Christina, bring me the brown tote I left in the living room." Grans looked at Mia. "Where's your laptop? I need you to look up something."

Mia went over and opened the roll top desk she used to hide the papers and mess that came with trying to run a business. She opened the laptop and booted the system. The Wi-Fi connection to the internet still worked, but she didn't know if it would hold up with the storm in full swing now. All it took was the loss of one cell tower and she'd be back in the Stone Age, cut off from the world.

Trent's phone rang. He glanced at the display and answered it. "Levi, what's going on?"

Mia watched Trent's face as he listened to the other side of the conversation. He definitely didn't like what Levi was telling him.

"Just get back here." He clicked off the phone.

Mia raised her eyebrows. "Problems?"

"Baldwin thinks it's too dangerous to send out anyone tonight. Barney's on his own until tomorrow morning, if then." Trent tossed the phone on the table. "Maybe he turned back and is hunkered down in Twin Falls. If not . . ."

Trent didn't have to finish the sentence. They all knew the danger being out in a storm like this could be to someone who was in great shape. Barney didn't have a chance.

Mia heard Grans whisper a protection blessing under her breath for the stranded lawyer. Then she straightened her shoulders and waved her hand over the phone. "No use us worrying about something we don't know is true. Barney Mann isn't stupid. If he's out in the storm, he'll find shelter, just like the two of you did. He's been around these Magics too long to let some Arizona tenderfoot get the better of him."

Mia listened to Grans's words, but something about what she said bothered her. Not about Barney; she knew Grans was right about him. Knowledge of the Magic had saved many a stranded townsperson over the years. He might just make it. But William—something was wrong with what she'd said about William. She realized all three were staring at her.

"What do you want me to look up?" She opened a web browser.

Grans dug in the tote and pulled out a folder stuffed with papers and photos. She paged through the pile until she pulled out an old picture. Two boys sat on the side of the Lodge pool, feet in the water and arm in arm, grinning at the camera. She turned over the picture. "Here it is. Look up Samuel Jacobs."

"Just Samuel Jacobs? There must be a million people by that name." Mia typed it into her search line hit Enter. As she suspected, pages and pages of entries. "Can you narrow it down a bit?"

Grans pushed the photo to her and pointed to one. "There are two boys."

Mia stared at the boy's face. A young William grinned back at her. "So that looks like William. I don't understand."

"Now look at this one." Grans handed her a school picture taken at the same age.

Mia held up the second photo to the first. "So, this is Sam?"

"Turn it over." Grans sat back, waiting.

Christina leaned closer as Mia turned over the photo. William Danforth III was scribbled in fading ink. Mia turned the picture back over. "This is William—not Samuel."

"And the man here in town is not William, but Samuel, posing as William." Grans nodded. "Adele must have recognized him from the pictures and that's why she was digging through the stuff on her desk. The man posing as William Danforth is a fraud."

"Which is why he was pushing to have the estate finalized," Trent added.

Christina picked up the two photos, "So if Samuel Jacobs is here, where is William Danforth?"

CHAPTER 17

"The biscuits are in the oven keeping warm and there's clam chowder on the stove." Grans pointed Levi to the kitchen when he arrived from the police station.

Levi smiled, but gestured to Trent to meet him at the door. "We need to talk."

"Where's James?" Trent left the couch, where he'd been sitting with Mia, watching her search the internet for any sign of either of the two men. After graduating from University of Utah together they both seemed to drop off the radar.

"The dude said he felt safer at City Hall, so he's hanging with Baldwin for the duration. Did you know the two of them went to college together?"

"There seems to be a lot of that going around lately." Trent glanced at Mia as she followed him to the door.

"Would you go with me through the school to make sure everything's okay?" She grabbed a sweater. "I'd feel better knowing we were alone in the building before we turned in for the night."

Trent slapped his brother on the back. "You stay here. Levi and I will do it."

"I can walk through my own building." Mia narrowed her eyes at the men.

"Yeah, but it gives us something to do to feel busy. You don't want us to feel like we're not helping, right?" Levi grinned at her, his dimples showing.

"What are you worried about?" Christina watched the exchange.

Trent shook his head. "Not worried, just taking precautions. We'll be right back, and in the meantime I'll catch Levi up on the William issue."

"Okay, but there's the front door, one in the kitchen, and one in the solarium. But I think there might be some other door or window open. Mr. Darcy seems like he's disappearing at times." Mia counted off the possible exits on her fingers. "Maybe I should just go."

"Stay here and stay warm. We'll find the exits. Remember, I used to help with the construction here." He put his hands on her arms. "Trust me, okay?"

She nodded and let the two men leave through the doorway. "I'm locking the door after you, so call us if we don't hear you knock."

"What William issue?" Levi followed him into the hallway.

Trent shushed his brother. He leaned through the crack between the door and the doorjamb. "Don't let anyone in until we get back."

"Like who?" Mia called out after him.

"I don't know, but with tonight's surprises already, it could be anyone." He grinned at her. "I didn't expect William to show up at the fishing lodge, did you?"

Mia returned to her laptop. "Men," she grumbled as she tried a new search tag, hoping to get a new hit on the two friends.

"It's nice having someone to watch over you. Your grandfather used to fuss over me at times. I miss that." Grans stood. "I'm due for a warm-up of my tea. You want some?"

Mia shook her head, already lost in thought as she paged through the search results, looking for the needle in the cyber haystack. From what they'd found, she didn't think Samuel or fake William, as she thought of him now, had a chance in a court fight. Barney would make sure of that. Mia hadn't gotten along with Adele, but that didn't mean she didn't want her money to go to the rightful heir.

Christina followed Grans into the kitchen. "Is there enough water for some hot chocolate?"

Mia smiled. Christina's piercings made it look like she was a badass, but really, deep down, she was still a young woman who enjoyed drinking cocoa.

Mia watched as a glow grew on the rocking chair. The glow slowly materialized into a shape, and then Dorothy Purcell sat in Mia's living room. Mr. Darcy, or maybe Dorian, moved over to sit by the chair.

"Hi, Dorothy." Mia leaned back, the computer forgotten. She should have been frightened by the presence, but the woman didn't seem spooky; in fact, during Mia's hospital stay, she'd calmed her. Not the normal ghost sighting, but what in her life was normal? She pulled her sweater closer; the temperature in the room had dropped a good ten degrees when the ghost materialized. Mia had thought the hospital room had just been cold, but now she realized Dorothy's presence had been to blame.

"What a lovely cat." Dorothy glanced around the room, reaching down to stroke Mr. Darcy's coat. Her hand jerked away from him almost immediately. "Did you know your cat has a human spirit sharing his body?"

Mia nodded. "Long story. So what are you doing here? I thought you only visited the hospital and the nursing home."

Dorothy leaned back into the rocker, studying Mia. "So, you've heard the stories about me."

"A few." Mia waited, but the woman seemed content to rock and look around the room. "Is there a reason you stopped by?"

"People your age are very direct. It's almost rude. What happened to polite conversation?" Dorothy shook her head. "No matter, you need to know this. The front door isn't the only way into the school."

"I have several doors here, front, back, side." Mia held up her hands. "Exactly what are you trying to say? Is someone coming?"

Dorothy's face contorted, and for a minute Mia thought the ghost might just cry. Then she sat still. "I said I'd tell you, so I will. There's a secret passage on the second floor that leads to a tunnel. The tunnel dead-ends into the woods. People can still get in even if the men lock the doors. You must be careful."

"How do you know about the tunnel?" Mia leaned forward, trying to will Dorothy to stay until she'd gotten a straight answer.

"I'm sure I mentioned that I went to school here. We used the tunnel to sneak out at night. 'Meet up,' I believe, is the modern term." Dorothy sighed, and Mia wondered who the woman was remembering meeting as a young girl.

"I get your drift." Mia smiled. "Where will we find the tunnel? And who told you to tell us?"

"Honestly, do you think after all these years I know where the entrance is? It seems to me it started in a class-room. Then the memory swirls into a book I read during junior year." Dorothy looked up and cocked her head at Mia. "Memories are like precious stones: hard to come by and easy to lose or have stolen from you. Don't let him steal your memories, dear girl."

Noise from the kitchen diverted Mia's attention, and when she looked back Dorothy was fading. "Wait, you didn't tell me who sent you."

"Your guardian," the whispered words echoed in the small room, keeping beat with the crackle of the fire on the logs.

The room quickly regained its heat as the rest of Dorothy disappeared into whatever spirit realm in which she existed. Mia curled her legs under her. A secret tun-nel? She wondered if Grans knew more about the tunnel. There had to be some type of local story, true or imag-ined. For the first time in her thirty years, Mia had been told she had a guardian.

Could the world get any stranger? Last summer she'd been an up-and-coming caterer living with her chef boy-friend and remodeling their dream house. Two months later she was unemployed, homeless, and learning her witch-ing history from a grandmother who believed in magic and saving the world, one spell at a time. Now she was talking to spirits and apparently had a guardian in the other world, wanting to help.

Oh, and she and the others were snowed in by the worst storm to hit Magic Springs in a decade.

"Don't forget to add poor Adele to your pity party. And Barney." Grans walked into the room alone.

"Not a pity party, just a reciting of the facts." Mia watched as Grans sat in the same rocker Dorothy had just vacated. "You need to stay out of my head. I like my privacy."

Grans snorted. "Child, you haven't had a private thought since you were born. Sorry, it doesn't work that way in our family. What you know, we know."

"So you knew I was stranded?"

She sipped her tea. "Of course, but Levi was already on the way to rescue the two of you." The elderly woman paused. "You could do worse than Trent. He's more like you than you believe."

"I'm not ready for a new relationship. Not after Isaac." Her stomach clenched as she thought about Isaac and his betrayal. How had she let herself get so blindsided? She hadn't protected her heart or her head in that relationship. Now, Grans wanted her to jump into the pool again. She shook her head. Arguing with her grandmother wasn't going to help them solve Adele's murder. "Dorothy was just here."

Grans set her tea cup on the table. "Dorothy Purcell? Why didn't I sense her?" She looked around the room, and Mia wondered if ghosts left trails that people with power could see.

"She materialized right there." Mia pointed to the chair where her grandmother sat. Grans stood and sat next to Mia on the couch. "Besides, weren't you the one saying I must have imagined her in my hospital room? What's up with that?"

"She and Adele had issues back in the day. I wasn't sure she was going to be honest with you, so I needed to figure out why she appeared." Grans shrugged. "Sorry I lied."

"That's it? 'Sorry I lied'? Are you kidding?" Mia stared at her grandmother.

"Don't worry about this. I'll explain later." She reached out and held Mia's hand. "I can't feel her. I always feel spirits. This is so strange. What did she say?"

"I'm in danger, my guardian sent her, there's a secret passage; you know, normal, ghost talk." Mia's laugh died in her throat. Grans's face had gone almost chalk white "What? What aren't you telling me?"

"It may not mean anything, but years ago a girl disappeared from the school. The whole town looked for her. The headmaster swore the doors were locked, but when they found her body in the woods, his alibi didn't hold up." Grans sighed. "I pulled your mother from the school the day after the girl's body was found. Even though everyone in town knew the headmaster had killed the girl, I never believed that. Your mother finished out school at Sun Valley High with the town kids."

"You think someone stole her through the tunnel?"

Grans nodded. "The headmaster was a sweet man. He couldn't step on a spider, let alone kill someone. Besides, his taste in life partners didn't include the female persuasion."

Mia's heart sank. "Which probably labeled him as different, so the town believed he committed the crime." How many people who had been falsely accused actually were convicted because of being different? Christina's words echoed in her ears. People are scared of different.

"The poor man died in prison. Put a label of a child

molester on someone, they won't survive long there." Grans stared at the chair. "So if someone came in through the tunnel and kidnapped that girl, he could still be around. Old, but around."

"He'd have to be in his fifties. Even if he was young for the first kill." Mia shuddered. "Very young."

"We don't know if he's even still alive, but according to Dorothy, someone knows about the tunnel. Someone who may see you as a loose end." Grans sipped her tea and Mia could see the thoughts racing through her head.

"I really can't see a connection between this murder and Adele's. Maybe Dorothy was confused. She said her memories kept swirling on her."

Grans shook her head back and forth. "No. There's a connection. Your guardian wouldn't have made them- selves known unless there was a problem. We just have to find it."

"About the guardian thing . . ." Mia was interrupted by a knock on the door. She glanced at her grandmother as she stood to let Trent and Levi in. "We're not done talk- ing about this."

"When the time's right," Grans agreed, postponing the discussion.

Mia didn't like her answer but knew it would be all she'd get until her grandmother thought she needed to know the facts. She checked the peephole, then opened the door.

The two men hurried inside, shutting and locking the door behind them. "Doors, windows, construction en- trances, all locked and sealed. No one is getting in the school tonight without you knowing."

She pointed to the chairs. "Well, maybe. You need to hear this."

For the second time she went through her visit with Dorothy and the hidden tunnel. By the time she was done, Christina had returned from the kitchen.

Christina's eyes widened. "You saw a real live ghost?"

Mia's lips curled into an involuntary smile. "Don't you mean a real *dead* ghost?"

Christina bounced in her seat. "Whatever. What did she look like? Did the room grow cold? Did she try to possess you?"

"Calm down, girl." Levi laughed. "You act like you've never seen a ghost in your life."

"Some of us didn't grow up in magical families," Christina shot back. "I'm a newcomer in the paranormal department. Besides, don't you have a party with your fawning admirers waiting for you to go to?"

Trent chuckled and Levi shot him a look.

"I chose to be here." Levi shrugged his shoulders. "Maybe I should choose differently."

"Maybe you should," Christina shot back.

Mia watched the interaction with interest. Apparently Christina and Levi knew each other before tonight. Could Levi be the guy she was dating? Mia glanced at Trent, who smiled.

"Are we done?" Trent glanced at his brother. When Levi nodded Trent focused on Grans. "Tell us the stories you heard about the tunnel. Anything you remember?"

Grans shook her head. "Except for where the body was found, I don't think they ever said anything about the tunnel. Malinda, Mia's mother, told me the other kids talked about the tunnel. The girl was meeting someone in the woods over by the entrance from the town square."

"Dorothy said the entrance was on the second floor. How is that even possible?" Mia frowned, thinking about the outside of the building. The rectangular shape didn't have any signs of an outside stairwell.

"Look, it's almost midnight." Trent looked around the room. "Let's build up the fire, bring in blankets and pillows, and get some sleep. Sorry about kicking you out of your rooms, but I'd rather have us together tonight, where we can watch over the group."

"I'll take first watch," Levi offered.

Trent shook his head. "You sleep. I'm so wired, I doubt I could relax. I'll wake you at three. You can finish off the night."

Mia grabbed blankets and pillows from the rooms and the linen closet. She set her grandmother up on the couch, shushing aside her protests that Mia or Christina should take the couch.

After everyone had a makeshift bed she followed Trent into the kitchen, where she made a fresh pot of coffee. She sat at the table.

Trent tapped the table with his fingers. "You should get some sleep."

"I will." Mia hesitated, trying to phrase the question. Finally she just blurted it out. "You think we're in danger?"

Trent sighed, playing with the spoon that sat next to his coffee cup. "Your grandmother thinks so. Your ghost friend thinks so. So, yeah, I think I'd be stupid not to listen."

"It just feels like we're missing something. I'm pretty sure if I called Officer Baldwin and asked for police protection because the local ghost is worried about my safety, I'd be locked up in the state mental hospital." Mia shook her head. "How do you live with this woo-woo surrounding you?"

"Like I said before, I leave that part of the family heritage to Levi. He likes the mystery." Trent stood and carried his cup over to the counter, where he poured fresh coffee. "I like running a grocery. Ordering supplies, paying bills, helping people. Normal stuff."

Mia nodded. "That's why I love cooking. You cook, people eat, you clean up. Rinse and repeat. The only magic involved is the food."

"I think you're selling yourself short." Trent sat back and sipped his coffee.

"What do you mean?"

"One of the ways our magic flows through us is through what we produce. For me, it's a cute little store that tourists want to stop and spend money at, even if they don't need something." He nodded at the kitchen. "For you, the magic is here, in your kitchen. And in the food you create."

"I like that." Mia considered his words and grinned. "I really am the kitchen witch."

"Something like that." Trent smiled. He leaned closer. "A very pretty kitchen witch."

Mia closed her eyes, waiting for the kiss. When it came Trent's lips were soft, teasing, making her want more, even with a living room filled with people next door. As she responded, a sound broke them apart. She stared at Trent. "Is that—?"

He nodded. "Someone is knocking on your apartment door."

CHAPTER 18

Mia stepped over Levi's sleeping body. His makeshift bed blocked the path to the door and, she noticed, kept him within reaching distance of Christina. No way those two weren't seeing each other. The girls would have a little talk as soon as they weren't snowed in with the testosterone.

Trent pushed her behind him with one arm; then, holding a broom he'd pulled out of the kitchen closet, he slowly opened the door. Mia couldn't see around his body or the door, but she heard the grunt when Trent shoved the broom forward. She followed him out of the door, where Isaac was sprawled on the floor with Trent sitting on top of him, pinning down his arms.

"Isaac? What are you doing here? I thought you went back to Boise." Mia stood over her ex-boyfriend. She felt a tad bit bad that she liked the fact that Trent had knocked him over so quickly.

"Let me up and I'll tell you." Isaac grunted. "This guy's crushing me."

"I don't think you're in a position to make any demands here." Trent looked up at Mia. "You tell me if you want me to let him up or not. I'm in no hurry."

"What are you doing here?" Mia asked again. "I know you don't have a key, and the guys made sure all the doors were locked. So either you were hiding in the school or . . ."

"Or he knows where the tunnel is," Trent added. "Maybe I should lean a little harder on him."

"You're crushing me now. I can barely breath." Isaac panted.

"Then talk." Mia waited. She couldn't believe she'd once loved the weasel.

"Christina told me where the tunnel started in the woods. I've been parked there since ten. She was supposed to meet me there and deliver—" Again, he paused.

"Deliver what?" Trent glanced at Mia.

Mia shook her head. "My cookbook. You conned Christina into helping you steal my recipes?"

"I owed him for getting me out of Vegas." Christina's voice cracked as she spoke. Mia turned to see her standing in the doorway, Levi's arm around her. "He said he wouldn't tell Mom what happened if I came here and got your book for him."

"What a crappy brother you are." Mia glared at him.

"It was a business arrangement." Isaac sneered. "You could have rotted in that jail for years if I hadn't rescued you. You owed me."

"No, you were her brother; she should have been able to depend on you without being in your debt. Family matters." Levi looked like he wanted to be the one sitting on Isaac's chest, choking the words out of him.

"Mia, I didn't know how to tell you. He said you'd kick me out if you knew what happened." Christina was sobbing now, the words hard to understand. "I only stole enough for dinner for my friend and me. We hadn't eaten in days and there was so much left over."

"You were arrested for stealing food?" Mia blanched. So much for the land of plenty. "What happened, Christina?"

"I got a job dancing at this party. A bachelor party or something. Carolyn, the girl I was staying with, well, she'd lost her job on the Strip and we couldn't pay the rent. So we were living in her car." Christina flushed and looked at Levi, "They didn't want just a dancer; the guy who set it up had promised more. Apparently he picked up girls off the street and, well, hired them out."

Isaac interrupted. "You were a prostitute. Tell them the truth."

Christina closed her eyes at the verbal assault. Pressing her lips together, she paused for a minute, then ignored her brother and focused her gaze on Mia. "As soon as I figured out what was really going on, I grabbed my tote, along with some roast beef, rolls, and appetizers in a plastic bag. Then I tried to leave. But the cops had been called, and all of a sudden I was in jail, charged with hooking."

"So when you called big brother, he made you an offer." Mia kicked Isaac in the leg. "How could you put her in this predicament? You're just as bad as that pimp."

"Ouch," Isaac roared at her. "She owed me. We cared for the brat for an entire summer. Who paid for her food or put a roof over her head? Me!"

"We did," Mia corrected. "But apparently I was taking care of family, while you were just racking up favors to be called in later."

"Mia, I'm sorry. I'll leave and you'll never see me again." Christina straightened.

"You're staying here. Isaac, on the other hand, can go to hell." Mia kicked him again for good measure.

"You could charge him for breaking and entering," Trent offered.

"I could. Then I'd have to see him in court." Mia shook her head. "Isaac isn't worth the time. If he ever contacts Christina again, I'll make him worth my time."

"Witch," Isaac muttered. "I want my recipes."

"Keep it up, loser, and I'll make you my personal project, even if Mia wants to let you sink back into the cesspool you crawled out of." Trent tightened his hold on Isaac's arms. "Got me?"

"Whatever. I can cook better than she can anyway. I don't need her or her recipes. I've got a hot piece waiting for me at home." Isaac stared at Trent. "You want to let me up?"

Trent looked at Mia. "Ready for Levi and me to take out the trash?"

"More than ready." Mia went over and pulled Christina into her arms. "You've been through so much. I'm so sorry."

Christina started sobbing in her arms. Mia led her back into the apartment, where Grans put a coverlet over her and slipped next to her on the couch.

"You don't have to be so nice to me," Christina choked

out. "I was planning on giving him your recipes. The copies are in my bag."

Mia grabbed the floral tote bag Christina had purchased at her weekly visit to the thrift store. She pulled out the rubber-banded pages. "You mean these?"

Christina nodded. "I found the book when you left with Trent to drive to Twin Falls and made a copy at the library."

"The book you copied wasn't my recipes. I made a new cookbook with recipes out of the old Betty Crocker cookbook I found in the kitchen. Isaac would have been bringing 1960s back to the hotel." Mia threw the paper copies into the fireplace.

"You knew?" Christina wiped her face with a tissue Grans had offered.

Mia pushed a lock of hair out of Christina's face. "I suspected. And when Isaac arrived in town I knew he wasn't here just to see if you were okay."

"You need to learn to trust the right people, Christina." Grans watched the fire spark around the pages.

"I know. I thought I could trust Isaac." Christina squared her shoulders. "I should have talked to you when he first sent me here."

Mia grabbed the envelope out of her purse. "And I should have given you this a long time ago. Things just kept happening."

"What is this?" Christina opened the manila envelope that Mia had kept in her purse until now.

"These are the papers from your lawyer in Vegas. All charges were dropped. I guess when you filed for your health department license, they picked up your new address." Mia glanced at her grandmother. "When Isaac came to town I had a feeling what was in the package was important. I planned on giving them to you once I got back from Twin Falls, but with everything that's happened, I forgot."

"Thank you."

"I shouldn't have opened your mail." Mia looked up when Trent and Levi returned to the apartment. Trent locked the dead bolts and his brother came over and stood near the couch.

Christina shook her head. "I knew you suspected something. You'd look at me so sad sometimes, it almost broke my heart. Opening my mail wasn't half as bad as what I was doing to you."

Mia stood to let Levi take her place. "I think I'll start us some breakfast." Mia smiled as she saw Levi take Christina's hand and whisper in her ear.

She stood in front of the sink watching the sun rise over the Magics when she sensed Trent come behind her. "Some night."

"Your ghost was right. We were expecting company. I just wasn't expecting Isaac." Trent smiled. "Can I help you with something? I'm excellent at peeling potatoes."

"You're hired. My sous chef is preoccupied by your brother at the moment." Mia pulled out some country sausage to brown and started chopping an onion.

"Yeah, I didn't see that one coming. I hope he doesn't break her heart." Trent glanced at the door to the living room. "He can be a bit flighty as far as women are concerned."

Grans came into the kitchen and headed to the coffee maker to brew a fresh pot. "Your brother was just sowing some wild oats. Now that he's found the one, they'll be fine."

"Grans, they're just dating." Mia dumped the chopped

onions into a bowl and started in on a mixture of sweet peppers.

"I know when true love hits someone. Those two have been shot with Cupid's arrow. We'll be having a wedding before you know it." Grans finished with the coffee and sat at the table. "Just like I told you that Isaac wasn't the one for you. When you first started dating you came up here for a Sunday dinner. I told you then that man was nothing but trouble."

"Thanks for the support." Mia smiled at Trent. "Can I help it if my heart thought I was in love?"

"Pshaw. You knew it wasn't real. You were just working too hard at the catering job to let your body catch up." Grans was studying Adele's family tree again. "I never thought he'd be this big of a pain, though. I should have started my wish therapy on your breakup sooner."

"You were spelling for our demise? If I wasn't so happy to be rid of him right now, I might be mad at you. You've got to stop meddling in relationships." Mia pulled a cup out of the cupboard and filled it with the fresh brew. She set the cup in front of her grandmother. When Grans reached for it Mia pulled it out of her reach. "Especially mine. Promise me."

"I only do these things because I love you." Grans reached for the cup again.

"Promise me," Mia urged, moving the cup farther away.

Her grandmother shot a glance up at Trent's back, then focused on Mia. She cocked her head, then sighed. "If that's what you truly want, I promise."

"Good. Now, let's talk about William Danforth again. Where were we when we gave up for the night?"

Trent turned. "Hold on, let me in on the discussion. I'm done peeling. You want these diced or shredded?"

"Diced. We'll mix them with the sausage, onions, and peppers and do an oven bake." She went back to the sink to finish the chopping. She sautéed the onions and peppers, then added the crumbled sausage.

When Trent finished chopping he put the potatoes in a greased baking dish. Mia drained the oil from the meat mixture into a collector pan and layered the mixture over the potatoes. She put an aluminum foil cover over the top, slipped the dish into the oven, and wiped off the cabinets. She joined Trent and Grans at the table, where he had already poured her a cup of coffee. She sipped the dark brew and sent up a blessing for the people who surrounded her. Thank the Goddess the men had been stranded here by the storm. If Isaac had figured out her recipe swap, he would have come back. A black cloud swirled around her mental picture of her ex-boyfriend. Grans was right; she should have seen the black sooner. She'd excused it away. Never again.

She realized she hadn't seen Mr. Darcy since the blowup with Isaac. Had the cat snuck out again? She stood from the table. "Hey, I'll be right back."

"We'll be here," Trent shot back.

The man knew the punch line, Mia thought as she checked the apartment for any sign of Mr. Darcy. When she didn't find him curled up next to Christina she knew the cat had snuck out again. She smiled, looking at the two lovers asleep on the couch. Levi had better be good to her or he'd have to answer to Mia. Christina was more than just a houseguest or a roommate, she was family.

She unlocked the apartment door and left it open a crack. The lights had been left on downstairs, giving the staircase an eerie glow. "Stupid cat," she muttered. *Stupid cat you love*, came Gloria's response in her head. At least now Mia knew where the cat had been disappearing to. He'd found the secret passage and probably was hunting in the woods as she spent time searching the house for him. She was on a fool's errand, but she hated to think of him locked up in a room all alone. When she reached the second story, a noise drew her toward the last classroom on the right. The rising sun lit the room with a soft glow.

"Mr. Darcy," she called. "Here kitty, kitty."

No response, no patter of little feet. Mia started to feel uncomfortable, like she was being watched. "Mr. Darcy, come here."

She glanced into one empty classroom, the desks still in little rows, waiting for the ghosts of past students to sit down for English class or, worse, chemistry. She'd check every room on the floor except the last one, where she assumed the secret passage started. Or ended. She'd have to have Brent seal the tunnel before she rented out this floor. No need asking for trouble.

But when she entered the last room it was too late. Mia kicked herself for being so stupid.

John Louis stood at the teacher's desk, holding a struggling Mr. Darcy. The cat clawed at his hand and the man dropped him. He kicked at the animal, who ran toward Mia and out the door, meowing.

"Stupid cat. But I guess I can thank him for bringing you down here."

Mia shook her head. "Get out of my house, John."

Instead of moving, he laughed. "Soon this 'house' will be a rubble of stone and brick. Then a nice, new, shiny supermarket will be built, and your buddy Trent will be begging to sell his corner lot for pennies on the dollar."

"I'm not selling to you." Mia glanced at the hallway. Could Trent and Levi hear her if she cried out for help?

"No need to yell, the apartment is soundproof. The last principal didn't like the sound of kids disturbing his afternoon naps." John pulled a gun out of his jacket. "You were thinking about screaming, weren't you?"

"You can't just kill me. There are people upstairs who know you've been stalking me." Mia shook her head. "You'll never get away with it."

"Honestly, I don't want you dead. I want you to sign this deed." He nodded to a pile of papers on the student desk closest to her. "Then I want you to pack up and move out of town."

"You think I'll just sign the school over to you and leave? What crazy world do you live in?" Mia laughed.

"The crazy world where I shoot your grandmother if you don't." The smile that accompanied the threat made Mia's blood run cold. "Look, let me tell you how it's going to go down if you don't sign here and now. I'll go home. My wife will testify that we were together making love this morning and Baldwin will believe my alibi over your crazy story. Then one day, maybe tomorrow, maybe next week, there will be an unfortunate home invasion at your grandmother's house and she'll be shot trying to defend her little dog. Hell, I'll probably shoot the dog too."

Mia's blood ran cold. "I'll tell Baldwin this too. Don't you think he'll be suspicious when it happens just like I said?"

"Maybe, but I'll have an alibi again. And your grandmother will be just as dead." He waved the gun toward the chair. "Have a seat while you read over the deed. A good real estate broker never lets his clients sign something they haven't read."

Mia called out to Grans through her link to Gloria. An answering wave of warmth flooded her body and she sank into the chair in relief. She'd been heard. Now all she had to do was stall until they could rescue her.

As she read the document, she kept an eye on John. He kept watching the secret passage instead of the classroom door. "Expecting someone?"

John laughed. "I watched a man go through the tunnel earlier this evening, then he wound up being thrown out of your front door by the Major brothers. Who was that? Your little friend sneaking in a lover?"

"Actually, he was my ex." Mia forced her eyes not to drift toward the classroom door. She felt Trent's presence, along with Levi's. "Why don't you put the gun away? You've already won. I'm signing the deed."

John chuckled. "You're right, probably overkill."

Mia heard the gun clunk on the wooden desk, then she spun toward the back of the room and sprinted to the secret passage opening.

"You little—" John roared. But instead of getting off a shot to stop her, he grunted, and Mia heard a loud bang—and not from a gun.

"We have him, it's okay," Trent called to her, and she turned back to see John on the floor under Trent's knee. Levi held the gun on the man.

Then Baldwin rushed into the room, Christina following behind.

"Levi, drop the weapon."

Levi smiled and put the gun on the desk next to the papers Mia had been pretending to read. "Calm down, Baldwin. We're the good guys here."

Trent called him over. "You want to cuff this piece of

crap before I punch him? Because I really feel like punching someone tonight."

Baldwin tossed the cuffs to Trent. "You can have the honors. I'll keep the gun aimed at him until he's secured."

Christina ran to Mia. "Are you okay? Mr. Darcy ran into the living room and started crying. Then Grans said you were in trouble, so we called the police."

Mia pulled her close. "Fine. I'm really, really done with all this drama, though. Let's go upstairs."

"I'll need your statement," Baldwin called after her.

Mia didn't even slow down, "Tomorrow. Come by tomorrow after breakfast."

Now, an hour later and with John secured in one of Magic Spring's jail cells, Mia sat at the kitchen table with Trent and Grans. They'd been working on something on the computer, but she'd been thinking about shrimp and grits and a trip to New Orleans she'd always wanted to take.

Trent's voice cut through the food daydream. "What do you think?"

Mia realized the question had been aimed at her. She didn't even pretend she knew what she'd been asked. "About?"

"I told you she wasn't listening." Grans pointed to the picture. "If this is William Danforth, Adele's nephew, that guy who's in town isn't."

"So we turn these pictures over to Baldwin," Trent offered.

Mia shook her head. "And the imposter will explain it away. Before we go to the police, we need more proof. Like what happened to the real William Danforth."

Trent nodded. "That makes sense. Besides, Baldwin has his hands full trying to track down Barney and now dealing with John. He doesn't need to be distracted with this."

Mia added good wishes for Barney to the white cloud of protection she'd created for her houseguests. No way the guy would survive another night out in the cold, Baldwin had to find him, and soon. "Then let's search the internet to see if we can find out anything else."

Grans glanced at the clock. "I'm calling Elizabeth at the library."

"It's not even six in the morning," Mia protested.

"I'm not calling her at work. I'm calling her at home." Grans pulled a small black notebook out of her purse. She thumbed through the pages, then keyed a number into her cell.

"You know you can save your numbers in the phone, right?" Trent leaned forward.

"Don't even start. It took me three years to get her to even carry it with her after I bought the cell. She still has a landline at the house." Mia focused on the list of William Danforths that her search engine had pulled up.

"I like my house phones. I have a Mickey Mouse phone in one room and Minnie in the other. I even have a phone in the bathroom, just like Elvis had."

"In 1970."

"You say that like it's a long time ago." Grans turned her head to the phone and Mia could hear the woman on the other end. She pointed her finger at Mia and put the phone on the table with the speaker on. "Be quiet, people. Elizabeth? Is that you?"

"Did you call me?" Elizabeth asked back.

"I did."

"Then that's who you got. This isn't some party line that gets the numbers mixed up, Mary Alice. A cell number is only answered by one person." Elizabeth sighed. "I'm writing. What do you want?"

"Oh, sorry. I wanted to know if Adele did any recent genealogy searches at the library. I mean before she died."

The line was quiet. Then Elizabeth came back on. "She had just finished her family tree, at least for the Simpson side. She traced those roots back to the Pilgrims who landed on Plymouth Rock. She even copied off a DAR application."

"Daughters of the American Revolution." Grans pointed to the notebook in front of Trent. "Write this down. Sorry, Elizabeth, go on."

"Well, I thought she was done, at least until next year. You know she likes to focus on her garden starting in April. Then, last week, she was in the library from the time it opened until I closed up. I had to kick her out a few times."

Mia traded glances with Trent. "Ask her if she knew what she was researching."

"Did you hear that?" Grans asked.

"Yes, I heard her. I don't know, but she was focused on newspapers from years ago. I must have pulled ten years of microfilm for her over the week."

"Do you remember what papers?" Mia called into the phone.

"I'm not senile, this only happened a couple of weeks ago."

When Elizabeth didn't respond Mia prompted, "What papers were they?"

"Three different ones. The *Phoenix Gazette*, the *Idaho Statesman* from Boise, and Sun Valley's *Daily*."

Trent wrote down the three names. "Time frames?"

"What dates . . ." Grans started to ask.

Elizabeth interrupted her. "I'm not deaf either. She started at ten years ago, then went back twenty years. Then stopped."

"Thanks for your help. Maybe we'll stop by to look at the microfilm later this week," Mia called out to Elizabeth.

"I can do you better. We did a Jumpdrive of everything she asked for print copies of. That way I could run the printer during slow times at the library. I still have the drive if you'd like it."

"I'll be there when you open." Trent leaned close to the phone.

Grans signed off the phone call and the trio looked at each other. "If Adele found out that William wasn't who he said he was, she would have been furious. She didn't like being made a fool of, even when she acted like one."

"And if she'd accused William of trying to cheat her—" Mia added, fear running up her spine. They'd been with the guy all afternoon. Alone in the cabin.

"He'd have plenty of motive to kill Adele before she ruined his inheritance scheme," Trent finished her thought.

CHAPTER 19

The sun broke through the snow clouds as Mia beat eggs in a bowl. She opened the oven and poured the egg-and-cheese mixture over the potatoes and sausage. Breakfast would be done in thirty minutes; then she and Trent would snowshoe to the library to pick up the Jumpdrive, leaving Levi with Grans and Christina. The weather reports given hourly on the local radio station said that temperatures would be skyrocketing into the low thirties today, and then dropping back into the teens at night.

She rinsed out the bowl and looked at the kitchen witch. "Please let Barney be found today, alive."

Mia heard a footfall behind her. She turned to find Trent leaning against the table watching her.

"Praying to your Goddess?"

Mia cocked her head. "Asking for favors, I guess. Barney needs all the good luck he can get right about now. It got pretty cold last night."

Trent walked closer and ran his finger down her cheekbone. "I'm sure he's fine."

Her breath caught and she wanted to reach up and run her fingers through that tousled hair. Her heartbeat quickened. *Not here, not now.* She held back from leaning into him, the musky smell of wood chips and peppermint toothpaste trying to draw her closer.

The beep of the second oven, where a batch of cinnamon rolls were baking, jerked her out of the spell he had over her. She ducked her head, then moved around him. "I didn't time breakfast right. The rolls will be cold before the egg dish is done."

Trent moved over to the coffeepot and poured another cup. He sat at the table and watched her pull out the pan. The smell of cinnamon and sugar filled the kitchen. "I guess we'll have to eat the rolls first."

Men. She hid a small smile as she pulled small plates from the cabinet and cut one of the rolls for Trent. "You first?"

He grinned, but accepted the plate. "Sorry, but it's been a while since we've eaten. You have to be hungry, right?"

"Why do you think I made cinnamon rolls? I'm addicted." Mia set her plate on the table and nodded to the door. "I'm sure the rest of the group will be showing up any time."

As if her words brought them rather than the smell of baked goods, Christina, Levi, and Grans piled into the room. Their chatter broke her uncomfortable draw toward Trent, but when she glanced at him, she saw the surprise on his face. So he'd felt the power too. She dropped her eyes and muttered a new mantra: *I don't need a new man in my life.* She heard a giggle from the Goddess.

As the baked goods disappeared and another pot of coffee was started, the timer on the oven announced that the casserole was done. Christina stood and retrieved a bowl of chopped fruit from the fridge. Trent grabbed larger plates for the main course, Grans poured fresh coffee, and Levi cleaned off the used plates to make room. The five of them moved as if meals together were a normal, everyday occurrence. Like a family.

As they passed the food around the table, Mia watched Christina bubble over. The way she had that summer, when her only worry was buying clothes for the new school year. A weight had been lifted from the girl. If calling Roxanne and ratting out Isaac would do any good, Mia would be on the phone in an instant. Instead, she knew Christina would be seen as the problem, not the golden boy. At least she had this makeshift family for now, until she made her own.

Grans patted her hand as if she knew the path Mia's thoughts were taking. Swallowing her tears, Mia focused on eating. She'd been starving, but with all the excitement, food just hadn't been a priority. Now they needed to refuel before they went to get the damaging evidence against the man known as William.

"After we get back we'll figure out what Adele had and then make a next step," Trent was outlining the morning for the others.

"What about the store?" Levi's words were garbled because his mouth was full of the last cinnamon roll.

"I've already called Sally. She's opening today." Trent smiled. "What about you? EMT duties?"

"I'm off this week." Levi snuck a glance at Christina. "I was planning on teaching someone to snowboard."

"I don't want you two disappearing up on that mountain before the police find Barney and we figure out if Danforth had anything to do with his disappearance. We don't need to be missing anyone else." Grans raised her eyebrows and waited.

"She's right. We need to stick together." Trent focused on his brother. "Agreed?"

Levi shrugged, then glanced at Christina. "Sorry, babe, we've been grounded."

"It's kind of nice to have someone worry about where you are," Christina added quietly.

And with that, everyone focused on their breakfast, with Christina's words floating around the room.

Trent and Mia bundled up in coats, gloves, hats, and scarves. Mia had to scrounge to find an appropriate scarf to wrap around Trent's neck.

He held it up. "Purple is not my color."

"You can wear pink instead," Mia offered. Everyone else was upstairs, focusing on chores. Levi and Christina had kitchen cleanup duty while Grans tried to piece together more of Adele's family tree puzzle.

"Purple will be fine."

They walked outside into a wonderland of snow. No snowplows had started clearing the streets. The sidewalks were still covered in several inches of snow. The town still appeared deserted. Mia glanced up at Trent, who walked next to her. "You think Elizabeth will even make it to the library?"

"She's never missed a day to open, even after the earthquake. She only lives a block away, so unless she's dead, yes, I think the library will be open." Trent reached over and took Mia's gloved hand.

Even through the material, Mia could feel the heat Trent's body put out. Unless it was just her imagination, the man should be melting the snow around them as they walked. This overflowing of emotion was getting way out of hand. She really needed to get a handle on her feelings before she did something really stupid, like kissing him. Again.

As if he'd read her thoughts, his face turned to meet her gaze. Smoldering hot. Oh, man, she needed to focus on something else. Like poor Barney. Poor, missing Barney.

Neither one of them spoke again until they reached the library. The snow had been swept away from the steps. When Trent pulled on the heavy oak door it opened easily. He grinned at her. "Told you."

Mia stomped the snow off her boots just a little too hard. As she walked into the marble foyer, her footing slipped and she started to fall. Strong arms caught her below her arms and pulled her into his body.

"Whoa there. You get all the way here and slip once we're in the building? Priceless." Trent's tone sparkled with humor.

"Bite me," she answered back.

Trent moved his lips closer to her ear and didn't let go, even though she had recovered her footing. "Where?" he whispered.

"Not the time," she responded, pulling away from him.

Trent chuckled and followed her into the library. "That's what you always say."

Elizabeth was at the checkout counter, watching them

enter. When they approached she tapped the flash drive on the counter. "About time you got here. I'm a busy woman. I can't be waiting around on you two all day."

Mia picked up the black drive. "So everything she was printing is on this?"

"You think I'm a liar?" The woman's retort was quick.

Mia choked. "No, I mean I was just wondering if Adele had access to email or another printer while she was here working."

Elizabeth seemed to consider that. "I guess she could have emailed herself a list of the references. She wrote all the days and pages in a notebook. There's no internet access on the microfilm scanners. She would have had to go to another computer. Really, what would be the point? She liked her paper."

Trent plucked the flash drive from Mia's hand. "Thanks a lot, Elizabeth. I'll bring you back a pack of new flash drives from the store later this week. My treat."

"You do so much for the library, Trent. You don't have to replace one flash drive." Elizabeth smiled at him, causing Mia to wonder what Trent did for the library. The man seemed to scatter goodwill throughout the town, like Magic Springs's personal Santa.

He glanced at his shoes. "Majors does a book drive every spring and fall for the library."

"And matches what's donated to allow us to buy new books. The city council has cut our budget for new purchases three years in a row. And don't get me started on ebooks. The council won't even talk to me about the need for a lending program." Elizabeth started stacking books on the counter to check in from a basket behind the desk.

"We'd better get going," Trent had started to squirm. "We'll see you around."

Elizabeth focused on Mia. "Have you got your library card yet? I understand you live in the district now."

"No, sorry, I haven't." At those words, a frown creased Elizabeth's forehead and Mia quickly added, "But I'll come in next week with the girl who's living with me. We'll get cards then."

Elizabeth nodded and Mia added one more thing on her already overcrowded to-do list: library cards.

They walked out the door and Trent laughed. "You looked like you were caught shoplifting back there. It's just a library card."

"I hadn't even thought about getting one," Mia admitted. "I'm so bad at returning books on time, it's cheaper for me to buy them than borrow."

"Humor her. Get a library card. You don't have to use the thing. I think she's out to make sure every town resident over three years old has a card. It's her life's ambition." Trent poked her with his elbow. "You don't want her to go to meet her maker one person short of her goal, now do you?"

"Guilt, the other white meat." Mia held up her hands in mock surrender. "Fine, as soon as I get the business opened, I'll get a library card."

"You're an angel in disguise."

"And you're a royal pain in the butt."

Mia followed Trent as they walked back to the school. She stopped in front of the store. "You need to check in?"

"Sally's fine. Besides, it's my day off.

Mia snorted.

"What?"

"I never knew any small business owner who wasn't on the clock twenty-four seven. Even when I catered at the hotel, Isaac and I were always running somewhere, fixing something." Mia brushed the snow from the fence surrounding the park as they passed by. "You never get time off."

"Then you were doing it wrong. Seriously, you have to have time to recharge or you're no good to anyone." He nodded to the park, covered in a blanket of white from the snow last night. "Nature knows how to take a rest, why don't humans?"

"Nature doesn't get calls from angry customers who wanted gluten-free lasagna and calorie-free desserts." Mia slowed her pace and looked at him. "You seriously take off a day a week?"

He raised his eyebrows and lowered his voice to a whisper. "I take off two."

"Sounds like heaven. Maybe after the business gets up and running, if I'm not in jail for killing Adele, I can learn from your slacker ways."

He pulled her close to his side. "You're not going to jail. At least I don't think you are. But maybe we should see if we're compatible in the sack before you're arrested. That way I won't lose one of my fishing days driving to Boise for a visit."

"Comforting." She pushed him away. "Besides, who said I wanted you to visit me anyway?"

"I can see it in your eyes when you look at my butt."

She slapped his arm with her gloved hand. "You are so bad."

He pulled her into a clench and stopped their forward movement. The cast iron of the park fence dug into her back, centering her as he reached under her chin. "You don't know how bad I can be. Yet."

Then he kissed her. Kisses that stole her breath away, and before she realized what she was doing, she kissed

him back. He pulled away from her and adjusted her hat
on her head, then took her hand and pulled her back onto
the sidewalk. Dazed, she followed him, wondering what
had just happened. She didn't need a new man in her life;
she'd just dumped Isaac. Of course, that didn't seem like
such a big loss now. In fact, she wasn't sure she could
even remember what he looked like.

By the time they got back to the school Trent was
humming and Mia felt torn. She didn't want to blurt out,
I don't want to date you, or anyone. Mostly because she
wasn't sure the words were true. She *shouldn't* want to
date him. She should focus on getting Mia's Morsels up
and going. She should help Christina figure out what she
was going to do about her brother and the Adams family.
She should be thinking about helping Grans deal with the
grief of losing Adele.

Instead, all she wanted to do was kiss Trent again. And
maybe again. Maybe something more personal, more private.

"Ready to find out what Adele was researching?"
Trent held the front door open for her.

Mia nodded, not trusting her voice. She sprinted up the
stairs to the apartment and banged the door open, star-
tling Grans, who was sitting on the couch, knitting.

"Something wrong?" Grans's head cocked and she
studied her.

Mia could feel her grandmother's magic floating over
her body, trying to determine if Mia was all right. Before
she could speak the tingles stopped and Grans smiled.

"Oh." Then she went back to her knitting.

Mia shook her head. She never had been able to hide
anything from the woman, even the night Ken Forrey got
to second base with her in the back seat of his Camaro

after the junior prom. That night Grans hadn't just said, "Oh." Mia'd gotten the birds and the bees speech, and the next morning a box of condoms sat on her beside with a note about a doctor's appointment if she wanted something more reliable.

"There's no *oh*." Mia sighed and headed to the kitchen. She felt rather than saw Trent following her. Like they were attached by a golden cord, invisible yet still strong. She wondered if that was what Grans saw.

CHAPTER 20

Mia set a fresh cup of coffee in front of Trent. "I can take over scanning if you're getting tired."

He put his arms in the air and, clasping his hands, he stretched. Then he accepted the cup and took a long sip. "This helps, thanks."

"Seriously, macho man, you don't have to solve the case all on your own." Mia slipped into the chair next to him, glancing at the screen. "You've gone through ten years already?"

"Yep. I'm kind of liking this detective role." He put a finger to his head, "Genius level IQ."

"Could have fooled me," Mia deadpanned.

"Jealousy doesn't become you." Trent leaned forward and pointed at the screen. "And bingo."

Mia stared at the screen. A death announcement for William Danforth III had been posted in the Boise paper.

She scanned the notice. He'd been living in Phoenix when he drowned in a backyard pool. Private services were held at the gravesite and donations were to be sent to the Friends of Steve community organization. "Friends of Steve?"

Trent shook his head. "No clue."

"Keep scanning; she must have found more." Mia watched as images of the Phoenix paper surfaced, and there was the full obituary. William Danforth had died at home. He was preceded in death by his parents and grandparents. Reading to the end, she frowned. "No wife, no kids."

"Just the Friends of Steve notation here again." Trent leaned back in his chair. "Sad."

"Sad? What the heck are you saying? We've found Adele's murderer. William Danforth can't be the guy staying at the Lodge because he died years ago. That guy must have killed her when she told him she knew he was a fraud."

"I think it's sad that the guy died alone with no family or friends. That's all." Trent pulled out his cell phone and stood. "I'm calling Levi, I want him to know, just in case."

Mia nodded and scrolled through the remaining pages. What she found on the last page made her gasp. Travis and Helen Marcum smiled out from the *Phoenix Gazette* with a twenty-million-dollar, oversize check in their hands. She scrolled the page. Helen, a lunch lady, and Travis, a retired construction worker, had bought the lottery ticket from their local Gas and Go. The paper quoted Helen saying, "I never liked Travis wasting our hard earned money on Lotto, but I guess he had the last laugh."

The Chicago couple wasn't who they said they were.

Mia studied the article, wondering why the two had come to Magic Springs incognito. Lottery winners weren't usual in their small town, but not impossible. New money spent just the same as old.

"Time to go. Levi's got some news and he wants us at the police station." Trent stood at the kitchen door. He nodded to the computer. "You find something else?"

"Nothing important." Mia shut the laptop and pulled out the flash drive, slipping it into her pocket. "Just some gossip about a local couple."

"A lot of our locals thrive on the gossip columns. It's a rite of passage around here. You're not someone until your worst actions are published in the society pages. Let's go take a walk." He opened the apartment door for her.

Leaving Grans and Christina upstairs, Trent and Mia headed downstairs to bundle up for the walk. The streets still weren't plowed. The county trucks were still cleaning off the major highways and, of course, Sun Valley. Magic Springs wasn't high on the plowing list. They slipped on snowshoes and headed off to meet Levi.

He stood outside the front door when they'd reached the building. Mia saw him crush out a cigarette in the snow. He held the door open for them as they slipped off their snowshoes. "You're not going to believe this."

As the door closed, Mia walked into a crowded lobby filled with townspeople. In the corner at a desk sat Barney. She crossed the room and enveloped the portly lawyer into a quick hug. "We were worried about you."

"I got myself stuck out there on those roads. Nearly froze to death, except I found a cabin." Barney shook his head. "I'm not going to incriminate myself, so let's just say the door was open when I got there." He held up his hand to stop Baldwin from speaking. "I'll reimburse the owner for any damage that happened prior to me arriving on the scene and, as luck may have it, probably saving my life." He winked at Mia.

"William said you were staying in town."

Barney sighed. "Would have been the best decision. I got a call from Sheila saying she'd found something on the estate. I ignored my inner warnings and drove back up the mountain, right into that snowstorm. Idiot."

Levi jumped into the conversation. "Want to guess what Sheila found?"

Mia held up the flash drive, "William's death certificate?"

The lawyer gasped. "How did you know? Sheila said that Adele had emailed her a copy that had gotten stuck in her spam box."

"We found Adele's research material." She handed over the flash drive to Baldwin. "That should help you find out who has been impersonating the late Mr. Danforth. I'd lay bets on his oldest friend, Samuel Jacobs."

Mia pulled out the two pictures they'd found in Adele's study. She just hoped he wouldn't ask how she came to have the pictures. She didn't want to have to explain her visit to Adele's with Grans. Although they had used a key, she figured entering the house of a murder victim was probably in bad taste, especially for one of the suspects.

"That's the name Adele sent to Sheila. She wanted her to research this guy because he was attending her party. I guess she planned on kicking him out during the festivities." Barney looked around the station. "Any chance I could get a ride home? I'm tired and cranky and I want a long bath."

"I'll take you in the cat." Levi looked at Baldwin. "Can we go now? Or do you want us to work on more of your unsolved cases?"

"Smart-ass," Baldwin mumbled. "Get out of here. Just . . ."

"Don't leave town?" He shook his head. "Seriously, dude, you have to come up with better material."

"Levi, let's go." Trent's voice held a warning. Even Mia could tell that Levi was on thin ice here.

"I'll warm up the cat." Levi tipped a mini salute to Baldwin and then walked out the door, Barney waddling behind him.

Baldwin glanced up at Trent. "That boy's trouble."

"No. He's rude to authority figures and mouthy, but he's not trouble."

Baldwin shook his head, "Let's just agree to disagree on your brother. Keep people close. If you're right, this Jacobs guy might be mad enough to do some more selective weeding in our little town." Baldwin tapped the pictures. "Thanks for this. Sheila's email was damning, but this is solid."

"Adele deserves to have her murderer caught." Mia leaned against Trent, her energy draining from her body. All of a sudden she was dead tired.

Baldwin stood. "I'll head over to the Lodge now and pick up our friend for questioning."

Trent put his hand on Mia's back, gently aiming her to the door. He called to Baldwin, "I'll check in later."

The sun shone bright on the snow when they left the courthouse. Climbing into the cat, she sat on the back seat next to Trent, her head on his shoulder.

"Tired?" His voice deep like dark chocolate.

Mia nodded. "Glad it's over."

An hour later Trent came back into the apartment, putting his phone away. "They have Samuel in custody. I guess when they went to his room he didn't even put up a fuss."

"He admitted to killing Adele?" Grans sounded tired. Mia reached over and patted her shoulder.

Trent sat on the couch next to Mia. "Actually, no. He admitted to running a scam, wanting to rip the 'old lady' off, as he called her. He said he was still playing the part when he found out she was dead."

Mia sat up. "Baldwin believes him?"

Trent shook his head. "No. He's got to find the holes in the guy's story first before he can charge him, but he's holding him until it checks out or not." He leaned forward, running his hands through his hair, "The guy's guilty; now all Baldwin has to do is prove it."

"But the pictures," Grans protested.

"Circumstantial, according to Baldwin." He stood. "Let me run you home and pick up some clothes and stuff. I think we need to continue the sleepover for a few days."

"I don't think that's necessary. I can go home."

Mia pulled Grans to her feet. "You can. But you're not going to. Let Trent take you and we'll do Mexican night when you get back. Tacos, burritos, Spanish rice, maybe even a few margaritas."

"Did I hear margaritas?" Levi and Christina walked into the apartment from taking Muffy out for walk. "Count me in."

Christina elbowed him. "Of course you're in. You don't even know if we are invited."

Mia smiled, watching the two. Christina had been sneaking out to see Levi. Not one of the rich kids whose main goal during their visit was to get in trouble. Of course, who knew what trouble Levi would bring? But the two looked happy, and for now that was all that mattered. Something about the night of Carrie's party niggled at her brain.

Trent nudged her. "Earth to Mia. Where are you?"

"Something doesn't make sense. If William, or Samuel, didn't kill Adele, who did?" She pushed on. "And who called and threatened me?"

"John, if I had my guess," Levi muttered. "The guy's a creep."

"But who had my knife?" Mia crossed her fingers, drawing her hands together and leaned into them. "All this doesn't make sense. I mean, I guess it could have been John. He admitted to having something to do with Adele's death."

"John was just trying to scare you into leaving. He underestimated how strong you really are." Trent held out his hand, as if to stop her musing. "Slow down. The only one saying William or Samuel didn't do the deed is him. I wouldn't trust the guy to babysit my pet goldfish."

"Wait, what? You have a pet goldfish?" Christina leaned against Levi, watching them. "I would have thought a German shepherd or a Saint Bernard. You definitely don't look like a pet fish type."

"Figure of speech." Trent sat back on the couch. "Okay, tell me what else is bothering you."

Mia held up her hand and pointed to her finger. "One, someone attacked me after Adele was murdered. Who?"

Trent shrugged. "My money's on Isaac."

Christina walked over and sat on the side of the couch. "Can't be Isaac. He was with me that night, trying to figure out where Mia had hidden her cookbook. We didn't leave the restaurant until nine, and she was already down when we pulled up in the driveway."

"See?" Mia pointed to her next finger. "Two, who locked me in Carrie's basement?"

"I thought you said the door slammed shut?" Christina looked worried now.

Mia ducked her head. "I didn't want you to worry."

"We need to start talking to one another." Grans shook her finger at Mia. "You've been keeping secrets."

"I don't know who to trust," Mia admitted. Seeing the shocked looks on everyone's faces, she amended her statement. "Outside of the four of you, that is."

"Almost a good catch," Trent said dryly. "Anyway, what else has happened?"

Mia went on to tell the assembled group about her missing, then returned knife, and the missing corkscrew. By the time she'd finished they were all gathered around her, lending moral support. Instead of feeling alone, she thought maybe, just maybe, everything would be all right.

Mia finished with the last question that had been bothering her. "Who are the Friends of Steve that William's obituary mentioned?"

Levi held up his hand. "I can answer that. It's a memorial fund that sponsors outreach for LGBT teens in the Phoenix area. It's been on the news lately because it's cut the rate of attempted suicide in the area down ten percent since its inception."

Everyone stared at Levi.

He shrugged. "What? There's a lot of downtime when you're an EMT. I hang out on the news web pages on my tablet most nights. There's talk about opening branches of the Friends of Steve in LA next year."

"You're always a surprise, little brother." Trent slapped Levi on the back and smiled at Mia. "One mystery solved. Now we just have a few more to work through."

"I'd just feel better if we knew more about a few things." Mia picked at a piece of lint on the couch.

"Well, listening to the rest of the story, now I know we should continue our little slumber party tonight. I'll drop Mary Alice off at her place, run and check on the store, then pick you back up on my way back here." Trent nodded to Grans. "Will you be okay for about an hour?"

"Dear, I've lived through worse storms than this one. I'm sure I can be by myself for an hour." The look on Grans's face had Mia biting her lip to keep from laughing.

"I'll get you a list of supplies I'll need for Mexican night." Mia stood.

Levi pulled Christina up as well. "I'm heading out to the ranch to check on Mom and Dad. As long as the roads are plowed out of town, we should be able to be back before sundown."

Christina looked at Mia. "Maybe I should stay here with you?"

Mia raised her eyebrows. "I'm pretty sure I can handle myself for a few hours today. Besides, it will give me time to check on the renovations, including when that inspector's going to be back in town. I've got plenty to do around here."

Trent pulled her close. She could feel the scruff on his cheek where his beard was growing; he hadn't shaved for a couple of days. The sensation made her shiver. He whispered, "Try to stay out of trouble, and if anything—" He paused and put his hands on her arms for emphasis. "*Anything* happens, you call me. I don't care if you lose

Mr. Darcy for a few minutes. Anything that's unexpected, I want to know."

Mia smiled. "I promise I will pretend I'm a princess enclosed in a tower, safe in my own little world."

"Not quite the analogy I was looking for, but it will do." He tapped her nose. "And once we get out of this, we need to talk."

Mia's stomach clenched. "Sounds like a date," she chirped, immediately regretting her choice of words.

Trent smiled and turned to Grans. "You ready?"

Thirty minutes later Mia was alone in the apartment. She'd walked through the school, writing down items on the clipboard that needed to be finished before she could open. She loved the way the bright sun beamed on the yellow walls where she'd finished painting. The remaining gray walls depressed her. "Finish painting" was the first thing she'd written on her list.

Something she could control. Not like the rest of her life. She stood and stretched, glancing at the clock as she pulled a soda out of the fridge. The gang would be back no later than five, ready for dinner, but until Trent came back with the groceries, she couldn't really start her prep. She glanced at her list. She had at least an hour before Trent came back, more than enough time if she hurried, to get the entryway painted, allowing her to check one item off her list.

She ran to her room, changed into her old jeans and painting T-shirt, and headed to the kitchen to grab her cell. When she picked it up the phone rang, and she fumbled to pick it up. Not taking the time to check the caller ID, she answered, "Hello?"

"Mia? Oh, God, come quick, your grandmother has fallen." The woman sounded out of breath.

"Grans? Where is she? The hospital?" Mia's heart beat faster, waiting for the answer.

"No. I've called the ambulance, but they're out on another run. You need to take her." The woman was insistent.

"I'll be right there. She's at her house, right?" Mia pulled on her coat as she left the kitchen. She glanced at the notepad, and scribbled, *Gone to help Grans*. As she shut the door to the apartment, the woman finally answered her question.

"No, she's at Adele's. She fell down the stairs."

CHAPTER 21

Mia stopped two feet from the front door. "Wait, why was she at Adele's? Who is this?" No answer; the phone call had been cut off. Mia dialed Grans's landline. Not surprisingly, Grans had left her cell on Mia's coffee table. A fast busy signal indicated that the phone lines were down, probably due to the storm. *Why would Grans be at Adele's?* Mia's thoughts went back to the discussion about Samuel. Grans had been sure that the photos should prove that the man killed Adele for the inheritance. Would she have walked over after Trent dropped her off just to make sure the dead woman hadn't left a diary or some other clue?

But then who had called Mia? This whole thing stunk. But then Mia saw a vision of her grandmother crumpled at the bottom of the stairs. It couldn't hurt just to make sure she was okay. She dialed Trent's cell. No answer.

She left a voice mail, explaining she'd gone to Adele's to check on Grans and asking him to call her as soon as possible. His words about staying put echoed in her head.

She shouldn't have let Trent drive Grans home. The woman was sneaky; Trent didn't know that. But she should have seen the look before they left. She would have stayed with Grans while she grabbed fresh clothes. She would have . . . but she hadn't. Now Grans needed her. She grabbed the spare keys to Grans's car, started the engine, turning the defroster on full blast, and scraped the windows as clear as she could. Hopefully the roads would be plowed and her windows would finish defrosting long before she arrived at Adele's, making the trip to the emergency room a bit safer for Grans.

Ten minutes later, after almost flying into a ditch not once, but twice, Mia pulled into a driveway filled with snow. No tire tracks, no other car. How had her grandmother even gotten over here? Who had called Mia? She pushed away the thought and ran up to the porch. The front door stood open. Fear gripped her, but she pushed through, her fingers brushing her cell in her pocket.

As she walked into the large foyer, she called out, "Grans? Are you here?" She listened to her voice echo in the hall, then heard the door slam and a lock click behind her.

A small woman stood by the door with a very large gun in her hand. Mia didn't know anything about guns, small or large, but she did know this one looked very, very real. "I take it Grans isn't here."

"Sorry, a bit of a lie. I'm so glad you could make it. If we hurry, we should be able to get this done and you won't be missed for days, living up in that old school by yourself." The woman actually smiled, and finally Mia recognized her. Helen Marcum.

"Now we're being polite? Like a real law professor from Chicago?" Mia tapped the screen on her cell, hoping she'd just dialed someone, anyone.

Helen stepped closer. "I figured once you found the old bat's notes about Sam, you'd figure me out pretty quickly. It's funny. You think if you only had money, everything would be fine. They'd treat you right. Be nice, but no. All those people in Arizona, all they remembered was my husband being a drunk and me feeding their brats at school." She shook her head violently. "Never once did they invite us to their crappy parties, even after we bought our way into that stupid country club."

"So you decided to move and take on a new life. Didn't you think someone might check up on you?" Mia glanced around the room, looking for something, anything, to use as a weapon or to duck under once Helen stopped being so chatty.

"Ha. Don't make me laugh. People don't bother the rich. All they do is talk about how they don't have any style or hate their choice of paint colors. Seriously, even when they didn't know I'd been poor, they still treated me like white trash. Nuevo rich, as Miss Adele called me. Oh, not to my face. Even she didn't have that kind of guts."

"Wait, let me get this straight. You're pointing a gun at me because people talk about you behind your back?" Mia spoke louder. "I don't think I ever heard anything about you, Helen, or your husband, Travis."

"Don't try all that hostage negotiation crap with me. Using my name isn't going to change the fact that you'll be dead in"—Helen glanced at her wristwatch—"maybe ten minutes? I want you to understand why I'm shooting you. It's the Christian thing to do."

"How in the hell is any of this Christian?" Mia felt the heat flow to her cheeks. The woman was even crazier than she'd thought. As soon as she saw Helen blanch, Mia wondered if she'd pushed too hard.

The gun waved toward her. "Now don't you be cussing in front of me. I'm not that kind of lady."

She'll shoot me, but she doesn't want to hear the word "hell?" What the heck? Mia prayed to the Goddess. Maybe this was all a dream and she'd wake up soon. Mia realized Helen was watching, waiting for a response. An apology? She'd be damned if . . . Mia swallowed her pride for a few more moments to figure out a plan, "I'm sorry. I'm a little stressed. I've never been threatened with a gun before. I'll listen to what you have to say." She hesitated, then added, "It's only right."

"Exactly. That's what I tried to tell Adele. When I told her I would kill her before I'd let her tell everyone I had been poor, she laughed. In my face." Helen's cheeks turned red at the memory. "She laughed at me. She said she was using the party to clear up a few misconceptions, one of them being me and my husband's rightful place in the community. That we were no better than the people who worked at the Lodge or the grocery."

"How did you kill her?" Mia felt drained, her energy being sapped by the heightened awareness she was putting out, trying to draw someone, anyone in. Okay, maybe not just anyone, but someone to take care of this crazy woman. All she had to do was keep her talking for a few more minutes. Then someone should arrive. She hoped.

"I had a carving knife I'd stolen from a buffet in Arizona. The chef there, well, I don't know if you could call someone who worked there a chef, but he's the one who told me about Magic Springs. That he was planning on moving here as soon as his probation was up."

"Probation?" Mia inched closer to the entry table. The antique wood may not stop a bullet, but maybe it would slow it, or deflect it away from her. She had to be talking about James. Why had James been on probation?

"See, even you are more intrigued by the bad parts of life than the good things we do. Yes, this guy was on probation, but he said the charges had been a big misunderstanding. He's too sweet a guy to be a thief. He said it was because he was gay. Gay people always get treated badly." Helen sagged a bit, the gun drooping in her hand. "I don't want to talk about that. It's confusing. When I saw him here I thought for sure he'd rat me out. But he never did. He may figure we held each other's secrets. But I wonder if he even recognized me. I'm a lot skinnier now. Hired my own trainer, just like the movie stars. I still work out three times a week."

We're talking about workouts? Mia jumped on the topic. "You can really tell. I mean, I didn't know you before, but you look so healthy."

Helen smiled, a cold smile that never reached her eyes. "Don't patronize me. I know you saw that interview we did with the newspaper reporter, just like Adele." She stopped and cocked her head toward Mia. "Now, did that person look 'healthy?'"

Mia decided to play dumb. "I don't understand why you keep saying I saw an article. I didn't see anything."

"The librarian said she gave you the flash drive. The woman's very disappointed that you didn't seem interested in setting up a library card." Helen shook her head.

"You aren't fitting in very well here; maybe they'll just think you moved home to live with that hunk of an ex-boyfriend." Helen smiled again, looking more like an alligator this time. "I could get lucky and some animal could drag off your carcass before you're found. That way we wouldn't have two murders in Magic Springs in less than a month."

"How about you just don't kill me—that would cut down the actual crime rate."

"Now, you know I can't do that." Helen nodded to the back of the house. "Where's the back door?"

"There isn't one. You're going to have to take me out the front." Something was going in her favor.

"What do you mean there isn't a back door? All houses have a back door." Helen frowned.

"You don't remember seeing one when you and Samuel toured the house, do you?" Mia pressed.

Helen cocked her head, "How did you know Samuel gave us a sneak peek?" She paused. "Never mind. I have to get back to the Lodge. We're playing bridge at four." She waved the gun toward Mia. "Go out the front door. I don't care; you'll still be just as dead as soon as we get to the trees in back."

Mia considered her options as she walked past Helen, but the woman kept the gun focused on her and Mia didn't think she'd be able to wrestle the firearm away without getting shot in the process.

As soon as she crossed the threshold, she was yanked to the left, a hand over her mouth. Helen had been pulled to the right, and then her gun was taken away. Mia watched as Baldwin cuffed the woman.

"You okay?" Trent's voice whispered in her ear and he removed his hand from her mouth.

"Luckily Helen didn't want blood all over the house just in case she still got to buy it." Mia squatted down, taking deep breaths, trying to keep from doing something stupid like passing out. She glanced up at Trent. "You're the one I called?"

"Actually, you dialed City Hall. The receptionist got your call to Baldwin and he called me to see where you would have gone. When you said it was Helen your grandmother knew exactly where the two of you were." Trent knelt close to her. "You want some water?"

Mia stood and shook off the dizziness. "I want to go home."

Baldwin nodded. "I'll stop by later to get your statement; there's no need for you to come to the station now."

Mia watched him walk Helen to the police cruiser that sat near the curb. "My, how things have changed."

"Stop giving him a hard time. He's just doing his job." Trent held her close. "I was worried."

"So was I."

"I told you to stay home. Locked in the apartment." Trent smoothed her hair with his hand. "Don't you ever listen?"

"She said Grans had fallen, I couldn't reach either of you. I thought she needed me."

Trent released her from his arms and the two walked to her grandmother's car. "Understandable, but not forgiven."

She handed him the keys. "You making the margaritas tonight?"

"I can; why?"

Mia slumped into the passenger seat of the car. "Make mine extra-strong."

CHAPTER 22

Forgiveness. Trent forgave her for not following orders after three margaritas that night, and the five of them played Scrabble until the fire died down. Then Mia slipped into her bedroom and slid between the covers, then fell asleep.

Now, it was two weeks later and both Samuel Jacobs and Helen Marcum were in jail, awaiting trial. And Mia couldn't sleep again. She had a few more things to deal with before her essence would be clear. Her daily chants and prayers had felt dull, as if her connection to the Goddess was blocked. Then Gloria told her why.

She read the handwritten list one more time. Taking a pen out of her jacket pocket, she added one more item. She sat cross-legged in front of the fire, calming herself. Gloria, the rag doll, sat on her lap, helping her to focus.

Mr. Darcy even sat next to her, reaching out one paw to rest it on her leg. She had a feeling from the way the cat was watching her that Dorian was the one doing the comforting.

She read the list again, wondering why she was stalling. Every slight, every hurt, every pain her heart had felt while she was with Isaac and after they broke up was on the paper. She needed to forgive him for these things so she could give up the hurt.

A noise behind her caused her to turn. Christina stood behind the couch watching her. She walked over to the hearth and dropped to the floor beside Mia. "What are you doing? You've got a big day tomorrow; you should be sleeping."

Mia smiled at the mothering tone from someone twelve years her junior. "You know me. I can't sleep before an event. Besides, it's time to do something."

Christina's gaze fell on the paper on the floor in front of her. "What's this?" She picked it up and silently read the list. When she finished she set it back down. "I told you that you were too good for my brother. This list more than proves it."

"Thanks, but that's not why I wrote the list." Mia started tearing the paper into strips. "I'm forgiving him."

Christina stopped her from tearing the paper with both hands. "Wait, you can't go back to him. He's not worth it. You won't be happy. No matter what he says, he's not sorry."

Mia pulled Christina into a hug. "I'm not going back. I'm releasing myself from the responsibility of hating him." She looked into the girl's eyes. "Don't you understand? Forgiveness isn't for the person doing the wronging. It's for the people he or she wrongs. I can't move on with my life until I release the past. And forgiving Isaac is part of that release."

Christina wiped her hand over her brow in an exaggerated gesture. "Whew. I thought you'd lost your mind there for a minute." She watched for a while as Mia finished tearing the sheet and had a small pile of strips sitting in front of them. "Mia?"

Mia turned to her, "Yes?" She sensed Christina's hesitation but thought she knew what she would ask her.

She picked up a piece of paper. "Can I add some things to the pile before we burn them?"

"Are you ready to forgive him?" Mia put her hand on Christina's shoulder. "It's okay to be mad as hell. He used you. Used your fear."

Christina flipped back her hair, and Mia noticed the bar in her eyebrow had been taken out. No more piercings. She'd grown up so quickly in the last month, Mia didn't want her to force the reconciliation of the Adams family. "I know. But you're forgiving him. And honestly, I don't want to hurt anymore. I'm ready to let go and just live."

Mia handed her the pen. "As long as you really mean it, get writing."

She watched the fire as Christina wrote out two pages of items, then, mimicking Mia's actions, she reread the papers and added some more lines. Satisfied, she started ripping.

The floor was covered in transgressions when she stopped.

"Take a deep breath; then, in your mind, start chanting, 'I forgive you, Isaac Adams.' Don't list out the whats or the whys. Just let it be as it is. 'I forgive you.' When we're ready we'll start throwing handfuls of strips onto the fire. When we're done we jump over the broom backward three times and sing 'Kumbaya.'"

Christina's eyes widened. "Really?"

"No," Mia said, chuckling. "I just wanted to see how far I could make you go. Throwing the paper into the fire ends it."

"You're mean." Christina sat quietly for a moment, watching the fire. "Levi told me about the coven. He wants me to visit."

"How do you feel about going?" Mia watched Christina's face, wondering what Mama Adams would think about her daughter dating a witch. Of course, her son had lived with one for years and the woman had been clueless. But she'd hidden her power from Isaac, not trusting him with that part of her. Logically, a good idea, especially now that they'd broken up, but a part of Mia had wondered if her holding back her secrets had caused Isaac to have his own.

Christina played with the ripped-up paper. "I don't know. I mean, I like him, really, really like him. But dating a witch? Wow, that seems like I've stepped into a paperback novel. Or one of those movies with all the sparkly vampires. Maybe he's cast a spell on me and that's why I like him." Christina stared at her. "You think he's handsome, right? It's not some glamour or something?"

"The guy could stop traffic." Mia smiled and tossed another handful of strips onto the fire. She pushed another wave of forgiveness toward Isaac and his troubled life before she continued. "No one can keep up a glamour that long. It's impossible."

"What if I'm always questioning, wondering if my feelings are true?" Christina stared at the fire where her Isaac faults were flaming.

Mia thought for a long time before she answered. "Magic happens. Especially around people in love. Who are we to say what's real and what's conjured? Human or witch, you'll always wonder about what brought you two together. It's just the nature of a true relationship."

The two women sat and watched the last of the strips curl in the fire before bursting into flame. Then Christina put her hands behind her and leaned back. "And that's it?"

Mia nodded. Inside she felt the grip of Isaac's actions release her heart. She'd forgiven him for the things he'd done to her, to Christina. Forgive, but not forget. He'd never be allowed close enough to hurt her again. Christina would have to set her own boundaries with her brother. Mia sent a silent prayer to the Goddess that she would find her way sooner rather than later.

She stood and brushed the dust from her pajama bottoms. She pulled Christina up to meet her. "You'll find your way with Levi. Take it slow. Visit the coven before you make any decisions. Just be warned: I think you'll have some women there not too happy to see he's chosen you."

Mia could see Christina blushing, even in the dim light. "He does like me."

As they walked back to the bedrooms, Mia checked the lock on the apartment door one more time. "That I know without using a drop of magic."

The smell of freshly baked bread and cinnamon-spiced apple cider floated through the crowded lobby. Mia couldn't believe how many people had come out for her open house. Free food and curiosity brought out the townspeople, now that the snow was beginning to recede up the Magics. Hyacinths pushed their way up through the flower beds closest to the building. Tulips would be arriving next. Trent had brought boxes of tulips up from Boise as part of her supply order, even though she hadn't asked. The man sometimes acted like he could read her mind. Though, if that was true, the two of them wouldn't be standing in this crowd of people right now.

She waved at Trent across the room. He and Grans were manning the menu table, handing out order sheets. Grans caught her eye and made a two thumbs-up gesture. Orders must be going well. Mia mingled through the crowd, nodding and smiling like she was actually listening to the well wishes and congratulations flowing around her. Christina put her arm through Mia's.

"It's amazing. I can't believe it's all real now. Grans said everyone loves the names." Christina beamed. "Al Capone's Last Meal is selling like hotcakes. We're going to be plenty busy for the next few months."

Mia studied the young woman standing next to her. Her blond hair was braided, and wearing the dress she'd chosen for the event, Christina looked more like Heidi in the Alps than the Goth princess who'd arrived in town less than three months before. Mia liked this version better than the dark one, but she was convinced even this persona was just that, a show. Someday Christina would find her essence. Today just wasn't that day.

"So you're staying around?" Mia nudged her.

"Yeah. I can take classes in Twin Falls and make Mom happy and still work full-time for you." Christina blushed. "That is, if you want me to."

"I told you, you're welcome as long as you want. I'm enjoying having someone around to talk to." Mia watched the mayor chatting with Grans. She sure loved the spotlight.

"You mean besides the ghosts?"

Mia shook her head. "One ghost, one time. Okay, maybe two times. However, Dorothy is as much a part of Magic Springs's history as the library or City Hall. I don't think she truly counts as a spirit."

"Whatever you have to tell yourself." Christina leaned closer. "Don't look now, but Baldwin's on his way over here. And he looks mad."

"Now what?" Mia groaned as she saw the cop face on the man. Maybe there were too many vehicles parked on the road for the open house. She had a permit from the city council somewhere. Mia racked her brain, trying to remember what she'd done with the event permit she'd gotten in the mail last week. It had to be on her desk upstairs. Or in her purse. Too late to dodge the man, she'd just have to bluff it if he asked to see the paper. She put on what she hoped was a welcoming smile and steeled herself for the interaction.

"Miss Malone, may I have a word with you?" Mark Baldwin raised his voice loud enough to be heard over the crowd noise. Mia assumed it was so the others could hear him. He focused his beady glare on Christina. "I would have thought you would have left town by now. Don't tell me you're planning on extending your visit."

"I've got to go check on something in the kitchen," Christina squeaked and sprinted away from Mia.

"Why do you torture her?" Mia sighed, watching her weave through the guests and disappear through the double doors leading to the kitchen, where she had staff from the hotel James had recommended working on appetizers and sample plates.

Baldwin grabbed a canapé from a passing tray. Popping the miniature shrimp wonton into his mouth, he wiped his hands on his pants. "She's fun. No one else sees me as a real cop around here. I'm just Mark Baldwin who got okay grades during high school and couldn't pass the state police exam after college. She fears me. It's good to be feared."

"She's young. And worse, she had a bad experience in Vegas not too long ago, so stop messing with her." Mia pointed a finger at the man whose chubby figure was straining the buttons on his uniform. "Now, what do you want?"

He shrugged. "I just came to visit. The wife says we're going to order from you as soon as you open, so I thought I'd better see what the big deal is before I pay an arm and a leg just for dinner." He grabbed a bacon-wrapped jalapeño pepper from a waiter's tray. "Although these puppies are good. I can't believe they have peanut butter in the center."

"I'm glad you like them." Mia glanced around the room, looking for the woman who must be Mrs. Baldwin. "Is your wife here? I'd like to meet her."

"We couldn't get a sitter, so she's stuck at home with the kids." Baldwin watched a tray of miniature quiche turn away from him. He headed toward the escaping waiter, "I've got to grab some menus."

Mia felt the warmth from Trent's hand on her back before he spoke. "Looks like the way to a man's heart is his stomach."

Mia bit her lip to keep from laughing. "The guy is totally in love, with my food. I hope he leaves enough for the rest of the customers."

"At least he's not trying to put you in jail. Did he tell you Helen's attorney is claiming self-defense? The story now is Adele attacked her and all she was doing was trying to stay alive." Trent put the back of his hand up to his forehead. "Oh, the injustice."

"So what's her excuse for trying to kill me? I didn't even get closer than ten feet to the woman during the whole escapade." Mia watched as people laughed and talked. In a way, the group mirrored the people who had attended Adele's wake, but this occasion was lighter, and there was an ease in the tone of the conversations that hadn't been there that night.

"You misunderstood her intention. She was holding the gun to protect the two of you, not kill you."

"From wandering wolves in the middle of Adele's living room?"

Trent chuckled. "Something like that. You can't blame her for trying."

Mia waved at Carrie Jones, who had just arrived. "I don't blame her for defending herself; I blame her for trying to kill me. Her husband must have been in on the whole thing; he was the one who called and threatened me."

"He's denying it, and Baldwin says the phone records are sketchy. I guess I'm just going to have to hang around and make sure you're safe."

Mia saw a shadow cross the floor. "Hold that thought. I'll be right back."

She followed the shadow into the little alcove where she'd be selling her own brand of Mia's Morsels condiments and seasonings soon. The place was coming to-gether.

Dorothy Purcell sat or hovered over the empty cabinet where the school secretary used to sort mail not so long ago, when the building was a bustling school. "The place looks good."

Mia smiled. "I'm glad you approve. You just visit-ing?" A part of her worried that Dorothy had brought an-other message from beyond. Things were settling down; Mia felt like a member of the community.

The woman's smile was sad. Even though she was transparent, Mia could see the pain on the ghost's face. "Sorry to ruin your special day. But the spirits aren't set-tled yet. There's a storm coming. A storm you need to stop before it swamps everything good out of Magic Springs."

"I don't understand." Mia's hand reached out to touch the counter to settle herself.

"The balance of power here has been noticed. You, your grandmother, Levi's coven—you're all focused on the good. But a town has to be balanced. If not, the posi-tive atmosphere is noticed and even the humans can see the magic." Dorothy paused. "Your guardian says the dark side is going to target Magic Springs. And you have to be ready."

"You never told me the rest of the story about my guardian. Who or what is she? The Goddess?" Mia felt like her head was going to explode. All she wanted was a calm, happy business here in Magic Springs. Not a war with the dark side.

Dorothy started fading. "We don't have time. Just be careful."

And then Mia was alone in the oversize closet. Not a

trace of Dorothy remained. Mia needed to find time to talk to her grandmother. Grans had held something back when she'd mentioned Dorothy before. Now it was time to find out what.

She walked back into the happy party crowd. Well, tomorrow. Tomorrow would be soon enough.

She returned to where she'd left Trent.

"You okay?" he whispered.

Mia nodded. "Lots to talk about, but not today. Today we celebrate."

He pulled her into a hug and planted a kiss on the top of her head. Mia heard the Goddess's laughter.

"I think we can arrange that." She looked up into his eyes and he leaned in for a real kiss, pulling away as he heard the click of stilettos approaching.

"Don't let me interrupt." Carrie giggled. "I just wanted to give you this package. Someone must have gifted and run; it was sitting outside on your front porch." Carrie handed Mia a silver gift bag. "My, you have been busy in here. We did a senior sneak here a few years ago and the place was a mess. Trent, you were in my class; tell her."

"The place was a mess," Trent deadpanned.

Carrie slapped him on the arm. "Anyway, I'm very glad you've decided to make Magic Springs your new home. I may not have to cook ever again." Carrie waved at someone across the room. "There's Amy. I simply must see who she's wearing."

Mia watched Carrie head for a younger woman across the room. "Amy?"

Trent nodded as they watched Amy and Carrie greet each other with air kisses and twirls to check out the fashion. "The mayor's wife. I'm pretty sure your little open house is going to hit the society page on Sunday."

"As long as it brings in orders, I don't care." Mia opened the gift bag and pulled out a corkscrew with a red bow around it. The corkscrew she'd lost when she catered for the Joneses. She glanced around the room, looking to see if anyone was watching her open the gift bag. Wouldn't the giver want to see her reaction? Had Carrie pretended to "find" the bag?

"What's wrong?" Trent was the only person paying any attention to her.

"This is my corkscrew. The one I lost at Carrie's." Mia held up the utensil for Trent to see it. "And it's wrapped, just like my knife was when it came back."

"Someone messing with you?" Trent pressed his hand possessively on the small of her back.

"Creeping me out." Mia saw her grandmother walking toward them. She shoved the corkscrew back into the bag, then tucked it on a side table, out of sight.

"Quite the coming-out party." Grans beamed. "I'm so glad you've decided to make Magic Springs home. I won't be quite as lonely now that Adele's gone."

Mia pulled her grandmother into a long hug. No one, nothing was going to ruin today. Not some weird stalker's gifts, not Baldwin, nothing. Today was to celebrate the opening of Mia's Morsels. Nothing more or less.

There'd be plenty of time to worry tomorrow. Mia released her grandmother and smiled. "Why don't we go mingle and you can introduce me to your friends?"

"Sounds divine. Trent?"

He shook his head. "You two go ahead. I've got some things to take care of."

He stood, on guard, as Mia walked around the room. The man didn't even blink as far as Mia knew.

James tapped her on the shoulder. He looked like someone had kicked his last puppy. "Can we talk?"

Mia nodded and walked over to the kitchen. They'd made the area off limits to the party crowd for safety reasons. A group of cooks hired from James's staff at the Lodge for the day nodded as we entered. "What's up?"

James glanced around and lowered his voice. "I guess Helen told you about my past?"

She put her hand on his arm. "Not really, but I guessed you were who she was talking about. There's a small pool of talented chefs in the local area."

"I didn't steal anything. I was set up by my lover's new boyfriend. The guy hated seeing my face and made sure I took the blame. He even was the one who suggested the lady hire me for her private party. When her jewels wound up in my knife case a few days later, I was toast." James wrinkled his nose remembering the incident.

"Because chefs always keep their knives close." Mia could see how easy it would be for someone to frame James. "I'm not going to tell anyone. But Helen might throw you under the bus if she thinks it will help her case."

"I've done my time. Even if I didn't do it, I was found guilty. Anything she says won't affect me here. The guys who hired me at the Lodge know about my past. I didn't hide anything."

Mia put her hand on his arm. "Then don't worry about it. Your real friends will stand by you no matter what."

James hugged her. "Thank you for understanding."

When she returned to the party Trent was still watching her. She wandered through the guests, stopping to answer questions and greet newcomers.

As she talked about the school's historic past and the new usage the building would have as a cooking school, Mia was aware of Trent's attention as she talked with her guests. And even with the craziness of the last few months, she knew one true thing.

She went back and stood next to him. He slipped his arm around her waist and she leaned into his body. The one true thing? She was finally home.

Recipe

Magic Springs's Easy Apple Pie

Pastry:
- 2 cups flour
- 1 tsp salt
- ⅔ cup shortening (I use butter)
- 4–6 Tbsp cold water

Mix the salt into the flour. If you use butter, use right out of the fridge and cut into squares. Fork the butter into the flour until you don't see any butter and it's all crumbling. Once you do that, dribble the water into the mix until you can hand mix it into a ball. Divide these into two balls and wrap in plastic. Then refrigerate for at least 45 minutes.

Roll out the bottom pastry and fit into a pie plate.

Preheat oven to 425 degrees.

Filling:
Peel, core, and slice 6–8 tart apples (Granny Smiths are great)

In a bowl mix the following dry ingredients:

- ¾ cup sugar
- 2 tsp cinnamon
- ½ cup flour

Put the apple slices into a large bowl, then sprinkle with 1 Tbsp lemon juice. Then add dry ingredients and stir well to coat the apple slices. Pour into the bottom pie shell. Top with 1 Tbsp of butter.

Roll out the second ball of pastry into a circle. Cut a design into the middle of the circle to allow steam to vent (I like a stem and leaves).

Put top circle on pie and seal the edges with a crimping motion.

Sprinkle top of crust with sugar or brush with an egg white.

Bake 35–40 minutes until filling bubbles inside the crust.

Serve at room temperature with ice cream or warm with a slice of sharp cheddar cheese.